Praise for Sean Doolittle

Burn

"An exceptionally well-crafted and well-told tale of arson, police work, misplaced zeal, bad relationships, good relationships, family bonds and, oh yes, exercise videos. Quirky, compelling, intelligent, and funny . . . If you like Elmore Leonard, do yourself a favor and pick up *Burn*."
                                        —*Lincoln Journal Star*

"Sean Doolittle has been winning high praise from crime fiction readers, and *Burn* will show you why—it's deftly written, tense and intelligent, and bound to make you scramble to find his other work."
                    —Jan Burke, author of *Nine*

"A cult writer for the masses—hip, smart and so mordantly funny that the casual reader might be laughing too hard to realize just how thoughtful Doolittle's work is. Get on the bandwagon now."
        —Laura Lippman, author of *By a Spider's Thread*

"[A] twist-filled crime caper."   —*Publishers Weekly*

"Dryly funny . . . [a] writer to watch."
                            —*Omaha World-Herald*

"Sean Doolittle combines wit, good humor, and a generosity of spirit rare in mystery fiction to create novels

that are both engrossing and strangely uplifting. He deserves to take his place among the best in the genre."
—John Connolly, author of *The White Road*

"Doolittle's prose style is smooth, his plotting fast-paced and addictive."
—*January Magazine* (Best Crime Fiction of 2003 pick)

"A pleasure to read."   —*Drood Review of Mystery*

"Textured and tasty . . . far beyond the typical thrillers . . . Doolittle is a true Crimedog, and *Burn* is his thesis. And you can see it all over this nine millimeter of a novel that his best is yet to come."   —*Plots With Guns*

"Doolittle expertly weaves [his] themes into a tight plot populated by memorable characters. . . . Having read hard-boiled mysteries for over thirty years, it has been exciting to watch young turks become grand masters. I certainly hope that Sean Doolittle has a long, exciting career."   —*Mystery News*

"Doolittle has managed a somewhat genre-bending feat in the mystery realm—he's written a feel-good hard-boiled mystery . . . that is wholly original. Smooth and stylish, combining wit and intelligence . . . Doolittle is adept at balancing a suspenseful, well-paced mystery story with realistic and humanistic characters."   —trashotron.com

"The cast of characters [here] is second to none in diversity, peculiarity, and hilarity. The dialogue is sharp and energetic, and the narrative is spare and spot-on. . . . Sean Doolittle shrugs off the sophomore curse without so

much as a stuttering blink. . . . If you want something new to read, something fun, something *good*, then your search is over. *Burn* is the book for you. Highly recommended."
—Cemetery Dance

"An estimable addition not only to the publisher's list but also to crime fiction . . . Doolittle delivers a briskly plotted, hard-boiled mystery that has its roots in the Elmore Leonard school of dark comedy."
—South Florida Sun-Sentinel

Winner of the gold medal in the mystery category of *ForeWord Magazine*'s Book of the Year Award.

Dirt

"Uproarious."
—Publishers Weekly

"It's very rare for a first novel to be perfect; to have a great story, sparkling writing, interesting layered characters, a carefully balanced and realized setting, a beautifully modulated pace, and not a single misstep. This first novel comes very close. . . . Doolittle is a writer with a story to tell and the skills to tell it well—clearly a writer to watch."
—ForeWord Magazine

"A really top-notch thriller . . . the book is a delight."
—Lincoln Journal Star

"Doolittle gives us a great comic-noir romp . . . one of the best noir novels of the year. It's a creative and quirky tour de force."
—Plots with Guns

"[Doolittle] balances realism and authenticity with the twists and turns of a mystery thriller. . . ."—*The Reader*

"Ferocious, smart, original and funny. What more do you want?"
—Jack Ketchum, author of *The Girl Next Door* and *The Lost*

"In a passionate flurry of curious motives, seedy characters, and a touch of the heroic, Doolittle delivers an A+ effort that should be considered one of the top crime novels of the year. . . . Highly recommended."
—*Cemetery Dance*

An Amazon.com Top 100 Editor's Pick.

SEAN DOOLITTLE

A DELL BOOK

BURN
A Dell Book

PUBLISHING HISTORY
UglyTown edition published 2003
Dell mass market edition / April 2005

Published by
Bantam Dell
A Division of Random House, Inc.
New York, New York

Book design by Glen M. Edelstein

Library of Congress Catalog Card Number: 2003012953

Dell is a registered trademark of Random House, Inc., and the
colophon is a trademark of Random House, Inc.

ISBN 0-440-24227-4

Printed in the United States of America
Published simultaneously in Canada

www.bantamdell.com

OPM 10   9   8   7   6   5   4   3   2   1

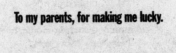

To my parents, for making me lucky.

Chorus:
And have frail mortals now the flame-bright fire?
Prometheus:
Yea, and shall master many arts thereby.
—*Aeschylus*

Love is a burning thing.
—*Johnny Cash*

BURN

12:29 P.M. | 103.6°F

THE morgue felt nice.

Detective Adrian Timms lingered in the bracing chill before pushing on into the long afternoon ahead. He stood beside the cold steel tray and pondered the fresh Y stitching the dead man's torso closed. He thought: *that's not maximum health.*

On his way out, Timms found the deputy coroner eating lunch at his cluttered office desk.

"This is the preliminary tox?"

The county M.E.'s man, an intuitive stickler named Washburn, looked over his Hunan chicken at the stapled pages Timms held in his hands.

"Yep."

"No blood alcohol."

"Nope," Washburn said. "So?"

Timms hadn't intended to think aloud. He pulled the

next sheet from the folder and slipped the toxicology report behind it.

Washburn pointed with his chopsticks. "Vic worked for Doren Lomax? That what I'm hearing?"

"Used to." Timms met Washburn's grin. "Yeah. I know."

The victim's name was Gregor Tavlin. He'd stopped breathing at forty-seven years of age, a Los Angeles County resident, a former Olympic decathlete, and a fitness guru of national renown. Timms had known of the man; his first ex-wife had owned all of Tavlin's aerobics videos. And you could still find barroom pundits around town who believed that back in the summer of 1976, Gregor Tavlin would have brought home Bruce Jenner's gold if a blown anterior cruciate ligament hadn't scuttled the young star's trip to the games in Montreal.

Cut to Mandeville Canyon, ten days ago, where Gregor Tavlin was discovered with a broken neck, a shattered pelvis, a collapsed rib cage, and dead tree branches in his eyes.

"Entertain me," Washburn said. "It's been nothing but heat-rage GSWs around here."

Timms chuckled, but he didn't have much to offer. He knew this so far:

On the morning of August 2, a forest ranger named Dean Barrow had lifted his respirator and motioned to a Los Angeles Fire Department captain standing next to him. The LAFD vet immediately rounded up the nearest three guys from a team of fifteen tending a controlled burn between the ridgeline and the embankment below the unimproved stretch of road known as Dirt Mulholland.

This sweat-streaked, ash-caked group of five had made their way as quickly as possible through the dense underbrush of the valley floor. The flashes Barrow had spotted two hundred yards in the distance could have been an injured hiker signaling with a pocket reflector.

What could have been an injured hiker turned out to be the wreckage of a vintage-model Alfa Romeo convertible. Barrow had glimpsed the car's twisted side-view mirror glinting in the sun.

The team found neither driver nor passenger in the remains of the shelled two-seater, which hadn't rested on the spot long. Long enough to get a nice 325-gallon rinse from the sky, courtesy of the California Department of Forestry's big red Huey tanker, but not long enough for the surrounding chaparral to heal from the crash.

Barrow had been the one who discovered the broken body of a middle-aged Caucasian male tangled in a nearby deadfall.

It was plain lucky, the ranger had told Adrian Timms, that the wind had shifted when it did. *We were about to pull back.* Barrow had explained how the gusts had broken the northern edge of their fire line, driving the flames too far too fast. *Down in the corridors like that, you get that wind tunnel effect, you're on the losing end. Another couple hours, nobody ever would have found this guy.*

Timms didn't know if "lucky" was the term for it, but he tried to look on the bright side: At least they'd been able to ID the victim without hunting up dental records.

"This," Timms said, pointing at a page. "This is SID's prelim?"

"Mm."

"And this," Timms said, pointing again, "is what you're saying?"

"All I'm saying," the deputy coroner said, "is the guy

somehow managed to leak blood and cerebrospinal fluid all over his own trunk."

Timms looked at the draft report, not really reading. He said, "Wonder how he managed that."

"Hey." Washburn scooped rice into his mouth. "You're the detective. You tell me."

1

COMMON sense told Andrew Kindler that a surprise visitor at the beach house didn't necessarily mean bad news. Instinct changed his mind long before the stranger with the sport coat on his arm got around to showing his badge.

"Hello up there."

Andrew hadn't realized he'd dozed off in the lounge chair until the voice startled him awake. He sat up and blinked against the sunlight, slowly regaining his sense of place. After all these weeks, he still sometimes woke up disoriented. He'd gotten to like the feeling.

Most of the time.

"Sorry. Over here."

Andrew looked toward the owner of the voice, who stood near the top of the long run of stairs leading up to the deck. When the stranger saw that he'd gotten Andrew's attention, he raised a rolled newspaper in greeting. "Anybody home?"

Andrew looked at his watch. Not quite nine o'clock. He reached to turn down the radio, suddenly wishing he had a dog.

"Morning," he said.

"Morning," said the stranger. "I rang the bell but nobody answered. Heard the radio, noticed the gate was open, thought I'd poke my head around. Mind if I come up?"

A German shepherd, Andrew thought. *Maybe a Doberman.*

"Watch that top step," he said. "It's cracked through the middle."

The guy acknowledged the tip with a short wave of the newspaper and a long stride over the offending tread. He strolled across the deck, scuffed cowboy boots sounding a hollow knock that echoed beneath the planks. Andrew watched from the lounge chair, evaluating possibilities.

Besides the gulls, and the occasional gutsy pelican, he didn't get many callers here. His cousin Caroline dropped by every so often with one of her foil-wrapped care packages, usually something new she'd learned in her gourmet cooking class. Andrew had begun to grow optimistic that anybody else who had reason to look for him probably would have found him before now.

The guy coming toward him wore rolled shirtsleeves and black denim slacks in spite of the heat wave in progress. He carried the sport coat over the crook of one elbow. Andrew saw big shoulders, weathered features, and a clean-shaved jaw. He guessed mid-forties, but the sunglasses made it hard to tell.

"Your paper was in a bush around back," the guy said, holding out the morning *Times.*

"I knew that kid's aim was improving. Thanks."

On the radio, the morning jock had just launched the hour with the daily Hot Spot report. Andrew leaned over and turned the volume back up a notch.

It had been almost two weeks since air and ground crews had reined in an out-of-control brush fire that had blackened nearly 2,500 acres of state parkland a few miles up the coast. According to the radio, smoldering pockets had flared up again during the night.

Meanwhile, farther north, separate wildfires in Topanga and Calabasas had been devouring parched scrub since late yesterday afternoon. Hot, dry Santa Ana gusts threatened to drive one fire into the other, pushing both through the mountain passes toward Malibu. Andrew had taken to spending his mornings on the deck, watching the forest department planes pass overhead on tag-team runs.

The stranger listened along for a moment, turning to gaze at the thick brown haze parked above Topanga Canyon to the north.

"Lifestyles of the rich and famous," he mused.

Andrew said, "Mm."

"Early in the year for this stuff, though. Dry summer."

"That's what they're saying."

"Sorry again for the drop-in, Mr. Borland." The stranger grinned easily and extended a palm. "I came by to see you yesterday, but you weren't around."

Mr. Borland. Andrew smiled and decided to let that one hang for now. He didn't explain to the stranger that he was not his jackass cousin-in-law, Lane, who owned the beach house. He reached to meet the man's grip, which felt calloused and solid.

"Detective, is it?"

The guy cocked his head without losing the grin. He watched Andrew from behind the shades. "You must be reading those papers."

"When I can find where they landed. Have you been in the papers?"

"Oh, I seem to be a regular celebrity lately."

"That must be it," Andrew said. "I probably saw your picture somewhere."

The detective nodded along, but Andrew could tell he wasn't buying it. Especially when the cop leaned forward and said, "Just between you and me, what really gave me away?"

Andrew thought: *I started it.* He shielded sun with his hand, starting over with the boots and working his way up.

"Put it this way," he said. "Are you much of a drinker?"

The detective—who had yet to state his business, Andrew couldn't help but note—seemed happy enough to play along. "I've been known to rest my feet on a rail from time to time."

"You know how when you're talking to a woman at a bar, one of the first things she notices is that spot where the wedding ring used to be on your left hand there?"

Now the detective looked at the hand he'd used to deliver the newspaper. His grin widened. "I do."

"For what it's worth," Andrew told him, "those sweat stains on your shirt say 'shoulder holster' to me."

The detective barked out a laugh that seemed to come back to them from beneath the deck. Without further chitchat, he folded open the jacket, reached inside, and said, "Not bad. Maybe you should have one of these."

Andrew set the newspaper aside and accepted the wallet. He flipped it open, checked the shield and ID.

Adrian Timms, LAPD. Robbery-Homicide Division. When Andrew handed the wallet back, Timms finally took off the shades and slipped them into his shirt pocket. His eyes seemed friendly, direct. Andrew got the feeling they didn't miss much.

"Mind if I sit down?"

"Help yourself." Andrew held up his coffee mug. "I've got a pot on in the house."

"Too hot for coffee, but thanks. I don't want to take much of your time."

"I'm not really on a tight schedule," Andrew said. "What brings you to the beach, Detective?"

Timms took the nearest sling chair, propped a boot across his knee, and draped the jacket over it. "I'm investigating this Gregor Tavlin business you've probably been hearing about."

Andrew was not aware of any Gregor Tavlin business. He hadn't really looked at the newspaper in a couple of weeks. Lane and Caroline had a television at the beach house, but he rarely turned it on. And except for the daily Hot Spot, he mostly just kept the radio around for company.

"No kidding? That's some business."

"Yes, I guess it is."

"Look," Andrew finally said. "I have a confession to make."

"Now there's something I don't hear every day."

He ran over with wit, this cop. Andrew gestured toward the house. "Lane Borland is my cousin's husband. I just moved to town a couple months ago. Lane owns the house. They don't use the place much, so I get a view of the ocean while I pretend to be hunting for my own shower and toilet."

The truth: He probably should have packed up and

moved on weeks ago. He knew better than to let himself get attached to the place, but he couldn't seem to help it.

Andrew liked the view of sand and water. He liked the coastline at dusk, the soft lap of the surf at night. He liked making coffee before sunrise, taking a hot mug out to the deck, and waiting for the salty mists to clear.

Lately, he'd grown to find something reassuring about the sight of a new horizon line.

He'd grown to like measuring out the days according to the rhythm of the tides.

Andrew didn't bother telling the detective how much he disliked the philandering greaseball his cousin Caroline had married, or how fiercely Lane Borland opposed the idea of Andrew anywhere near his property.

Lane, a talent manager who specialized in spokesmodels, had bought the beach house during a dip in the real estate market last year. He'd claimed it was a resale investment until Caroline had caught him here celebrating their anniversary with a buxom twenty-two-year-old Maybelline girl.

Caroline had offered her husband two options: get rid of the place, or hire a lawyer and get ready to pay up. Lane had caved without argument at the time, though he'd been citing soft real estate numbers ever since. He blamed the stock market.

But Andrew's kid cousin was no dummy, despite her inexplicable taste in men. Which meant that until Lane decided to stop dragging his feet and give up his million-dollar whoopie pad, Andrew had a fantastic rent-free view of the Pacific.

He was happy to help.

"I'll be honest," Detective Timms said. "That explains a thing or two."

"Oh?"

"I was thinking you didn't seem to be from around here."

It appeared to be Andrew's turn. "What gave me away?"

The detective started with Andrew's sandals and worked his way up from there.

"The tan, for starters," he said. "No offense, but you're a little on the pale side for a fellow who spends mornings on a sundeck."

Andrew held up the tube of SPF 60 he generally kept with him when he planned to be outside for any length of time. "These rays you've got out here are hell on scar tissue."

As if he'd been granted permission, the detective now nodded toward the first thing most people noticed about Andrew's face.

"I've been wondering what you tangled with," he admitted. "Left a little mark."

Andrew supposed the detective was being polite. The worst of the scars was thick as a pencil and ran half the length of his jawline. The jagged hook at the corner of his eye had been quickest to heal; its sibling, which trailed from the opposite corner of his mouth, had puckered as it sealed, leaving him with a permanent smirk. Caroline told him it looked cute. *Kind of aw-shucksy,* she said. Andrew thought it looked like he'd shaved with a Cuisinart.

"It was a concrete abutment," he lied. "The car looked worse."

Timms gave a low whistle.

"Probably should have kept my feet on that bar rail," Andrew said. "Gas pedal turned out to be a bad idea."

"Hindsight's always twenty-twenty."

"So they say."

"I'm sorry," the detective said. "What did you say your name was, again?"

"I didn't. It's Andrew. I can get you Lane's office number if you need to talk to him. I think I've got it in the house somewhere."

"Don't bother, I've already got it," Timms said. "I was just in the neighborhood, thought I'd try to catch him at home."

Andrew didn't ask the detective what had led him to assume he might find Lane at the beach house on a weekday morning. He planned to ask Lane that question personally. With any luck, he'd be forced to choke the answer out of the little weasel.

"But as long as I'm here, maybe you can save me some shoe leather," Timms said. "David Lomax is the person I'm actually looking for. He's a hard guy to find lately. We were told he might have stayed here recently. Have you spoken with him?"

"Lomax?"

The detective nodded. "David. I don't suppose you've seen him around."

Andrew shook his head and told the truth. "Never even heard of him."

"I see." Timms gathered up his jacket and stood. "Thanks for your time. I'll get out of your hair, give your cousin a call. Sorry again for the bother."

"Cousin-in-law. And it's no bother. Hope you track down your guy."

"That makes two of us."

Timms stuck out his hand again, and Andrew shook it. He was about to wish the detective luck, maybe say something conciliatory about the heat, when he noticed Timms glancing off toward the water. The detective seemed to be considering something.

"Before I go," he said, "mind if I ask one more question?"

"Not at all."

"Don't look now. But have you noticed the guy with the turned-up visor over there? Scooting the metal detector around that pile of driftwood. Hundred yards out."

Casually, Andrew moved his gaze down the beach.

"You mean the guy pointing the rocket launcher at us?"

"Looks like about a 400-millimeter zoom lens to me," Timms said. "Just so you know, he's been sneaking peeks over this way ever since I got here."

Andrew waited before glancing toward the guy with the camera again. The guy had turned his back to the house. He swept the metal detector's circular antenna coil from side to side over the sand a few feet in front of him.

It wasn't easy to be sure from this distance, but Andrew didn't think he'd ever seen the person before. He watched the guy pretend to inspect a fist-sized stalk of dried kelp. He thought: *This might not be my day.*

"I'm really starting to wish these pikers would update their maps," he said, spinning out the first thing that came to mind.

Timms lifted an eyebrow.

"You know who I'm talking about? I see them sitting around in lawn chairs all the time. I guess they sell 'em to the tourists?"

"Ah," Timms said. "Homes of the Stars."

"Right, right." Andrew gestured toward the house again. "My cousin tells me a Baldwin used to own the place before Lane bought it. That's the third guy with a camera since I've been here."

This time, when the detective laughed, the whole deck seemed to vibrate beneath Andrew's chair. Timms fished his sunglasses out of his shirt pocket and put them on again.

"It's a little unnerving," Andrew said.

"Well," said Timms. "In that case, I can only think of one thing to tell you."

"What's that?"

"Welcome to Los Angeles, Mr. Kindler."

Andrew laughed politely. He and Timms exchanged final pleasantries. With that, the detective strolled back across the deck, remembering the top step as he descended the stairs.

For a long time after he'd gone, Andrew stayed out on the deck, listening to the radio. He pondered the smoke banks blotting the pale blue sky above the Santa Monica Mountains.

Over the sound of the radio, Andrew could hear young kids kicking a ball around behind the tall privacy fence encircling the adjacent property. Three long blonde rollerbladers in thong tankinis threaded joggers on the strip. Across the busy highway, atop the rail-lined cliffs, the tall palms along Ocean Avenue hung their fronds in the heat.

By the time the guy with the beachcombing rig had wandered out of view, Andrew had decided only two things for sure.

He was out of ideas.

And he was absolutely positive that he'd never told the big detective with the cowboy boots his last name.

2

AFTER the detective left, Andrew stayed out on the deck and debated his first item of business for almost an hour. At a quarter past ten, he finally gave up, collected the newspaper, tossed the tube of sunblock into his empty coffee mug, and gathered up the radio.

He went inside long enough to throw on a shirt and a clean pair of chinos. When he returned to the deck, Andrew stood at the rail for a minute. He twirled his car keys on his finger as he looked out over the water. Then he turned away and headed down the stairs. He made a point of leaving the sliding glass door to the house unlocked behind him.

Despite heavy mid-morning traffic, Andrew made it to the customer counter at the Cal Fed branch on 5th Street and Santa Monica Boulevard in a little under ten minutes. He showed his key, along with the bogus ID he'd used to reserve a safety-deposit box a few days after he'd arrived in Los Angeles. The teller smiled and showed him to a private access room. Andrew made a withdrawal, which he tucked into his waistband beneath his shirt. Then he left the bank and drove home.

Andrew paid eight dollars to park in the public lot a quarter mile up the beach. He walked the distance back to the house at a leisurely pace. At the bottom of the stairs to the deck, he took off his sandals and headed up quietly on the balls of his feet.

The first thing he noted as he reached the landing was the metal detector leaning against the side of the house. That, and the two-foot gap between the sliding screen and the jamb.

Andrew took a moment, then reached under his shirt.

When he slid the screen open the rest of the way and stepped inside, the beachcomber looked up from the breakfast bar, where he'd been rummaging through a stack of utility bills. Wisps of thinning hair floated above the brim of the guy's sun visor in breeze-blown question marks. His eyes widened, and he opened his mouth, but he didn't make a sound.

"Morning," Andrew said.

The guy said, "Oh."

"Listen, help me out, I'm new to the area. Do people shoot trespassers around here?"

The guy didn't answer. He didn't even appear to breathe. He stood like a lamppost with lips, palms hovering six inches above the countertop. The gun in Andrew's hand seemed to hold his attention.

"I can explain," he finally said. "I . . . okay. I can explain."

"Great." Andrew closed the distance between them

and performed a quick one-handed frisk: armpits and waistband. Clean. "I'm all ears."

The guy opened his mouth and closed it again. Andrew noticed the camera sitting on one of the barstools. While he waited for the guy to get his story in order, he walked over, picked up the camera, tilted the big lens toward the guy, and snapped off a couple of exposures.

"Did you want to do the honors?"

The guy exhaled. "You've got the gun."

"Good point."

Andrew popped the back of the camera and stripped out the film in long glossy coils. When he was finished, he stepped back to the open door, gripped the camera by the lens, and sent it flying with a hard underhanded toss. The camera made a lazy, tumbling arc over the deck and disappeared beyond the rail.

Andrew watched it go. When he looked back, he saw the photographer wincing as though in pain.

Running to the bank for the gun was beginning to seem zealous in retrospect. Over the long lazy weeks, Andrew had imagined a hundred ways trouble might one day present itself; none of those scenarios had included the paunchy guy with the sun-reddened scalp standing before him now. But then, nothing about this morning made much sense so far.

"Don't worry," he said. "You can tack it on your fee. Now tell me who you work for."

Andrew noted a half-hearted resistance in the man's eyes. He tipped the barrel of the gun forward, letting the hammer click back beneath his thumb. The man's eyes dulled.

He said, "I'm looking for David Lomax, okay? I was hired by the family. Sort of. That's all I can tell you."

David Lomax. Andrew shook his head. He was really starting to wonder if he ought to know somebody named David Lomax after all. He narrowed his eyes and raised the muzzle an inch.

"Look, I'm not playing games. I can verify. Would it be okay if I used my phone?"

Andrew held out his hand. "Allow me."

The guy fished in the front pocket of his shorts, then reached across the counter to hand Andrew a cellular telephone the size of a credit card. When Andrew prompted, the guy began reciting digits. Andrew punched them in with his pinky fingernail. A local number.

After three rings, a male voice picked up the line. It did not have East Coast in it, Andrew noted. Under the circumstances, this came more as a puzzlement than a relief.

"This is Benjy."

"Hey there, Benjy. How are you?"

"Who is this?"

"Listen. Benjy. I've got somebody here who needs to talk to you."

Andrew handed over the phone. The guy accepted it wearily.

"It's me," he said. "Yeah. No. That was him just now." Pause. "I mean that was *him*. The *guy*." A pause, another sigh. "Because he caught me in his house, okay?"

Andrew leaned forward. "Tell him he has an hour to come get you."

The guy looked at Andrew. Closed his eyes.

"He says. . . ."

Pause.

"Look, does it really matter at this point? What do you want me to say? He's pointing a friggin' gun at me."

Pause. "I realize that. But thanks for the bulletin. Yeah. The address I gave you yesterday."

Without further exchange, the guy folded the phone in his palm and turned to face Andrew again.

Andrew waggled the gun barrel. "Okay, Marlowe. Good job. Here we go."

"Here we go where? That was my client. He's on his way. He'll tell you everything you want to know."

"Left, right, left," Andrew said. "You can do it."

"But I don't understand what. . . ."

Andrew raised a finger to his lips. When the man stopped speaking, Andrew directed him out from behind the breakfast bar, into the living room, and over to the sofa.

"On your stomach," he instructed.

"What? Why?"

Andrew removed the throw pillows and pointed. The guy looked at the short designer couch. Caroline had chosen it, she'd explained when she'd first showed Andrew around the place, to balance a negative space problem in the room. It had been part of her class project in the feng shui minicourse she'd taken at the Design Center last year.

"On that? I'm too tall."

"You flatter yourself."

The guy looked at Andrew with a dubious expression. Andrew wagged the gun. The guy sighed. After much shifting and squirming, he finally settled. His shins rested at a bent-knee angle against one sloped armrest.

"Come on," he said into the cushions. "Seriously."

"You'd be more comfortable if you stopped fidgeting."

"What are you going to do to me?"

"Don't worry," Andrew told him. "This won't hurt. Now be still."

Keeping an eye on the guy, Andrew went to the sliding door and reached out around the corner. He brought the metal detector back to the living room with him and sat down in one of Caroline's rattan accent chairs. He stripped the headphones and the antenna coil and tied the guy's wrists and ankles with the cords.

"What are you doing?"

Andrew removed the snoop's mashed sun visor for him and straightened.

"Comfy?"

The snoop turned his face toward Andrew's kneecaps. "Is this really necessary?"

"It makes me feel better." Andrew nodded toward the tightly rolled newspapers he'd gotten into the habit of stacking in the woodbin near the fireplace. "Now. I'm a week behind on my current events, so I'm going to read while we wait for your ride to get here. If I were you, I'd use this time to think about the downside of your chosen career field. Holler if you need anything."

The snoop wriggled onto his side and looked up. "Who *are* you?"

Andrew had to grin. "You're not very good at this job, are you, pal?"

Thursday, August 9

HEALTH CLUB HEIR SOUGHT IN TAVLIN CASE

By MELANIE ROTH
TIMES staff writer

Local businessman David Lomax is being sought for questioning in the suspected murder of former Lomax Enterprises employee Gregor Tavlin, police said Thursday.

"There are discrepancies we believe Mr. Lomax may be able to help us sort out," LAPD Detective Adrian Timms said. "We are examining all possible sources of information."

Gregor Tavlin, the noted exercise innovator who helped establish the Club Maximum chain of health clubs owned by Lomax Enterprises, was found dead near his overturned automobile off the unpaved Mulholland Drive extension near Topanga State Park on August 2. Autopsy findings overruled preliminary indications of accidental death.

David Lomax, 29, is the son of Doren Lomax, founder and CEO of Lomax Enterprises. The elder Lomax currently is serving his second term as an appointed member of the LAPD Board of Police Commissioners.

David Lomax, a junior vice president at his father's corporation, has not reported to work since the end of July, according to company spokesperson and Lomax family friend Todd Todman. Authorities also have been unable to locate the younger Lomax at his Silver Lake home.

"David is somewhat notorious for his unannounced vacations," Todman said. "Naturally, we are concerned for his well-being, but we fully expect to locate him in short order. In the meantime, the entire Lomax Enterprises family intends to cooperate with law enforcement without reservation."

Detective Timms declined to confirm whether David Lomax will be questioned as a suspect in the murder investigation at the present time.

3

"**THIS** is Todman. Go."

"Mr. Todman, this is Adrian Timms."

"Oh . . . Detective Timms. Hello there. Excuse my tone, I assumed this was a work call. What can I do for you?"

"Well, I was just hoping to hook up with you again sometime in the next day or two. I stopped by your office, but your secretary told me you were going to be hard to catch. Think you could find a few spare minutes at some point?"

"Absolutely. Is there information about David?"

"Nothing new. I'd just like to go over a couple of things."

"Yes, absolutely. Of course. Fire away."

"I'd just as soon speak in person. It's nothing that can't wait."

"I see. Let me track down Doren and get back to you. I'm sure he'd want to make himself available."

"That's fine. I probably won't be at my desk today. Let me give you my cell number."

"No need, Detective. I have it programmed into my phone."

"I'll talk to you soon, then."

Todd Todman assured the detective that he'd be in touch the minute he talked to his employer. Then he snapped his phone closed, brushed a fleck of lint from his company oxford, and turned to look for the next challenge waiting in the queue.

From where he stood, he saw at least two. One could wait. The other was called Lenhoff.

"I'm telling my guys to pack up," Lenhoff said. He practically stomped his feet as he crossed the soundstage. "We're out of here. Give me a call when you get your shit together. Better yet: Don't."

Todd raised his palms. "Rory, I know. If you could just hang in there a few—"

"A few? You do realize we're already two and a half hours behind fucking schedule on this fucking shoot?"

"I appreciate that, Rory. I just got word from Mr. Marvalis. He's on his way now."

Lenhoff snorted and swept his hand toward the set behind him, which had been designed to convey the general idea of a high-tech, futuristic warehouse interior. The scruffy twenty-eight-year-old director, fresh off a Grammy nomination for his work in pop music videos, brought just the brand of hip young energy Todd felt the project needed. Sadly, he also brought a budding auteur complex the size of his going rate, which was getting to be considerable.

"Rod Marvalis," Lenhoff muttered. "You know, Todman, I still don't know what you expect me to do with that tubby son of a bitch if he does manage to drag his bloated ass in here before noon. Tavlin's corpse would look better on camera."

Todd finally regarded Lenhoff with a frown.

"Gregor Tavlin was an important member of the Maximum Health family," he said. "We all feel the loss. I understand that you're agitated, Rory, but try to show a little common respect."

"Respect? You want to talk about respect? This is horseshit."

Out of the corner of his eye, Todd saw his other challenge heading over and put his reply on hold. This challenge wore a lime green cycle shirt with the word SECURITY in white block letters across his broad back. His name was Luther Vines. Lenhoff saw him coming, too. The director smirked.

"Oh, this is cute. I guess I'm supposed to go back to my designated area and be a good little boy now?"

Vines had been glowering in Todd's direction from his post by the stage door for approximately an hour. Now he moved toward them with an athletic, purposeful grace. Todd could understand why Lenhoff might be under the impression that he was about to be handled in a manner somewhat less accommodating than Todd's own.

A striking, V-shaped wedge of muscle from waist to shoulders. That was Luther Vines. He kept his head shaved to a clean black dome, and his hooded eyes seemed to smolder, even when he was in a good mood. Which was not often. In fact, Todd Todman couldn't recall if he'd ever seen Luther smile.

He didn't start with Lenhoff. "Problem over here?"

"Yeah, there's a problem." Lenhoff barely looked at

him. "It's called gross fucking unprofessionalism. Is it any of your concern? Gee. I don't think so."

"Yo, Spielberg," Luther said. "Here's a news flash. You're shooting an aerobics video. You can chill."

"Luther." Todd held up a hand, but he could see that it was too late. Luther's uninvited input had nudged Lenhoff's needle into the red zone.

"Who *exactly* do you think you're talking to?" The director wheeled on Todd. "Do you really have the sac to tell me you'd let this walking meat slab speak to Spike Jonze this way?"

"Wouldn't matter to me if you was Spike Lee," Luther said. "And you ain't either one of 'em."

Behind them, the other members of the production had begun to whisper amongst themselves as they observed the developing scene. The extras had stopped flirting with each other. The sound guy peered out from behind his mixing console. The lighting crew stood in a loose huddle, furtively passing folded bills to one of the cable pullers. They were taking bets, Todd realized. He was beginning to fear that Rory Lenhoff might actually blow a hose.

Just then, the stage door opened. A bright shaft of sunlight pierced the moment; everybody turned. Accompanied by the sounds of street traffic, the other half of the security detail appeared.

This one's name was Denny Hoyle. Everyone watched as he stood aside and held the door.

When Rodney Marvalis finally sauntered through—sunglass perched atop his head, frosted blond mane tousled cinematically by the draft from an overhead HVAC duct—Lenhoff glared at Todd. Then he glared at Luther Vines. Then he applauded sarcastically and stalked away.

Todd sighed.

"Well," he said. "That was diplomatic of you."

Luther Vines didn't answer. He was too busy scowling at their star, Rod Marvalis, who had already begun to graze the craft services table. Even from this distance, Marvalis looked like a case study in hangover.

Denny Hoyle jogged toward them.

"I miss anything?"

"We were beginning to think you got lost," Todd said.

"Sorry, boss. Got jammed up on the 405. Hey, Luthe."

Vines crossed his bulging arms without acknowledging his junior associate. Hoyle didn't seem to notice.

"Plus we had to turn around and go back on account of Rod forgot his back brace."

Vines snorted. "Brace, shit. That's a girdle."

Denny Hoyle shrugged absently. His attention had already been captured by the sight of long brunette hair falling over the shoulder straps of a sleek white unitard. Without blinking, he watched the slim-waisted extra as she leaned into a full-body stretch against a nearby prop crate.

"Denny, why don't you take the door while Luther and I finish up here?" Todd said.

"Huh? Oh. Yeah."

Todd could feel Luther's stare as he watched Hoyle hustle back toward the stage door. He counted to five, took a deep breath, and turned.

"Okay, Luther. Okay. What's on your mind?"

"I want a meeting."

"You've made yourself clear on that point. I told you we'd work it in."

"You keep tellin' me."

Todd nodded patiently, flipped open his phone, and moved on to challenge number three: getting the founder and president of Lomax Enterprises on the line before lunch on his tennis day.

"A little patience," he said. "That's all I'm asking. These things take time."

Luther's stormy expression didn't change. Todd sent the first number on his speed dial and raised the phone to his ear. "Deal?"

Luther Vines took a step forward and spoke directly into Todd's other ear.

"You and me already got a deal," he said. His breath was hot enough to steam Todd's ear canal.

"Doren," Todd said quickly. "It's me."

Without looking at Luther, he plugged his ear with a finger and moved away.

A few seconds later, Doren Lomax's unanswered phone finally routed him to the voice mail system. Todd Todman sighed. There were days, he thought, and then there were days.

Still feeling Luther's eyes on his back, Todd strolled to the quietest spot he could find, still pretending to be deep in conversation long after Doren's mailbox beeped and hung up on him.

4

"**HEY**. That thing's not even loaded."

Andrew looked over a corner of the newspaper to find the snoop studying the gun on the coffee table between them. It seemed he'd finally noticed the hollow space in the base of the grip where a clip was supposed to go.

"You know what they say." Andrew turned to the next article, which he'd just found in the August 6 edition at the bottom of the woodbin: FOUL PLAY SUSPECTED IN TAVLIN DEATH. "Guns don't kill people. It's the bullets."

"I don't believe this."

"You'd feel better if I loaded it?"

"I didn't say that."

Andrew was actually starting to like the guy he'd tied up on Caroline's couch, in spite of their rocky start. Travis Plum, according to the driver's license. So he chose not to add insult to bondage by revealing that he'd left the clip and the box of extra rounds back at the bank.

Andrew wasn't scared of guns, but he didn't particularly like them either. As far as he was concerned, every gun he'd ever met seemed to have a personality, and not the kind he cared to have around. So he generally avoided their company.

The Glock on the coffee table was the first and only firearm Andrew had ever owned. He'd bought it on his way out of Baltimore from an aging Czech who ran a neighborhood bakery known for its kolaches and untraceable small arms. It had been a last-minute decision, a reluctant concession to a lingering bit of wisdom an old crewhand had once passed along. *Better to have one and never need it.*

Andrew had always planned to toss the gun into the Pacific one day as a symbolic gesture. He kept telling himself he'd get around to it.

"Listen," Plum said. "Would you mind if I asked you a personal question?"

Somewhere outside, a car door slammed.

"Hold that thought," Andrew said.

After a few empty moments, the intercom crackled. A voice said, "Hello?"

Andrew stood and went to the nearest wall unit. He thumbed the button. "Say your name."

"Benjamin. Benjy. We talked on the phone."

"Anybody else out there with you, Benjamin?"

"Benjy. Just me."

"I'm going to take your word on that."

"You can."

"Okay, Benjy. Look to your left, you'll see a gate. It's open. Come on up to the deck and follow it around. You can use the sliding door. That's also open."

"Gate, deck, sliding door."

"A-plus. We'll be waiting for you." Andrew released the button, then turned back and pressed it again. "Benjy?"

"Yes."

"Skip over the top step when you come up the stairs. I need to fix it."

Andrew buzzed out without waiting for a reply. He went to the tall windows overlooking Pacific Coast Highway and peeked around the edge of the pull shade. Down below, he saw a charcoal Town Car parked askew on the narrow brick-paved strip in front of the garage.

He went back to the chair, sat down again, and nodded at Plum.

"You wanted to ask me something?"

The snoop had wrangled his way into a sitting position, arms still behind his back, bound legs kicked out to one side. As muffled footfalls climbed the stairs and crossed the deck outside, he looked at Andrew's face, seemed to reconsider, and finally said, "Never mind."

Andrew shrugged as a figure appeared in the open doorframe, backlit by the high morning sun.

"Come on in," Andrew said.

The silhouette stepped across the door track and became a sun-bleached, thirty-something guy in business casual attire: dark green polo shirt tucked into pressed khaki trousers, black dress belt to match the tassled shoes. He glanced at the snarl of exposed film on the floor. Then he stopped in place and raised his hands, as if to acknowledge that some sort of gun had been mentioned.

"You can relax," Andrew said.

Benjy lowered his hands. "You're the boss."

"Ironic, considering I seem to be the only guy in the room who doesn't know why we're all here."

"I can help with that."

"That's what Trav here tells me."

The man named Benjy took a moment to regard the man named Plum. "Nice," he said.

"Kiss my ass," Plum told him. "I didn't sign up for this."

"Five hundred a day plus expenses," Benjy said. "What a joke."

"I resent that."

"A metal detector and Bermuda shorts?" Benjy looked at the stripped apparatus on the floor and snorted. "Where'd you learn surveillance, *Simon and Simon* reruns?"

"Okay, people," Andrew said. "This is getting us nowhere."

Benjy dismissed Plum and turned back to Andrew. "I owe you an apology. And an explanation, obviously."

"You can just skip to the explanation."

Benjy nodded as though that suited him fine. "Can I assume by the fact that you haven't picked up that gun yet that we're starting on friendly terms?"

"It isn't even loaded," Plum said from the couch.

Benjy shot him a look.

"Well, it isn't."

"Then that makes you even sadder, doesn't it?"

"You and I can start right where we are," Andrew said. "We'll see how it goes."

"Fair enough." Benjy closed the distance between them, extending a hand. "The last name's Corbin."

"Andrew. But I'm guessing you know that already."

"I didn't. Hello."

Andrew noticed a few things as he shook the hand. Faint scars on the knuckles. A workingman's forearms covered by thick brambles of wheat-colored hair. The polo shirt had what looked like some kind of corporate logo embroidered on the sleeve.

"Nice Lincoln outside," Andrew said. "Do you lease or own?"

"I just drive it."

Andrew nodded. "I thought that outfit of yours looked mandatory. No offense."

"None taken."

"I'm listening."

Benjy said, "I'm going to reach around my back and take something out of my pocket. We're still friendly?"

"Sure."

Benjy made his reach and brought back a fat envelope. He handed the envelope to Andrew.

"What's this?"

"That's the apology," Corbin said.

Andrew could smell the ink even before he slipped the rubber band from around the envelope. He ran his thumb along the edge of the bundle inside and estimated somewhere in the neighborhood of five grand in crisp new bills.

"I think you'd better get back to the explanation."

"The first thing I need to let you know is that Ace over there wasn't spying on you," Corbin said. "At least not you in particular. We had him following a cop who seemed to be interested in this address. We wondered why. That's as far as it goes."

"He was here again this morning," Plum said. "They shook hands, talked on the deck for about fifteen minutes."

"You're fired," Benjy said, "so you can shut up anytime."

Andrew said, "Who's we?"

"I retained Mr. Plum as a favor to my employer's daughter," Benjy said. "Heather Lomax."

Andrew filed away the name. "And this?"

"Miss Lomax has asked me to offer that in exchange for any information you might be able to supply regarding the whereabouts of her brother, David."

Andrew extended his arm, offering back the cash.

"You can tell Miss Lomax to keep her money," he said. "I don't know her brother. Or his whereabouts. I told the cop the same thing when he asked me this morning. And he wasn't paying."

"The money's still yours."

Andrew tossed the package. It slid across the bare floor and stopped against the sole of Benjy's shoe. Corbin looked at it. He didn't bend to retrieve it.

"If you don't mind me saying so, I get the feeling you've got more on the ball than this, Benjamin."

"Sorry?"

"Come on," Andrew said. "Say I really did know this guy everybody seems to think I know. Coming around here asking seems like a good idea to you?"

"I'm only here on behalf of Miss Lomax," Benjy said.

"Part of your job description?"

"A favor." Benjy finally offered a tight grin. "Do I think this is a good idea? No. Have I told Heather that? A couple of times. But she's worried about her brother. And she's a friend."

"So you go around behind the cops offering cash to strangers?"

"So I find a guy who came recommended." He flicked his gaze toward the couch. "You get the rest of what he had coming to him. Consider it a token of our regret."

"Oh, that's fair," Plum said.

Andrew just looked at Corbin.

"If you want," Benjy said, "I'll put you in touch with my boss right now. His name is Doren. You can get me fired and put Heather in the doghouse with daddy for a few days." He shrugged. "Or you can keep the money for your trouble, and I'll deliver your message. I'll leave you a number, just in case you decide you want to use it at some point after this. But you won't be bothered again."

"You can leave any number you want," Andrew told him. "I still don't know anything about your boy."

"As long as that's settled," Plum said from the couch, "could somebody go ahead and untie me now?"

While Benjy stood by, Andrew picked up the Glock from the coffee table and stuck it back in his waistband. He went to the kitchen and rummaged through drawers. He found a pair of pizza shears and brought the giant scissors back with him.

Without turning his back on Benjy, Andrew did Plum's ankles first. He said, "Hop up."

Plum dragged his feet beneath him and rose. As he steadied himself, Andrew snipped the knot where the headphones dangled from Plum's wrists. Then he rounded up the severed cords and handed them over.

"More for the 'plus expenses' column," he said.

"Gee. Thanks."

Andrew looked at Benjy again. "I may end up regretting this, but I'm going to choose to believe this is all what you say it is. Because frankly, if it wasn't, it would have to make a hell of a lot more sense than it does."

"I guess I follow that."

"Then I guess I'm willing to pretend this never happened," Andrew said. "You can return your little payoff when you deliver the message. Tell your friend Heather I hope she finds her brother. But don't ever send anybody around here again."

Benjy looked at Andrew for a long moment. Then he picked up the envelope from the floor and looked at Plum. "What are *you* waiting for? A ride to your car?"

"There's going to be a contingency fee on this," Plum said. He stooped, snatched his fallen visor, picked up the disabled metal detector by the shaft, and headed for the open doorway to the deck.

Benjy mouthed something to himself as he watched Plum go. Then he turned back to Andrew one last time.

"No hard feelings, I hope."

Before Andrew could respond, the driver pivoted on a heel. Andrew watched him follow Plum out the door.

Corbin stopped only long enough to produce a pen from somewhere on his person. He used it to scribble something on the envelope.

Then he walked out the way he'd walked in, leaving the bundle sitting on the edge of the breakfast bar like a brick on a ledge, waiting to fall.

5

"**TEAM** one finished rerunning the financials."

Timms glanced across the table at his partner as he squirted more ketchup on his fries. When it came to lunch, they had a standing agreement not to talk about anything case-related until they were finished eating their food. Timms believed the downtime promoted digestion. Drea Munoz always finished eating first.

"Any idea how much these movie stars pay to get buff?" She washed down the last of her pastrami on rye. "I'm thinking about switching careers. Get myself one of those gigs as a consultant for the movies. You know? Show J.Lo what kind of backup piece goes with slacks."

"I didn't know you followed fashion."

"Never wear a .45 after Labor Day is my rule. And by the way, screw you, cowboy. This is a Donna Karan suit. D.A. couldn't keep his eyes off me in court this morning."

Timms smirked and munched a fry. "Anything we didn't know on the money end?"

"Nothing new. Guy's tight on paper. Took a nice income bump with the private gigs, but we knew that already."

"Greener pastures." According to Todd Todman, the official talking head for Lomax Enterprises, Gregor Tavlin had bought out his own contract with the company last year due to late-blooming irreconcilable differences with executive management. He'd spent the interim freelancing as a personal trainer to several Hollywood A-listers.

"So what happened with our mystery man?"

"He was having himself a little snooze outside when I showed up," Timms said. "Claims he's never heard of David Lomax."

"No kidding," Drea said. She mimed a yawn. "How'd you make him?"

"Haven't figured that out yet," Timms said. "But I'll bet you a paycheck he's got a jacket somewhere."

"Yeah?"

"Knew I was on the job before I even flashed the tin. He just didn't know what. Like it could have been anything. Lets me act like I think he's the homeowner until he knows why I'm there, then he cops to the fact he's only a houseguest. Offers me coffee and his landlord's phone number." Timms polished off his fries and wiped his hands on a napkin. "Says he's been in town a couple months, I'd say that looks about right. Somebody did a number on his face about that long ago, by the look. Same paycheck says he needed a place to hole up and lick a few wounds."

Drea nodded along. The vague smile on her face suggested she had a story of her own.

Timms sipped his coffee, which had gone cold. "You get a read on the homeowner?"

"Borland? I didn't have to read him. He was an audio book. Couldn't shut him up. Kindler's his wife's cousin, he says."

"Kindler gave me that," Timms said. "I make him from back East somewhere."

"Yeah? How far east have you ever been?"

"I knew a guy at SMPD from South Boston. Pronounced his Rs the same way."

"Not bad. Baltimore." Drea began to gesture with her hands while she spoke. "Borland, he's like, 'Anything I can do to help, Detective. I don't know what he did, but I told Caroline'—that's the wife—'I told her I don't want the guy around. I don't care if he's family. He should be in prison. Instead, he's living in my beach house.'"

"Was this before or after you showed Borland the letter?"

"Didn't even mention the letter."

"No kidding." Timms folded his arms on the table. "Should be in prison, huh?"

"That seems to be Borland's opinion."

"He give a reason why?"

"Oh, you'll love this," Drea said. "I called a pal of mine in the Bureau field office, asked him to run Kindler through NCIC for me while I was in court. Haven't heard back yet. But Borland mentions a juvie beef that never stuck. He's all, like, hey, you didn't hear it from me."

Timms had learned to listen patiently. With Drea, it usually paid off in the end.

"I made some calls," she said. "No record in Maryland. But here's Borland's story. You ready?"

"More than."

"Put it this way." Drea seemed to be savoring her punch line. "Does 'Kindler' sound like an occupational name to you?"

Timms narrowed his eyes. "What'd he do?"

"Nothing much. Burned his stepfather's house down. Allegedly. Like, allegedly to the ground. Stepdad happened to be home at the time."

Timms leaned back in the booth.

"Guy made it out. Middle of the night, shitfaced drunk, no serious injuries. But I haven't even told you the best part."

"What's the best part?"

"The stepfather? He was an arson investigator." Drea beamed and clapped her hands. "Baltimore Life and Casualty. Twelve years!"

"Please."

"The way Borland tells it, the guy's running around in his BVDs screaming stepkid's name in the streets. Local cops hauled the kid in, worked him through the drill—he's fourteen—but he sails with flying colors. Sleeping over at a friend's house, he tells 'em. The friend checks out, parents back it up. Meanwhile, the fire guys rule the house accidental. Said the stepdad fell asleep smoking a cigarette. Whoomp!"

"And Borland's just laying this all out."

"Like he's driving the tram at Universal Studios. Says the stepfather got canned at the insurance company before the week was out. Left the mother, moved to the Meadowlands to sell Jacuzzis."

Timms shook his head again.

"Some story, huh?"

"Some story."

"That's about where Borland leaves it. Says everybody

in the neighborhood knew the Kindler kid did it, but nobody was crying over the stepdad leaving town, and the cops and the marshals had no reason not to be satisfied with the cigarette theory. Guy was a known boozer. He gets plowed, passes out watching television in the chair, drops his Camel on a pile of newspapers, should be counting his blessings he's alive. Next case."

She leaned forward, still acting out her meeting with Lane Borland. Though he hadn't known Drea Munoz a great deal of time, Timms had come to enjoy his partner's demonstrative narrative style. She was the original Type A personality. The A stood for Attitude.

"Then he gets all hush-hush, right? I mean he actually looks this way, looks that way." She looked to her left and to her right as she spoke. "Walks over and shuts his office door. I mean, he's playing this for all it's worth, trying to show me how serious he is. Says he really can't tell me much more. For personal safety reasons, he says. It could be that Kindler ended up getting recruited by some pros later on, he tells me. But he really wouldn't know."

"Interesting," Timms said.

"I thought you'd like it." Drea settled back to her side of the booth again. "So what do you think?"

Timms didn't need to think about it. "I think the whole thing stinks. That letter sticks in my craw."

Monday morning, after putting in his own court appearance for a previous case, Timms had gone home to lose the suit and the tie and found an unmarked, dun-colored business envelope with his personal mail. The envelope contained a plain white sheet of paper with a typed note. Not printed from a computer: actually typed on a typewriter. The note read:

Detective Timms,

The man you need to speak with is named Andrew Kindler. He's staying at the enclosed address. He will not be expecting you.

> *Yours,*
> *David Lomax*

If not for the signature at the bottom, Timms would have tossed the letter on the pile along with the thousand other bogus tips and cheap pranks they'd received so far. But at a glance, compared to documents they'd collected from Lomax's office files, the sig looked close enough to earn a flag and a follow-up.

"I swung by the lab on my way here," Drea said. "No prints. They're still looking at it."

Timms nodded. "I already checked in."

"Say we're taking this guy Kindler seriously. Theoretically, what? An OC angle, maybe?"

Timms shrugged. Nothing about the case had pointed to an organized-crime connection before now. "Possibility."

"Possible enough to haul him in?"

"Don't see what good it would do us at this point," Timms said. "Theoretically, he'd just play dumb and go home. Or take off."

"We could put Reese and Carvajal on the Baltimore thing. See if they can dig up any ties with Lomax or Tavlin there."

"Somebody besides us is already looking into Kindler," he said. "Guy was snapping photos of the house while I was there."

"No shit."

"Nope. Kindler came up with a story. Said the house is on celebrity maps."

"And?"

"Not on any I could find."

"He's quick on his feet, though," Drea said. "How'd you leave it?"

"I dropped a bug in his ear when I left," Timms said. "Hung back and watched awhile, see if it got him moving."

"And?"

"He might have taken another nap."

"I love it."

"Went somewhere after about an hour," Timms said.

"Driving fast?"

"Not particularly."

Even if he'd been inclined, Timms had no hope of tailing, given the logistics. Kindler's borrowed neighborhood consisted of a short row of expensive beachfront homes fifteen feet off the beachside shoulder of PCH. Sandstone cliffs for an eastern shoulder and two lanes of fast traffic in either direction. After talking with Kindler, Timms had to move his car to a nearby pay lot and decide between the beach side of the property or the highway side. From the highway side, he'd had a fantastic view of a gated brick wall and a closed garage door. So he'd found a spot on the beach path that offered decent line-of-sight through the field binoculars he kept in the glovebox of the Oldsmobile. What the position had lacked in cover it made up for in immobility.

"So are we calling this guy a player?"

"Don't have much choice until the lab on that letter comes back," Timms said. "I'll say this, though. Kindler may have a cool streak, but he's a shitty liar."

"Think he's holding something?"

"That's just it," Timms said. "When he said he didn't know our guy, I believed him."

"Then what?"

"You want to know the only time I really knew for sure this guy Kindler was full of shit?"

Drea watched as he dumped back the last of his cold coffee. She didn't bother making a guess.

Timms popped a breath mint and said, "When he pretended he knew what I was talking about when I mentioned the Tavlin thing."

6

BORLAND Management hung its shingle on the fifth floor
of an unimaginative high rise downtown. Andrew had
never been to the place, but it wasn't hard to find. He
took the elevator up, followed the floor directory, and
arrived in Lane's neo-primitive reception area a little after one o'clock.

After giving his name, Andrew stood and absorbed
the decor, which featured lots of brushed aluminum,
glass, burnished cherrywood, trendy earth tones, and
mass-produced totems meant to look imported from
dark exotic locales. He doubted very much that Caroline had anything to do with the scheme.

At a desk made of improbable angles sat an attractive
middle-aged woman with a spiky platinum crew cut.
Without looking at Andrew, she poked a button with a
gunmetal fingernail, repeated his name, and told him to
have a seat.

Andrew had a seat.

He didn't intend to get into a conversation in the process. But the ponytailed guy already waiting tipped a nod, which Andrew returned. The guy asked if Andrew had the time, which Andrew did. After that, the guy just sort of kept on chatting.

Before long, Andrew found himself leaning forward with his elbows on his knees. He figured he had a few minutes to spare.

"Wait, back up a minute," he said. "Tell me again about the det cord?"

The guy, who had introduced himself as Kyle, claimed to own his own business. *Crash and Burn Productions.* He was—of all things—a special-effects technician for Hollywood.

Andrew couldn't help but enjoy the professional coincidence. By the time Kyle started naming off a few of the movies he'd worked on, Andrew was hooked. He'd actually seen a few of them.

"Okay," Kyle said, re-explaining the type of detonating fuse he'd already described. "It's frequency-activated. Right? *Frequency-activated.* As in, you use padded plastic snips to cut it if you wanna keep all your hands attached."

He waggled his fingers for emphasis. Andrew grinned and shook his head, imagining the scenario.

Kyle said he'd been working on a small-budget horror flick when the incident occurred. According to Kyle, his first mistake had been putting moves on the female day player who had gotten hacked apart in a dormitory shower sequence earlier that morning.

"But come on," he said. "This girl's like twenty-two, and she's stacked, like, bam. Cutest little flirt, right? I'm a human being. So we're on the lot, back of my van. I'm just getting my freak on, and I get a buzz on my pager.

Great. So I climb out and use my cell. For like a minute."
He held his fingers an inch apart. "A *minute*."

Long enough, apparently, for the girl to decide that
when Kyle returned to the van, tying each other up
might be fun. She'd rummaged around amongst his
supplies until she'd found a spool of what she'd believed
to be yellow rope. And a pair of bolt cutters.

"I don't even know how she found the stuff," Kyle
said for the third time. "I keep it in a reinforced trunk.
Wrapped up in blast blankets."

Andrew didn't mean to laugh. "But she's okay?"

"Sonja? Nothing a little vascular surgery couldn't
fix," he said. "If the girl ever gets engaged, okay, she's
probably gonna wear the ring on her other hand. But
I'd say she came through pretty lucky."

"Wow."

"Yeah. And now she's suing me. You believe that?"

"Not so lucky for you," Andrew said.

"Tell me about it. Here I sit. Supposed to meet the
lawyers here for the deposition today." He looked at his
wrist, which still wore no watch, and shrugged. "Guess
I'm early."

Andrew looked up at the big double doors closed on
Lane's office at the end of the short track-lighted hallway opposite the waiting area. He decided that was his
cue. He stuck out his hand.

"Well, hey," he said, "good luck to you. Hope everything works out."

Kyle blew out a breath. "Yeah."

As Andrew strode past the desk on his way toward
Lane's office, the receptionist sat up in her chair and
took the phone away from her ear.

"Sir? Mr. Borland is in a meeting. You need to
wait . . . hey. . . ."

He used both hands, one on each knob, and left the big doors open behind him as he passed through.

Lane sat behind a blond wood desk the size of a basketball court. When Andrew walked in, Lane's eyes snapped open, and he lurched forward. From beneath the desk there came a hollow thud, followed by a muffled yelp.

"Jesus, take it easy," said a female voice.

Lane plunged his hands beneath the desk, glared at Andrew, and said, "What the hell do you think you're doing? Margot!"

Margot—the tall receptionist, Andrew surmised— had followed him into the office. When she saw Lane, her expression flared like a match. Her green eyes smoldered a moment before narrowing to predatory slits. She said: "You sorry son of a bitch."

By the time Andrew turned to agree, Margot had already disappeared in a swirl of citrus perfume.

"Just a minute," Lane whispered to somebody, then hung on to his pants. His fancy black mesh office chair scooted back from the desk as though operating under its own power.

Andrew heard a shifting, another thump, and a soft grunt as a petite young woman with copper-colored spiral curls appeared as if crawling from a cave. She kicked Lane once in the ankle as she smoothed a snug blue minidress over her bottom with one palm. Lane worked to fasten his belt as quickly as he could without standing up from the chair.

Andrew folded his arms and observed the display without comment. The girl gave him a demure sideways glance as she corrected the corner of her lipstick with a fingernail. She had a tiny waist and slender hips and breasts like soccer balls. Andrew couldn't help but notice the padded white club of gauze encasing the girl's left hand from fingertips to mid-forearm. An elaborate framework of pins and wires stood over the bandages like bionic scaffolding.

"You must be Sonja," Andrew said.

She smiled brightly. "That's right! Do we know each other?"

"Nah. But I met your friend Kyle outside."

"Oh."

"He seems like a nice guy. Very regretful."

Lane said, "Sonja, could you excuse us?"

"Excuse you where? I'm not sitting out there with that jerk."

"You can go now." Lane gestured to the open doorway. "Shut the doors on your way out."

Sonja looked at him as though he'd just sprouted a snout and tusks. He looked back at her as if to say, *which word didn't you understand?* She cocked a hip and held it a moment. Then she pivoted like a runway model for surgical hardware. Using her good hand, Sonja slammed Lane's doors one at a time with a force that startled even Andrew.

He turned back to Lane.

"Maybe I'm reading too much into it, but Margot seemed angrier overall," he said. "I guess she considers dictation to be her turf, huh?"

Lane stood and tucked in his shirttails with violent thrusts. "That's very funny."

"Lane, I'm afraid I might end up beating you to death one of these days."

Lane faltered, took one look at Andrew, then wrestled open his middle desk drawer. He retrieved a letter opener and took a step back. "I've got a year and a half of Kenpo, pal. Green belt with a stripe. Don't think I won't defend myself."

Andrew rolled his eyes and walked toward the desk. Lane bent at the knees and tracked him with the blunted point of the letter opener. When Andrew sat down in one of the chairs, Lane relaxed his posture and exhaled.

"Margot's right," Andrew said. "You really are one sorry son of a bitch."

"Your opinion means so much to me I could just shit my pants." Lane tossed the letter opener back into the drawer and pushed the drawer shut with his thigh. "Take your foot off my desk."

Andrew left his foot where it was. "We need to talk, Lane."

"We do?" Lane folded his arms and leaned forward. "What could you and I possibly have to talk about? I said everything I needed to say this morning. When the police came here asking about you."

"The cops came *here*?" Andrew put a hand to his heart. "Asking about *me*? Gosh. I hope you said nice things."

"Oh, Detective Munoz and I had quite a conversation. She had all sorts of questions. I had Margot clear my nine o'clock so we could talk without interruption."

"Civic of you," Andrew said.

On the way over, he'd mentally outlined a basic interrogation plan based on the handful of possible responses he'd expected from Lane. But Lane had already wandered from the script.

When the police came here asking about you. Munoz, he'd said. Who would have been here talking with Lane right about the time Andrew had been talking with Timms at the beach house. Which meant the cops must have gotten Andrew's name somewhere else and split their leads. Assuming Lane was telling the truth.

"So," Andrew said. "What did you and Detective Munoz talk about?"

"You mean when she asked me what I could tell her about a person named Andrew Kindler, did I mention that I just so happened to have a dirtbag criminal by that name living in my house? Oh, never."

"That's a relief."

"Let me tell you something," Lane said. He put his knuckles on the desk and leaned over them. "I don't know what this is about. I don't know what you're involved in."

Andrew thought: *Join the club, you little nerd.*

"And do you know what? I don't give a runny crap. I've been telling Caroline something like this was bound to happen ever since you showed up here. Just a matter of when. Once a dirtbag, always a dirtbag."

"Can't argue with an authority," Andrew said.

"Keep laughing, tough guy." Lane finally sat down in the chair and pressed his lips into a smug, bloodless crease. "Maybe you were the big swinging dick around the neighborhood when we were kids, but you're on my turf now. And your little credit line at Bank of Borland just ran out. I already called your cousin and told her I want you out of the beach house by morning. You're history, Jack."

"You called Caroline? That must have been before your afternoon hum job."

Lane's face reddened in a descending flush, starting at the hairline and deepening all the way to his collar.

"That," he said, "is none of your goddamned business."

"Listen, I'm heading over to see Caroline myself after this. Want me to tell her anything for you?"

"You can tell her anything you want," Lane said. He still looked smug, but his voice had lost a bit of its pomp. "It won't change anything."

"Gee, Lane. You sound so sure."

Lane said nothing to this. But after a long, silent moment, he took his feet off the desk and sat up.

"You want to know what I'm sure about?"

"Do share."

Lane squared his shoulders and looked at Andrew as though he were finally getting the chance he'd been waiting for to get this one thing off his chest.

"Caroline may be your cousin. But she's my wife. And you being here puts her in danger. It's that simple." He raised his empty hands to indicate how simple it was. "She can choose to ignore that if she wants to. I'll just keep looking out for both of us."

Watching him, Andrew suddenly realized that for all his petty, self-obsessed ooze, Lane genuinely believed what he'd just said. Worse: He was right.

Even worse: He knew it.

"Having you in the same family tree is bad enough," Lane said. "But that doesn't mean you hug the goddamned trunk in an electrical storm."

"Good one."

"And if she thinks I'm putting that house on the market with these property values, she's got another think coming. I'll tell you that right now."

"Say," Andrew said. "What's your homeowner's policy on that place, anyway?"

Lane looked at him. "What kind of question is that?"

"Just curious, Lane, that's all."

"None of your business," he said. But he narrowed his eyes. "Why did you ask me that?"

"I'm just concerned. I mean, this weather. Plus that salty air you get out there at the beach. Dries everything out, corrodes that older wiring. And that exterior electrical panel under the deck? The insurance inspector really should have made you reroute that inside. Their mistake, I guess."

"What are you talking about?"

"I'm not talking about anything," Andrew said. "I'm just thinking out loud. I mean, market being what it is, I don't blame you for not wanting to sell the place."

"You might as well stop right there," Lane said. "Because I'm not listening to another word."

"You're the one who keeps bringing up what I used to do for a living, Lane. I'm only trying to be helpful."

"I'm not having this conversation."

"Yeah, I suppose you're right," Andrew said. "With Caroline's name on the title and insurance, she'd end up getting half the payout. In a settlement situation—God forbid you two should ever come to that—that'd mean you'd be out . . . what . . . half a mil or so? That hardly seems fair."

Lane looked at him for a long time, expressionless. By now, his color had drained; his suntan had taken on an ashy cast. "Are you threatening me?"

"Whoa," Andrew said. He held up his palms. "Who's making threats?"

"You wouldn't." Lane straightened in his chair. He seemed to be working out a math problem in his head. "Hell, you *couldn't*."

"Wouldn't, couldn't, let's not get into theoreticals. I just came to see what you and the police talked about. Relax, Lane. We're just a couple of dirtbags here."

"I want you to leave," Lane said quietly.

Andrew shrugged. "It's your turf."

Just before Andrew reached the doors, Lane spoke one last time. It was more a mumble than an assertion.

"I think I deserve to know what you plan to say to Caroline about this."

Andrew paused. Behind the enormous desk, Lane sat with a sag in his shoulders. He looked like a child with adult furniture.

"Tell you what," Andrew said. "You lay off my new buddy Kyle out there, I'll spend some time thinking about it."

7

"ALL I'm sayin'," said Denny Hoyle, "is you'd be a lot happier if you weren't so negative about everything."

"Be a lot happier," Luther Vines told him, "if you quit tellin' me how happy I'm supposed to be."

From where they sat by the door, Luther looked across the soundstage toward Rodney Marvalis. Just the sight of the phony lardass darkened Luther's mood. Marvalis stood with his hands on his hips, chatting up a pair of lycra-wrapped backup chicks left over from the video shoot. Tall curvy blonde, short perky brunette. Stagehands dismantled the set around them. Lenhoff's camera crew had packed up and disappeared an hour ago.

Denny shook his head. "I'm just saying I don't get it is all. The mood lately."

Luther didn't expect Denny to get it. The guy never had a better gig in his whole life than this; he'd been happy as a clam in a butter tub since the day Luther had gotten him the job. Denny had it in his head they were bodyguards for some kind of celebrity. Goofy cracker figured it was bound to get him laid one of these days.

They were glorified babysitters, Luther didn't kid himself. When he'd first heard about the opening over here, he'd mostly just liked the idea of a pay jump and free access to all the top-end workout gear he could use. Few weeks on the job, his delts never looked so good. Triceps? The size of chuck roasts. Eight percent body fat. Plus his own parking spot.

But ever since Rod Marvalis had showed up to take over Gregor Tavlin's spot around here, Luther Vines had started to look at things with a whole new attitude.

"I don't know what you got against the guy," Hoyle said.

Luther snorted. Sometimes he had to wonder how a guy like Denny Hoyle got by.

Couple years back, they'd worked together as bouncers at what at the time had been one of Dominic Sackin's it-spot clubs. At least they'd worked together until the night Denny got fired for busting some hotshot movie producer's head open with a Dos Equis for talking trash.

Denny had gotten lucky; the hotshot had been too embarrassed to press charges, and all that ever came out of it was losing his job. But Luther had always kind of liked that about the guy. No fear. Not a lot of brains, but no fear.

"You want my opinion," Denny muttered, "I think you're just jealous Rod's got his own TV show."

Luther looked at him hard.

"Check him out," Denny said. "Say what you want, but my boy is smooth."

Across the room, blondie tossed her hair and laughed. Marvalis made a picture frame with his hands and sized her with it. She batted at his elbow with her fingertips.

Luther stood. With his right palm on the crown of his smooth scalp, he pulled his head to the side until his neck popped. He rolled his shoulders in a circle.

"Luthe?" Denny said. "Aww, hell."

Luther had already crossed the floor. He said, "That's a wrap, kids."

Marvalis glanced over and flashed the girls his camera grin. "Here's trouble. Ladies, meet Luther Vines. He's big and he's bad. Vines, this is Cammie, and this is Vivian. They're not bad at all. Are you, girls?"

"That depends," said the short one, grinning at Rod.

Vines looked at her. Cammie. Or maybe it was Vivian. He didn't particularly give a rat's ass.

"Gotta have you bad girls clear the facility," he said. "Security policy."

Rod gave him a look, then winked at the girls.

"It's okay, Vines. Cammie and Vivian have backstage passes."

"That a fact."

Rod started explaining how Cammie and Vivian were interested in auditioning for spots on the daily television show.

Luther wasn't listening. He reached forward and jerked the front of Rod's tank top high in one fist. He thought: *You want backstage?* With his other hand, he grabbed the cuff of the neoprene band at Rod's waist and yanked. Velcro gave way with a loud rip. Unfettered, the moist, wrinkled flesh around Rod's midsection quivered briefly, then puddled over his hip bones.

Rod's eyes flew open wide. He grabbed his shirt and tugged it back down. The tall one looked at the short one. The short one just put a hand over her mouth.

"Welcome to the locker room," Vines told them. "Tour's over, y'all. Shake ass."

Cammie and Vivian exchanged looks one more time. Then they checked Luther, dropped their eyes, and retreated to the changing area to grab their gear.

Marvalis snatched the band away and started rolling it into a tight bundle. He'd gone so red he looked purple, and a vein pulsed in his neck. Which made him look, Luther thought, a lot like what he was: a throbbing dickhead.

"You unbelievable *asshole*," he hissed. "What the hell is your problem?"

"No pussy on the job, dog," Luther said. He was starting to feel a little better. "Lawsuits and shit."

"You think this is funny?"

"Take it up with Todman if you got a problem. Just earnin' my pay."

Marvalis looked around and shoved the rolled waist control down the front of his tight black shorts. He glared at the stage guys until they hopped back to work. He glared at Luther.

Luther stepped toward him and crossed his arms.

"Um . . . hey, guys," Denny said. "What's shakin'?"

Marvalis tried to stay eyeball-to-eyeball with Luther, but he couldn't keep the nerve up. So he turned his glare on Denny instead.

Denny said, "Rod, good shoot, man. Hot stuff. How about I go get the car?"

"You do that," Rod said.

Marvalis brushed past Luther with his shoulder. Luther stood solid, and the impact bumped Rod off balance. Marvalis tried to cover, walk off tough, but he was still packing the fatty wrap in his shorts, and it affected his stride. From where Luther and Denny stood, it looked like his ass was screwed on sideways.

Denny looked at Luther, shaking his head.

"Oh, he's smooth," Luther told him, loud enough for Marvalis to hear.

A few feet away, Cammie and Vivian passed by, now decked in cute swishy warm-ups, their club bags looped over their shoulders. Luther happened to catch a snip of the conversation as they whispered to each other on their way toward the exit.

Did he seem kind of out of shape to you? The short one.

Viv. Please. The tall one. *My Hyundai has a smaller spare tire.*

"You know what, Luthe?" said Denny. "When you want, you can be a damn cold guy."

"Guess I'm just jealous," Luther said, smiling for the first time all day.

8

EVEN as kids, Andrew had never been able to fool Caroline completely. It was only one of the things he loved about her.

"Did you really threaten to burn down the beach house?"

"He must have misunderstood my meaning."

She smirked at him. "You two."

"I just needed to know where to find the fuse box. He can be obsessively suspicious, your husband. Sometimes I get the feeling he doesn't like me."

"You could try harder yourself, you know."

"Kiddo, I hate to say it, but I'm starting to think I've tried about as hard as I can."

They sat poking their forks at a large plate of leftover Penne Diavolo that Caroline had rewarmed in a skillet on the stove. From his side of the small wooden table where they shared lunch, Andrew surveyed Caroline's new-and-improved sunroom. She'd spent the weekend making the place over, just because the mood had struck: cheerful new colors, airier spaces, young potted bamboo sprigs growing on high windowsills.

He liked it. Caroline had an undeniable knack for making a room seem like it wanted you in it.

"He's not a bad person, Drew. He's not even a bad husband, all in all."

Andrew tried to hold his tongue. He'd only meddled in Caroline's romantic affairs one time that he could remember, and it had turned out to be a colossally foolish decision in the long run. He'd tried to take a lesson.

Still, he couldn't help but ponder the irony. After all this time, Caroline had ended up with a guy like Lane Borland instead of a guy Andrew had once considered family.

"He's a conniving horndog, and he doesn't deserve you," Andrew told her. "I swear, I don't know why you stay."

"Deserve. Now there's a concept." She chewed her food. "You'll have to tell me all about it sometime."

"Here we go."

"Look, nobody's arguing he's got his flaws. He's not perfect, believe me, I know. But I'm not Aunt Shirley, God rest her. As for Lane . . . come on. Whatever Lane might be, he isn't your dad."

Andrew took a pause at that one, surprised by this uncharacteristic turn in her usual sphinx-like rhetoric where her husband was concerned. Caroline only shrugged and waited.

"First of all," he said, "the sorry prick you must be talking about wasn't my dad. You know that."

"He adopted you when you were born, Drew. He might as well have been. He was a sorry prick, no argument. I wish he'd gone away sooner. That isn't the point."

"Then why bring it up?"

"Because I always get this feeling you're making some kind of comparison that isn't really fair." She quickly held up her palm. "Don't even bother, I know you think I'm full of it. But give me some credit. I'm aware that Lane has issues, okay? There are things he does."

Caroline scraped a bite off her fork with her teeth and pointed at him with the tines.

"But there's plenty he doesn't do. He doesn't drink. Not so you'd notice, anyway. He doesn't gamble. He doesn't yell. And he'd jump in front of a bus before he raised a hand to me."

"That puts him in the running for hubby of the year? Those aren't credentials, Care. They're prerequisites."

"Okay. But you don't know him. Not really."

"That's funny. He says you tell him the same thing about me."

"He doesn't listen, either."

Andrew rolled his eyes.

"Do you want to know what I think? I don't think it's even about you with Lane. I mean, you've always intimidated him, that's no big secret. But that's only part of it."

"My favorite part."

"Make fun if you want to. But I think what it really boils down to is, you're like this constant reminder of the Lane he wants to believe he put behind years ago. All of this?" She swept her hand around her head, indicating the redecorated sunroom, but more: the room, the house, the Brentwood address, the bean-shaped swimming pool landscaped into the backyard. "This is Lane trying to prove how far beyond that person he's grown. But here you come, back from the old neighborhood. The place where he felt like this inadequate little reject growing up. He'd never admit it, but it's the truth. And you remind him that the neighborhood didn't disappear. He just doesn't happen to live there anymore."

Caroline obviously meant for him to understand what she was trying to explain, so Andrew resisted the urge to scoff.

Back home, the Borland family had lived next door to Caroline and Aunt Judy, his mother's sister. Which made them Andrew's neighbors for a while, when Mom and Aunt Judy had combined what remained of their respective households after the fire. Aunt Judy had been widowed going on six years by then; it had been just her and Caroline since Uncle Phil died of bone cancer, and they'd had plenty of room to spare. After the fire, it only made sense to go to Aunt Judy's. Andrew had been fourteen at the time, Caroline almost nine.

As for Lane—the kid from Caroline's grade the next row house over—Andrew didn't think the neighborhood had been his biggest problem. Lane Borland's biggest problem was that he'd never quite figured out how to be a neighbor. Or a hood. It helped if you could be a little of both, but you at least had to be one or the other.

Andrew couldn't even remember noticing the kid had gone off to college until he came back for Thanksgiving one year, a big shot from California, and surprised everybody by sweeping Caroline off her feet.

"I don't care why Lane doesn't like me," Andrew said. "I'm talking about how he treats you."

"And don't think I don't love you for it. But you don't know everything." She pointed again with the fork. "Would you like to know how much Lane donated to the shelter last year?" She was talking about one of the many organizations for which she volunteered: a safe house in Gardena for battered women and their children. "I think you'd be surprised."

"So he gets 'philandering' and 'philanthropy' confused sometimes. Big deal."

"Clever you. But I'll tell you something. Lane helped keep that place operating last year. And just for the record, wifey never asked him to contribute a dime."

"Let's talk about something else."

"My pleasure." Caroline finally put down her silverware and faced him. "It's time you stopped stalling anyway. Tell me what's going on."

He'd already told her that an LAPD detective had been around to visit that morning. She'd heard a similar story from Lane. Andrew decided not to fill her in on what few details remained, at least not for now. He didn't see the point.

"Is it bad?"

"I have no idea what it is," he said.

She didn't say anything.

"But until I find out, I want you to do something for me."

"Anything I can. You know that."

He reached around his back, pulled the Glock from his waistband, placed it on the table, and slid it across. He'd stopped by the bank again on his way to Brentwood. For the clip this time.

"I want you to keep this somewhere handy."

Caroline looked at the gun. She looked at Andrew. She raised her eyebrows.

"I don't want to argue about it, Care. You said you took that class at Lane's gun club, right? So you probably know more about how to run one of these than I do."

"There's nothing to argue about," she said. "Because

I'm not touching that thing. God, what are you thinking, carrying a gun around?"

"Do we really have to make a production out of
this?"

"Apparently. Because you obviously know more than
you're telling me, and I want to hear it. Right now."

"I *don't* know more than I'm telling you," Andrew
said. "That's what bothers me. Something's definitely
cooking. If it was going to get bad, my guess is it would
have gotten bad already." He shook his head. "But things
aren't adding up. So take the gun until I get it sorted.
And if somebody you don't know comes to the door,
looking for me . . ."

"I don't like the sound of this. What did the police
want to talk to you about?"

Andrew said nothing. After a beat, he reached out
and slid the gun toward her another inch.

"I already told you," she said.

He looked her in the eye. "You're the one who convinced me to come out here."

An opposite coast, she'd argued. *It's symbolic. Besides. If
you really want to start over? Become something new? Sweetie,
where else but L.A.? This town reinvents everybody.*

"And I'm delighted you did," she said. "But if this is
your idea of a thank-you gift, let me give you two
words for future reference: pearl earrings."

"Please." He nodded once toward the Glock. "For
me."

Caroline eyed him across the table for a long time.
Eventually, she looked at the gun again. "This would
make you feel better."

"Not better enough. But better than nothing."

"I'll say it one more time for the record. I don't like
this. Not one bit."

"I know."

Caroline watched him. She glanced again at the gun. After a minute of silence, the corner of her mouth twitched.

"What's the matter?"

"Nothing," she said. "I was just imagining the look on Lane's face when he sees me cleaning a handgun when he gets home."

Andrew grinned back at her. "That's my girl."

9

BUT he kind of wished he still had the gun when he finally returned to the beach house after dark.

The faint smell of leather was Andrew's first clue that he had company. That, and the light that turned on when he came in.

He hadn't bothered flipping any switches; he'd come straight up from the garage and headed toward the kitchen, making his way by the last of the dusky light still seeping in through the blinds. He was tired. He wanted a beer.

He stopped in his tracks instead, car keys still in hand.

Reading lamp. The one beside Caroline's antique wooden rocker near the dark empty fireplace. Andrew identified the source by the sound of the pull chain, the low-wattage corona suddenly rimming the boundaries of his peripheral view.

He tensed, mind suddenly roaring. He tried to imagine the layout of the space behind him. He prepared to move.

"Torch," a familiar voice said. "I was starting to think you weren't ever coming home."

10

A mean Baltimore night, cold and wet.

Torch stood outside a warehouse down by the docks. A razor wind raked his back, spun salt and spring frost through his hair. He stared at the grimy door for almost twenty minutes before he finally took a breath and grabbed the handle. Rusty wheels wailed in their tracks as he slid the big door open and stepped on through.

He heard the hammer clicks a half-second before he felt cool metal pressed in three places against the back of his skull.

"Blink," somebody behind him said. "Wiggle something."

The place smelled like oil, dust, wet steel. A single fire burning in a trash barrel provided the only light inside. Slowly, Torch raised his hands where he stood.

First came silence. Then a laugh.

"Man, we figured you was stupid. But this settles it."

Without turning his head, Torch spoke to the gun under his left ear. "How you doing, Louis?"

"Better'n you, I guess."

Torch said, "Guess so."

Something popped inside the trash barrel and pinged against the can's metal hide. Flames lapped above the rim, trailing acrid smoke toward the high open windows above. As Torch's eyes adjusted to the dimness, he could see the rest of the crew hanging in the shadows, slouched against shelving and crates.

The tallest of them straightened and detached from the others.

"Look who's here," Eyebrow Larry said, stepping out of the flickering gloom and into the light of the fire.

They called him Eyebrow because he had only one left. Torch had burned off the other himself with a Zippo, and it never had grown back.

It was hard to believe they'd once been like brothers, but it was true. He and Larry had watched each other's backs and rambled together for years. All that remained of those days now was the legendary pale twist of scar above Larry's left eye.

"Thanks for meeting me."

"Get to the point, Torchie. This is getting boring fast."

Torch dropped his hands. "I'm out. For good. That's not what I came to tell you, I just figured you'd be interested to know."

"I'm interested to know where you scored whatever you were smoking when you decided it'd be a good idea to come down here just to say hey."

Torch heard chuckles from the boys with the guns behind him.

"'Cause I gotta tell you, Torch." Larry crossed his

arms. "You got me a little concerned for your mental shit right about now."

"Save it. I'm only here because I never told you I was sorry for burning off your eyebrow that time." He shrugged. "That whole thing . . . that just got out of hand."

The snickers started again behind him, this time spreading to the peanut gallery like an oil fire. Larry just shook his head.

"Retiring," he said. "You don't say."

"I do."

"Mama Mingo know that yet?"

"I assume she'll put it together eventually."

Larry nodded along. Torch waited patiently.

"So, what? Gonna move to Florida? Open up a bait shop? Screw cocktail waitresses?"

"Something like that."

"And you just woke up and decided this, I guess."

"It's been a while coming," Torch said.

"Burnout's a bitch, huh?"

More snickers from the shadows.

"I'm just getting out. That's all."

To this, Larry offered the thinnest of grins. "Hate to be the one to say it, Torch. But you ought to know better than that by now."

"That's not my name anymore. The rest is my problem."

"Bold words coming from a guy who just crossed his own name off the protected species list."

"This doesn't have anything to do with that."

"You don't think?"

A long moment passed.

"Look. I just wanted to tell you I was sorry. It needed to be said. I said it."

At first, he'd thought Larry's nod was for him. But then he felt the muzzles lift from his scalp. All around the warehouse, Larry's crew erupted with loud hoots and gibes.

Torch watched his old pal Larry take off his long leather coat and drop it in a pile by his boot.

A hand shoved Torch forward. He tripped on his own feet but managed to untangle himself before he went down. Somebody howled; somebody else echoed. Soon the warehouse thrummed with the sound of fists pounding on shipping crates all around the fire can.

Torch tuned out the noise. He concentrated on not falling down. When he finally recovered his balance, he couldn't help but note the Louisville Slugger on which Larry now leaned.

"Well, hey," Eyebrow Larry said, kicking up the ball bat with a boot heel and giving it a twirl. "We got history. I appreciate the fact you came forward."

As if to prove it, Larry reached around behind him and found a pair of pliers in the back pocket of his jeans.

For the sake of history, Andrew assumed, he'd pulled most of the nails out of the slugging end of the bat first.

"Lawrence."

In the darkness of the living room, low golden lamplight illuminated half of the last face in the world Andrew expected to find waiting for him at the end of this long, outrageous day.

The eyebrow half got the light; the other half remained in shadow. The unmistakable grin overlapped both hemispheres.

"Gee, Torch. Try not to sound so happy to see me."

"You should have called first."

"Yeah, funny thing. You don't seem to be listed."

Andrew's left hand began to ache; he realized he'd instinctively made a fist around his keyring, arranging the keys so that they poked out between his knuckles. He relaxed his grip. But not completely.

"How long have you been in town?"

Black leather creaked as Larry shifted. "Few days."

Andrew said nothing to that. The coat Larry wore looked new and expensive. Andrew could still smell the leather from where he stood. He kept standing there.

Larry glanced toward the pulled window shades to his right. "What's that street above the highway? Palm trees all up and down both sides? Runs next to a little park with a footpath through it, has a railing so you don't fall off the cliff?"

"Ocean Avenue."

"Ocean. I guess that makes sense." Larry scratched his nose. "You might want to have a peek out the window. Couple plainclothes types up there with binocs. I think they might be watching you."

Andrew had already spotted the men Larry meant. One white, one black, both in jeans and short-sleeved weekender shirts. It wasn't the weekend. He'd bought a sandwich and a paperback novel and watched them from a distant park bench for most of the afternoon and evening. After they'd ridden out the sunset without vacating their position, Andrew had finally given up and vacated his.

So the cops were staking out the beach house. He didn't see much to be done about it. Except maybe wave, if he saw them again tomorrow.

"I went ahead and let myself in around the other side," Larry said. "Don't think they saw me from up there, but you never know."

"I take it the alarm system didn't give you much trouble."

Larry smirked. "You trying to hurt my feelings?"

"How'd you find the place?"

"That Laney Borland," Larry said, shaking his head. "I guess the little shit hasn't done so bad for himself out here in La La Land. Two addresses on the property rolls, and each of 'em almost a million tax value apiece. Go figure."

"I'm still trying to figure out what you're doing here."

Eyebrow Larry Tomiczek drummed his thumbs on the wide wooden arms of the chair.

"You know," he said, "I came three thousand miles to see you, and you still haven't even said hello."

"What do you want, Larry?"

Larry smiled. "That all depends what you got to drink around here."

On his way west, Andrew had heard a psychologist on some A.M. talk-radio program use a phrase that wound up sticking in his aching brain.

He'd been in the car at the time, trancing to the whine of tires on asphalt, the bone-white reach of highway in his high beams. This was several hours past the desolate beauty of the Nebraska Sandhills, the scrubby dunes and stubby derricks of northeastern Colorado behind him, Denver's pale glow low in the sky ahead, Los Angeles still two sunsets away. His broken ribs had yet to heal, and the stiletto ache still spiked his breath. The deep gashes at his eye and mouth and jaw still seeped hot, watery red fluid between the butterfly strips holding them closed.

Family of choice. That was the phrase the radio therapist had used. Forget the old saying about not being able to choose your family, the therapist had been telling the caller on the line; when it comes down to it, all families are bound by choice, not genetic code. Most of us happen to choose our blood relatives, or at least choose not to choose otherwise. Some of us choose to mix and match until some other combination works. Some of us even choose to sever all ties and start fresh, embracing our people where we find them. But we always choose.

It had been a notion Andrew couldn't help but ponder as he chewed his way through the miles. He found himself imagining the many possible ways things might have turned out differently if he and Larry had started out as brothers in the traditional sense of the term. If nothing else, being blood siblings almost certainly would have prevented the specific disagreement that had done them in.

It seemed silly, looking back at more than a decade in the rearview mirror.

The irony? Caroline—seventeen going on thirty back then—had already broken it off with Larry herself by the time Andrew had discovered through the grapevine that the two of them had been carrying on.

Of course Andrew hadn't known this the day he found Larry at their regular spot outside Warek's. Larry, because he was Larry, hadn't volunteered the information.

He'd simply given Andrew a canary-feather smirk, admitted, yeah, he'd been meaning to come clean about a couple things. Should have said something sooner about what had been going on between him and Caroline, never really planned it in the first place, but still. Wasn't right, keeping it quiet. It really had been bugging him. What could he say?

You can say so long, Casanova, Andrew had informed him. Because there's no way you're going out with my cousin. A: She's just a kid. B: She's going to college, not staying around this neighborhood. C: What's the matter with you?

He still remembered the way Larry had looked at him. Surprised. Slightly amused.

He'd said:

First of all, Caroline's no kid. Second of all, you'd think it'd set a guy at ease, seeing family with his oldest pal instead of some punk he didn't even know. Three, mind your own fucking business.

Andrew mentioned something about the problem being that his oldest pal happened to *be* a punk.

The conversation basically went off the rails from there.

Andrew hadn't intended for things to go loud with Larry right there on the sidewalk outside Warek's at three o'clock in the afternoon. He probably should have known better. So much for hindsight.

Once it was on, it was on. They'd made a mess of the place: clumsy, bullish, unstoppable. At one point, Andrew managed to find himself on the doling end of a headlock—but he was no match for Larry in a fair fight, and the tables had been about to turn. He remembered being flat on his back against a sewer grate, about to lose his hold. When Larry had begun to find leverage against the curb with his boots, Andrew had known he was through.

That was when he'd remembered the lighter in his jacket pocket . . .

. . . and so went up, in a sudden sizzle and a brief

stink of singed hair and skin, a friendship that went all the way back to the days when they'd still been grade school paperboys, delivering envelopes for the previous generation of guys who'd held down the chairs outside Warek's Café.

It had been a problematic situation, fraught with complications on many levels. Despite Andrew's fighting words, Larry Tomiczek was no punk. By then, Larry was known all over the harbor and beyond as the youngest guy ever to run his own crew for Cedric Zaganos. Technically, Larry had been Andrew's superior.

By nightfall, word of their tangle had spread to the far reaches of the kingdom and its rivals. The story was already mutating into different versions of itself, each one grander and gorier than the last.

Nobody but Andrew and Larry had known the pitiful truth about what had really sparked their rumble that day. Andrew had only gotten the better end because the cops had cleared the place before things could get any uglier. But the truth wouldn't have changed the reality of the situation.

Because losing an eyebrow was one thing. Losing face was something else entirely, and the thing at Warek's had been bad all around. Bad for Larry, bad for the organization. Very bad for Andrew, considering Larry rightfully had the organization on his side.

He'd given his friend little choice. Andrew had understood that even then. A guy in Larry's position didn't stay a guy in Larry's position by letting business like what had happened at Warek's slide. Friends were friends, but the food chain ruled.

Andrew had woken up the next morning hiding under a phony name in a Motel 6 near the airport. As for choices, under the circumstances he'd counted only two.

In Baltimore, the Zaganos organization dominated half the waterfront, plus anything worth dominating in the West that wasn't directly controlled by New York. Cedric Z had only one important competitor: a 260-pound sociopath named Henrietta Mingo, who controlled the other half of the waterfront and ran the rackets in East Baltimore. Inheritor of the organization her infamous father Henry had built, Henrietta Mingo had been successfully recruiting away Zaganos employees for years.

So Andrew—suddenly out of work, faced with the prospect of spending his days scanning the horizon for signs of Larry—had decided to make things easier for everybody.

He'd joined those who had already defected, exchanging asylum for what turned out to be more than a decade of indentured servitude to the scariest fairy godmother in all Baltimore.

Maybe you really did choose your family. But that didn't mean you always had appealing options.

"By the way, it's hotter than hell out here." Larry perched on a stool at the breakfast bar and sipped at the bourbon Andrew had poured. Two glasses, three fingers each, both neat. "The travel guide said seventy-five and sunny all year round."

"Did the travel guide recommend anything in terms of beachwear?"

"I didn't read that far. Why?"

"No reason."

"I get it." Larry tugged a black leather lapel and smoothed it with his fingers. "Like the skin? I bought it special for the trip. Figured I'd try to look like I fit in with all the movie stars."

"You look like a Polack goombah."

Larry held out a sleeve, considered it.

"Maybe you're right. I should borrow something of yours." He gestured with his drink. "Nice pants you got on there, J. Crew. Retired a couple months and already shopping outta the yuppie catalogs, huh?"

Andrew leaned against the corner of the refrigerator. "You never answered my question."

"Sorry, what was it again? I forgot."

Andrew sipped his whiskey.

"Oh, right. What am I doing here. That's easy." Larry made a gesture with his hand, pantomiming the act of aiming a remote control at a television. "I just turned on CNN, saw California was on fire, and thought to myself, hey, what do you know? The Torch must have gone to visit his cousin. Pretty simple from there. I just followed the smoke."

"Hilarious."

"Don't worry. Nobody else is coming to visit, if that's what you're wondering."

"All I'm wondering right now," Andrew said, "is why did you?"

Larry took a sip. Then he grinned and said, "Turns out life's got a sense of humor."

Andrew stood by, wondering when Larry was going to decide to let him in on the joke.

"And you owe me a favor," Larry said.

"I don't know how you're keeping score. By my count, you and me are just about even."

"You still owe me, by mine."

"You'll have to explain how you figure that."

Larry finished his first round and brought himself an-other from the bottle Andrew had left on the counter. He held the bottle up; Andrew declined by raising his glass, still two fingers full. Or one finger empty, depending on your viewpoint.

"What I said before? About nobody else coming to visit?" Larry tilted his head. "Why do you think that is?"

"Not worth the trouble, I assume."

"Man. I swear, Torchie. Only you." Larry took the top off his freshened drink and shook his head. "When you walked in naked that night and said you were quits, I figured you must be dumber than I realized. But in a million years, I never thought you'd be dumb enough to skip town with the advance cash from three open jobs. I gotta be honest, there's a part of me still doesn't believe it."

"Those were back wages," Andrew said. "Compensation for time served."

"Yeah, well, the way I heard it, Mama Mingo called it your hide. You may be dumb, but I don't think you're so dumb you expected that big greasy psycho to let a thing like that slide." Larry arched his eyebrow. "And I know you ain't so dumb to think I'm the only guy bright enough to figure the most likely place to start looking for your dumb ass."

What remained of the money still waited in the safety-deposit box at California Federal. Every last large bill of it, neatly bundled and stacked. Andrew had convinced himself he'd needed it if he really planned to make a fresh start, convinced himself he deserved it for all the earnings Henrietta Mingo had gouged from his cut over the years.

But he still didn't know what had possessed him to take the money with him. Probably the same reason he'd risked putting Caroline in harm's way, coming here to hide.

There had been a time not long ago when Andrew simply had not been thinking clearly.

"Call me sentimental," Larry said. "But I didn't let you keep breathing just so that fat bag Mingo could save you the trouble."

"Am I supposed to know what you're talking about?"

"All you need to know is some business got settled. We can leave it there."

Some business got settled. Andrew didn't know what that meant. He didn't know if he wanted to know. As he stood there, looking at Larry, sudden waves of conflicting sentiment began to lap at his conscience. He knocked back the whiskey in his glass and poured a refill.

"I never asked you to settle my business."

"What are friends for?"

"Jesus."

"Nah. Just me."

Andrew looked into the bottom of the glass and pondered the amber liquid there. For some reason, just then, the bourbon reminded him of nothing so much as kerosene. He stood there looking at it for a long while.

"By the way," Larry said. He peered inside his own glass as if wondering what was so interesting. "Last time you and me saw each other, wasn't really the time and place, right, but just so you know. I was . . . shit. I was sorry to hear about your ma."

It was the last thing Andrew expected to hear out of Larry at that particular moment, and it caught him off guard.

"Thanks," he said.

"She was some lady. Shoulda had more time."

"Yeah."

Andrew didn't know what else there was to say about it. She'd had a bad heart, that was all. It was hardly a surprise. God only knew it had been broken enough times.

"Things had been different, I would have been to the funeral," Larry said. "Whatever. Stopped by the cemetery once, paid my respects. You picked her out a nice stone."

"You should tell Henrietta Mingo," Andrew said. "She paid for it."

Larry chuckled at that.

"She always wished you and me had patched things up," Andrew told him. He didn't know why he suddenly felt the need. "Mom. She told me that once, toward the end."

Larry nodded. Then he just sat there for a minute or two.

"Wanna ask you something," he finally said.

"Yeah."

"That the reason you decided to come down the docks that night like the dumbest mutt in the free world?"

"Does it really matter?"

Larry shrugged. "Not really."

They sat awhile longer, listening to the surf, the hum of the refrigerator motor kicking in. Somewhere beyond the walls, they heard the brief distant Doppler effect of a car shooting PCH with its top down, stereo system pumping a drum-and-bass line like an amplified pulse. Neither of them said much of anything.

Andrew finally looked Larry in the eye.

"This business you settled. How much territory did it cost you?"

"Enough."

"I want to know."

"That ain't important."

"It is to me."

"Then you and Cedric got at least one thing in common." Larry grinned and drank. "Which brings us back to that favor you owe me."

Andrew sighed and finally took a stool. He reached for the bottle, poured another for each of them, and asked the same question once again.

"What are you doing here, Larry?"

One of these times, he figured he was bound to get an answer.

But Larry only said, "Hey. You been to Disneyland yet?"

"What does that have to do with anything?"

"I was just thinking about that ride they got there. Too bad I don't have more time. We could go check it out for laughs."

As he took a fresh sip, Larry began humming a tune. When Andrew finally placed the melody, he shook his head, crossed his arms, settled in.

And waited for Eyebrow Larry to explain exactly how it had turned out to be a small world after all.

11

"Guess what day it is?"

On the other end of the line, she cleared her sleep-croaked throat. It sounded like music.

"Hello?"

"Heather." He gave her another moment to absorb his voice. "I woke you."

"Todd?"

"Hey, sleepyhead."

"What time is it?"

"I have . . . let's see . . . midnight-oh-two. Sorry: oh-three."

"Is there news? Todd? Did somebody hear from David?"

At the bedside phone in his Westwood condo, Todd Todman sipped Beaujolais. He said, "Sweetie, I'm sorry.

There's no word. I didn't mean to put you on pins and needles."

In the pause on her end, he could hear the rustle of bedsheets. Satin? Silk?

"Todd?"

"Right here."

"Why are you calling me?"

"Hey. Somebody around here has to remember a girl's birthday, don't they?"

"Tell me you're joking."

"Did you really think I'd forget?"

"You? Todd, *I* even forgot I was thirty today. Thanks for waking me up just to depress me."

"Forget that," Todd said. "Thirty is sensational on you."

Her yawn: a symphony.

"You're sweet, Todd. I'm going back to sleep now."

"You do that, birthday girl. Just do me a favor: when you wake up, remember that you have plans for the evening."

"Mmm. Me, a tub of Häagen-Dazs, and a stack of John Cusack DVDs."

"Sorry. I'm taking you out."

"Are you, now?"

"Well, I would have brought your birthday present to you, but it was already booked."

"It's a little early in the morning for riddles, my friend." Another yawn.

"Okay, okay, have it your way, I'll blow the big surprise." He sipped more wine. "I was going to get you that Sam Phillips box set you wanted, then I found out she's playing Royce Hall this week. So I got tickets instead. Double C, right in the middle. We'll have some food at Le Dome first. What do you think?"

"I think my father pays you too much." Her voice had gone drowsy again. "If you're wasting your money on my stupid birthday."

"Listen, these past couple of weeks have been a hell of a strain for everybody. I know. But it's your birthday. I'm not going to let you spend it alone."

"Mm."

"I'll pick you up at the house around six. Okay?"

Heather Lomax said nothing.

He waited.

Silence.

Todd listened closely. After a few moments, he understood why Heather wasn't answering. He could just hear her on the other end of the line; her breathing had grown deep and regular.

She'd fallen back to sleep.

He took this as a yes. Todd smiled.

"Sweet dreams," he whispered.

Then he hung up the phone, finished his wine, turned out the lights, and slipped into dreams of his own.

"Luthe, you know, it ain't much fun for either of us if you ain't even gonna *try* and win your money back."

When Luther failed to acknowledge him, Denny Hoyle finally gave up and slouched over to the booth. He planted his pool cue in front of him and leaned on it.

Around them, there weren't but three or four other bodies taking up space, all of them regular as the furniture. Except for the usual chatter from the crappy television mounted on the wall behind the bar, and a little Marvin Gaye on the jukebox in the corner, the place was mostly quiet. Rudy's, being the shithole it was, was mostly quiet most of the time. Which was one of the reasons Denny and Luther came mostly to Rudy's when they wanted to have a few pops and shoot some pool at the end of a long day on the job.

God only knew they didn't come for the billiards. Denny was willing to bet that if they tried their hardest, they wouldn't be able to find a pool table in all Los Angeles County in worse shape than the scroungy, off-sized, coin-op beast Rudy Watson claimed. It had cigarette burns in the felt and cracks in the slate. You had to put bar coasters under one of the feet to account for the tilt, and you had to replace them every other game. Plus all Rudy's cue sticks were warped.

But Luther always picked Rudy's because it was close to his apartment in Inglewood, and Denny didn't usually care enough to argue about it. The fact was, on any kind of table, any kind of night, he could generally make an evening out of whipping Luther's ass when it came to shooting pool.

Except Luther wasn't doing much shooting tonight. For the past hour he'd just been sitting there in the booth, bulging in his tight blue cycle shirt and black Nike track pants, hunched over some kind of project involving the strangest bunch of materials Denny had seen anytime recently.

He finally had to ask. "You ever gonna tell me what exactly you're doing?"

Not a word.

"Come on, man, it's been your turn for like half an hour. You're solids. I spotted you two."

Luther just held up a narrow strip of leather and looked at it. He turned the strip this way and that way. Then he put it down in front of him and went back to work on it.

"Luthe."

"My stick's busted."

Denny looked at the cue stick Luther had left propped against the end of the booth. "Hell, it ain't either."

Without looking at him, Luther swung out from the table, grabbed the stick, took it in both hands, and snapped it in half over his knee with one quick crack.

From over behind the bar, Rudy stopped telling stories about the last Malibu fire, glared toward the back, and said, "Goddammit, Vines, I told you to quit that. That motherfucker's going on your tab."

Luther sent back a dark look that caused Rudy to scowl, mutter something, and turn back to his fire stories and mug wiping.

Luther handed the pieces of the busted stick to Denny. "Happy?"

Denny rolled his eyes and gave up. He went over and racked his own stick, tossed Luther's broken cue onto the table, came back to the booth, and slid in the other side. He debated commenting on Luther's mood but decided against it. He folded his arms and watched quietly.

Earlier in the day, after work, they'd walked to get tacos from the mobile stand they'd noticed the day before, one of those private rigs that had gotten a permit to come in and serve the workers at a construction site near the club. On their way past the barricades, Luther had noticed a hardhat sitting upside down on the packed dirt next to a Thermos bottle, presumably left there by one of the *hermanos* gone off to the nearby row of porta-crappers. For some reason Denny couldn't fathom, Luther had held up. He'd told Denny to keep a lookout while he went over, ducked under the chain, grabbed the hardhat, and carried it with them to the taco stand.

First thing he did with the hat was put it on his head

and score a Steelworkers Local #412 discount on a chicken chimichanga combo plate.

But that, apparently, wasn't why he'd wanted the hat. Denny didn't really start to figure this out until after they'd finished eating and headed back to the club for Luther's car.

Luther carried the hardhat all the way back with them and tossed it in the trunk of the Buick. Before heading over to La Cienega and taking it south, he swung by the Ralph's on Sunset and picked up two items: a slender chain-link dog leader with a leather loop for your wrist, and a roll of duct tape.

Into the trunk they went, alongside the hardhat.

On their way to Rudy's, Luther swung by a hardware store for a few more things: a utility razor, two pairs of pliers, a pop rivet set, and a rotary punch.

All of which now littered the scarred table between them. Denny looked at the scuffed yellow hardhat, which Luther had discarded after ripping out the adjustable plastic head strap from inside.

"Seriously. What you doing?"

"Ain't done doin' it yet."

From what Denny could see so far, Luther had used the utility knife to cut the leather loop from the dog chain into two equal lengths. Using the punch and the rivet tool, he'd already attached one of the leather pieces to the hardhat liner. Denny watched quietly as Luther attached the other leather strip directly opposite the first, creating what looked to Denny like a halo brace with sideburns.

Luther held up the whatever-it-was and checked it over. He gave a hard tug on each leather strap. Seeming satisfied, he grabbed the big roll of duct tape, skinned off a long strip, tore it with his teeth, and started wrapping.

Denny called over to the bar and ordered himself another beer.

He got the feeling they were going to be there awhile.

———————————

It was after one in the morning when Denny noticed that Luther had stopped fiddling with the dog chain. A half dozen empty, uncollected longnecks crowded the table on Denny's side of the booth. Luther, like always, had been drinking nothing but plain water, no ice. He was all focused and intense, which lately pretty much described Luther all the time. He'd been working on the dog chain with the pliers. Now he sat still, a pair of pliers in each hand, like he'd grown a set of drop-forged pincers.

Denny yawned and looked up to find Luther glaring at the television behind the bar. He recognized the voice coming out of the set at about the same time he noticed the vein bulging in Luther's forehead.

Denny sighed.

Programming had gone to infomercials. On the television, Rod Marvalis showed how you could get a rock-hard six-pack in just ten minutes a day using the only product on the market that carried the Maximum Health guarantee.

Many times as he'd seen the crazy thing, Denny still couldn't help but get sucked in. Because normally you had to do, like, twelve different exercises to get the same results. Or you could do your bod a favor and order The Abdominator™. It was light as a feather. It was durable as a dump truck. It folded up so you could keep it just about anywhere. It was so revolutionary you couldn't even believe it. And if you ordered now, you got a special

bonus DVD where Rod Marvalis personally demon-
strated the five basic movements that led to Maximum
Abs or your money back.

As they watched, Denny thought he heard a growl
rattle up from deep in Luther's big muscular chest. He
started gathering up empty bottles from the table, looking around for anything else within Luther's reach that
might be breakable. To Rudy, he called, "Yo, Rudimus.
Can't you find anything else to watch on that thing?"

Soggy bar towel over one shoulder, Rudy looked up
from the tap, where he pulled a beer to go with the shot
he'd already set up for one of the burnouts at the bar.

"Remote's up here where it always is," he said.
"Come change it yourself."

"Leave it," Luther said.

"Luthe. You gotta quit with this already. I told you, it
ain't healthy."

"Said leave it."

Denny shook his head as Luther went back to work
on the chain.

Fifteen numbing minutes later, Luther seemed to be
finished with his big masterpiece. Dog chains jingling,
he handed the whole perverted contraption across the
booth.

"Yo," he said. "You wanna help so bad, try this on."

Denny looked at the apparatus Luther had devised:
the head harness from the hardhat, every inch wrapped
in silver tape, with the dog chain hanging down from
the leather strips connected to either side.

"The hell is that supposed to be?"

"Just put it on your head."

"Um, no thanks."

"You want in on this idea I got or not?"

Looking at Luther's rig, Denny honestly couldn't

answer the question. But he finally took the thing out of Luther's hand, looked it over, and carefully settled it over his skull. The dog chain hung in a Y shape, looping under his chin with the tail nearly reaching his sternum. The harness wobbled against his crown.

"I feel like a gonad."

"Just fit it up with that knob there on the back."

Denny sighed and did as he was instructed, reaching back to twist the knob until the headband tightened to a snug fit. It wasn't totally uncomfortable.

"Now gimmee some resistance," Luther said.

"Say what?"

"Just hold your neck tight."

Denny still didn't know what Luther meant. But before he could say so, Luther reached across, grabbed the straight length of the chain, and pulled down hard. Denny's head bobbled on his neck. He braced himself with his hands on the table and tried to pull back, but Luther yanked too hard. Denny had enough time to see the table rising up to meet him before his forehead bounced off the rough wood between his hands. Empty Bud bottles clattered together.

"Hey!"

Luther let go of the chain, chuckling. Denny sat up, rubbing his forehead.

"What the hell?"

"See there? Works better'n I thought."

"Damn, dude. That ain't even funny."

"It was kinda funny."

"Yeah? Put this fucker on your head, we'll see how funny it is."

"Told you to give me some resistance." Luther motioned with his hand. "Give it here, Crash Test. I gotta tweak me a couple things."

Denny yanked off the stupid hat harness and tossed it back at Luther, still massaging his head. When he noticed a little smear of blood on his index finger, he touched the spot again, came back with another smear, then grabbed the napkin holder from the table and looked at his reflection in the metal.

"God*damn*," he said, pulling out a wad of napkins and dabbing the small gouge at his hairline.

Luther frowned, looked at Denny's head, then ran his finger around the inside of the headband.

"My bad," he said, showing Denny an exposed metal flange from one of the pop rivets he'd used to attach the leather straps.

"I don't believe this shit," Denny said. He felt a little bit like bouncing the heavy napkin holder off the top of Luther's shiny black dome.

But he waited for the urge to pass. He'd never gone around with Luther before, and he didn't see the point in getting it on over something as stupid as this. They were pretty much buds.

"It ain't nothing," Luther said. "Scratch is all."

"Yeah? You can scratch my ass. You happen to notice I'm bleeding?"

"So it ain't quite refined yet."

Denny pursed his lips and grumbled, pressing the napkins against his head. While Rod Marvalis showed a babe in an electric blue bikini how to use The Abdominator in the comfort of her own bedroom, Luther went back to examining his invention.

Suddenly, holding his napkins and watching, Denny began to get a vague idea of what Luther might be up to. He looked at Rod Marvalis up on the television. He looked at Luther.

He said, "Now this is just getting sad."

"Hand me over that tape."

"Tell me you don't think anybody's gonna actually try and sell that little torture rig you got there on TV," Denny said. "I can't even tell what you'd want it for. Outside some kinda crazy sex-dungeon shit."

"Tape."

"Here's your tape." Denny slapped the big roll into Luther's hand. "But I'm saying it this one time. You, big buddy, got issues. Oughta have that shit looked at 'fore it causes you trouble."

Luther tore of a length of tape and went hunting for more exposed rivets.

"I mean, what?" Denny said. "So Rod's a personality and you ain't. Big deal. When you all of a sudden get a bug up your butt about it, anyway?"

" 'Bout the time I found out what that sorry gutbag makes a year."

"Yeah, well. You want my opinion, obsessing about it ain't gonna improve your outlook on life."

"We'll see."

Denny Hoyle sighed.

Knowing Luther, he was afraid they probably would.

12

EARLY Wednesday morning, Eyebrow Larry Tomiczek slipped back into the past as the first flush of dawn began to lighten the sky.

Andrew watched the reflection of daybreak on the water. His head felt thick, and his mouth tasted sour. He felt like he'd been drained into the chaise lounge through a straw. But he didn't feel particularly sleepy, even though he hadn't had so much as a nap in the past twenty-four hours. Somehow, he couldn't get over the sensation that he'd been sleeping since he left Baltimore.

Andrew sat in the chair out on the deck, his mind strangely lucid, uncluttered. He looked out over the water. The pressure system behind the ongoing heat wave domed the entire basin like an overturned bowl. Even here at the ocean's edge, the nights stayed dense and warm. With the sunrise came dry breezes that stirred the palms, rustling the fronds like sandpaper blades. By the time Andrew spotted the day's first jogger shuffling past on the strip, the sky had brightened to a pale hazy blue. Sweat ran, mixed with sunblock, and stung his eyes. The temperature seemed to have already risen ten degrees.

He went inside, collected the glasses he and Larry had left behind, and rinsed them at the sink. He capped the bottle and put it back in the cupboard, wiped the counters with a damp paper towel.

Eventually, Andrew wandered into the bedroom, stripped down, and stood under a cool shower until his skin pulled tight. When he'd had enough, he scrubbed himself dry with one of Caroline's soft towels.

He found clean clothes and put them on. He went back to the kitchen, found coffee, and put that on, too.

Somewhere along the way, Andrew realized he was hungry. Ravenous. So he pulled a chef's knife and the cutting board, started chopping onions and green peppers for scrambled eggs. He sliced off a three-inch cube of butter, dropped it in a skillet with the peppers and the onions, and put the pan over a low flame.

As the kitchen began to fill with the smell of breakfast, Andrew went to Caroline's utensil drawer and retrieved a spatula. He paused there a moment before shutting the drawer with his hip.

Then he pulled the drawer open again.

The envelope of cash still waited where he'd stowed it yesterday. Andrew picked up the bundle and held it in his hand a minute before he finally traded it for the phone. On his way back to the stove, he dialed the number scrawled in black ink on the envelope's flap.

Three rings.

"This is Benjy."

"Morning," Andrew said. "This is Andrew Kindler."

During the pause on the other end, Andrew cranked up the heat, cracked four eggs into the pan, and started scrambling. He said, "Surprised?"

Over the sizzle, he heard Corbin say, "Hey, Mom. I'm at work. Can I call you back?"

"Boss in the backseat, huh?"

"Sure."

"Don't worry, I'll make this quick." Andrew cradled the phone with his shoulder, turning his eggs while he talked. "Tell your friend Heather I changed my mind. I want to meet with her. Tonight."

"I'll call you back in an hour."

"But I won't answer, so it won't do you any good." Andrew reached for the salt and pepper. A jolt of Tabasco sounded good; he swiveled toward the refrigerator and found the slender bottle in the door. "There's a place called Keegan's in Torrance. I'll be waiting there at ten P.M. Tell her to look for the guy with the pretty face."

"That's twenty miles away. Why don't you let me find someplace closer?"

"All you need to do is pass along the message," Andrew said. "You won't be joining us anyway. If she still wants to meet me, it'll be a party of two. Otherwise, no deal."

"I don't know, Ma."

"That's the message." Andrew killed the flame under the pan and added, in his best maternal mimic, "Have a nice day at work, dear."

Before Benjy could say more, Andrew hung up the phone. He grabbed a fork and leaned against the counter while he ate his eggs out of the pan.

He felt like he could have eaten a dozen more without

moving from the spot. Instead, he did up the dishes and put them away. He resumed his position against the counter and drank two cups of coffee, wondering how he should spend the hours ahead in light of the things he'd learned from Larry a few hours ago.

He thought about getting in the car and taking a drive up Ocean to see if the cops were still camped out in the park. He thought about taking them up some coffee, just to be neighborly.

He thought about calling Caroline and telling her about his unexpected visit from her long-ago Romeo. He thought about packing a suitcase and driving for Mexico. He thought about grabbing the radio, finding the newspaper wherever it had landed today, going out to the deck like usual, and making believe he'd dreamed the whole damned thing.

In the end, he found himself gazing across the kitchen at the bundle of cash on the counter. He looked at it for quite a while.

When he'd finally decided what he wanted to do with it, Andrew poured himself another cup of coffee and got out the yellow pages. It took him a minute to find the number he was looking for, but he finally found it. He dialed.

"Plum Investigations," said the voice on the other end of the line.

"I expected a receptionist," Andrew said. "Or at least an answering machine. I guess business must be slow."

"This is Travis Plum. Can I help you?"

"That's what I'm wondering," Andrew said.

"Who is this?"

"Listen," Andrew said. "You and I got off on the wrong foot yesterday. Sorry I got you fired. How about we call it water under the bridge and start over? Clean slate."

At first, Andrew heard only silence on Plum's end.

"What the hell," the snoop finally said, "do *you* want?"

"For starters," Andrew said, hefting the envelope in his hand, "I thought we could talk about your hiring fee."

13

THE longer Adrian Timms worked the job, the less he understood about what caused one person to put the life out of another. But over the years he'd learned that both murderers and their victims always had at least one thing in common: the higher their profile before the crime, the messier the aftermath.

This simple formula of proportion was the reason why Timms's boss, Captain Garland Graham, had been appointed by the chief to scramble a twelve-detective investigation into the murder of Gregor Tavlin. Tavlin's celebrity may have been modest by Tinseltown standards, but his ties to Doren Lomax—by extension, to the department itself—made the case a matter of high public scrutiny.

Doren Lomax, besides being Gregor Tavlin's former employer, happened to be the longest-sitting current member of the Civilian Board of Police Commissioners.

With aftershocks of Rodney King, O. J. Simpson, Rampart Division, and assorted lesser scandals still rippling from the epicenter of too-recent memory, the department intended to walk this case home and put it to bed without a peep.

Graham had divided his investigative force into two teams. Team One's focus: Gregor Tavlin's year post-Lomax Enterprises, including his scholarship foundation and his lengthy roster of Hollywood clientele.

Timms had been assigned to walk point on Team Two: the Lomax Enterprises era.

Late Wednesday morning, the crew assembled around an octagonal table in one of the new multiuse pods off the squad room. The murder book, a fat blue binder containing a record of everything collected in the Tavlin investigation so far, served as a centerpiece.

Detectives Joe Reese and Ruben Carvajal took the first turn. Their previous night's stakeout of the house on Palisades Beach Road had marked a possible new player. Timms studied color printouts of digital photos of the visitor who had climbed the gate to the property just after sundown.

"That's him leaving the property this morning, few minutes past five," Reese said. They'd obtained permission from a neighboring homeowner to park a few numbers up for the night. "Walks right past us without giving a glance. Had a rental parked in the pay lot up the beach."

Carvajal took it from there. "Guy checks out of the Hotel California on Ocean Ave around six. We talked to the desk on our way back. Night manager marked him right off, said he remembered the guy had an unusual scar above his eye."

"Must have been riding shotgun," Timms said,

thinking about the car accident story Kindler had fed him yesterday.

Carvajal said, "When?"

Timms shook his head. "Never mind. Scarface here, how was he registered?"

"Under the name Ronald McDonald. Paid cash for the room," Reese said. "Goes straight from there to LAX, checks in the rental under the name Guy Smiley, then hops a nonstop United flight to Baltimore."

Timms studied the photo a moment longer, then tossed it onto the table. He looked at the group. "Opinions?"

"We could cross-check the passenger list with NCIC, OCIS, definitely Baltimore PD," Reese suggested.

"Maybe we should go ahead and x-ref the Maryland telephone listings for Willy Wonka while we're at it," Aaron Keene said.

"I could put a Baltimore phone book up your ass," Drea offered. "You can x-ref it with a hand mirror."

"Children," Timms said.

"He started it."

Keene curled his hand and stroked it back and forth in front of him. Timms ignored the gesture. Every circle had a jerk; Aaron Keene just happened to be theirs. When it came to working a suspect, Timms had seen Aaron Keene play a hand as close to the vest as anybody. But around the shop, Keene pretty much wore his asshole on his sleeve.

"I talked to SID this morning," Drea said, moving on, repeating for the group what she'd already given Timms. Among other things, the Scientific Investigation Division performed forensic analyses of evidence items. Timms had handed over the Lomax letter, and the envelope containing it, to SID's Questioned Documents section, who had returned their findings to Drea Munoz two hours ago. "Computer workup of the handwriting samples basically clinches it. The signature's a forge."

"Big surprise," Keene said.

"Somebody wants to ding this guy Kindler for something," Timms said. "But whatever he's into, it smells to me like some other cop's problem."

Aaron Keene said, "So we can sign off on this zero now?"

"I'm not signing off anything yet," Timms told him. "What have you got?"

"How about an actual lead?" Keene opened the file folder he'd brought with him and passed a sheet of paper. "This is an arrest record for a Lomax Enterprises employee named Benjamin Corbin."

The name rang a bell. Timms pulled the murder book and flipped to the running index of conducted interviews. "That's the driver," he said for everybody's benefit, thumping the page with his finger. "Goes by Benjy. We talked to him August 8."

"I ran the employee files for priors and popped a flag on this guy," Keene said. "Dinged for misdemeanor possession in '89 and '91. Hammered April '95 for intent to distribute plus possession of an illegal firearm. Drew a dime at Chino, served three with good behavior."

Drea passed the arrest sheet to Timms. "So the guy's got a record. What's the flag?"

"Lomax Enterprises runs security checks on all new employees," Keene said. "But there's no background on this in Corbin's file. I just got off the phone with the flack."

"Todman," Timms said.

"Who explains to me that they're aware of the record, and the conviction, but Corbin is a special case,"

Keene went on. "Friend of the family. David's old high school buddy, roommate in college, even dated the sister Heather at one point."

"No kidding."

"According to Todman," said Keene. "Seems Benjamin hooked up with a bad crowd along the way, made some bad moves, got in a little trouble, but hey. Happens to the best of us, right? Everybody deserves another chance. So when Corbin makes his paper, David and Heather plead his case to Daddy, who brings him on at the company and gives him a shot. Guy's been clean since then, at least on the screens."

"Funny," Timms said. "I don't remember Mr. Corbin mentioning any of that in his interview. Or anybody else, come to think of it."

"Could be they closed ranks around Corbin because of the record," Carvajal said. "That'd sound about Todman's speed to me. Felon on the payroll, more dirty laundry they don't need aired, he'd want to keep it away from the reporters."

"I have a gut feeling," Keene said, "that says we put a tap and a tail on Corbin, we'll find our boy before long."

Timms nodded, despite his own gut feeling. He was learning to live with it; he'd had it ever since this case began.

The odds had been stacked against them from the start, even setting aside the family involved. Clearance statistics for dump cases—cases in which a victim was killed in one location but discovered in another—always suffered due to the absence of an immediate crime scene. Time was a perpetual enemy. Time between the murder and the discovery of the body. Time for weather, traffic, wildlife, and water-dropping helicopters to compromise the body and the dumpsite itself.

Based on the initial evidence, the picture they'd assembled looked something like this:

Somebody puts a large dent in Gregor Tavlin's brain pan and loads him into the trunk of his own car. They don't take special precautions—a drop cloth, for example—because they have a plan. The plan involves driving Tavlin's Alfa up into the smoke-filled hills. Removing the body from the trunk and situating it behind the wheel. Emptying a bottle of booze over everything and tossing it into the car for appearances, but doubting it will matter. Because they finish by sending the car over in a bashing, smashing tumble, leaving it where it finally comes to rest, directly in the path of the wildfire marching toward the sea.

The nature of the wound and the method of disposal sent mixed signals. The blow to the head—intimate, but delivered to a turned back—suggested anything from an altercation with a personal acquaintance to old-fashioned random assault. Neither scenario suggested a professional job.

The disposal of the body, however, was leagues beyond anything the average citizen generally thought to attempt after they'd snapped and killed somebody. The dump spot itself seemed interesting, less than a mile from state land. Drea believed the dumpers may have hoped to create jurisdictional confusion in the event somebody found the body before the fire did its job.

At least two perps seemed likely: one to drive the Alfa, one to follow in another vehicle. With Tavlin in the driver's seat and the Alfa's transmission in neutral, the second vehicle could have been used to push the convertible off the road toward oblivion.

Reese and Carvajal had turned up the most promising lead so far. On July 30, according to miscellaneous

Lomax Enterprises employees, Gregor Tavlin had paid his first return visit to Lomax corporate headquarters since leaving the company the previous year. He'd apparently demanded a meeting with Doren Lomax, who was not in the office at the time. According to Lomax's executive assistant, Doren's son David had fielded the call in his father's absence.

There had been rancor. According to the executive assistant, the two men had left the building together, taking their argument to lunch.

To the knowledge of the executive assistant, David Lomax did not return to the office from lunch that day. Neither did she know the specifics of his disagreement with Tavlin.

A search of the hard drive of the personal computer Tavlin kept at his home in Palos Verdes turned up a voice message from David Lomax in the inbox of Gregor Tavlin's answerphone software. The message was date-stamped July 30, 3:30 P.M. The same day they'd left the office together. In his message, Lomax had asked for a second meeting late that evening back at his office in the corporate building.

The building itself had no security cameras, but it did have a keycard entry system. Every full-time employee had a personal ID badge that allowed access to the facilities after regular business hours. According to the company's information technology department, each security card contained an embedded smart chip that allowed the system to record a log of all after-hours traffic in and out of the building. Daily records were backed up on a network server; at month-end, these logs were archived on CD-ROM and purged from the main system.

When Timms and his team had requested the archival

disc for the month of July, they'd waited two days before receiving word that said disc—the only existing
record for the night of July 30—seemed to have van-
ished into the same thin air David Lomax currently oc-
cupied.

An LAPD data recovery specialist had worked with
the company IT department to retrieve the purged files
from the network. No dice.

Meanwhile, a security manager for Club Maximum,
a man named Luther Vines, stated during an interview
with Timms and Drea that he'd personally checked out
the July archives to David Lomax on the morning of
August 1. When asked why he imagined a corporate executive had come to him with such a request, Vines had
been unable to speculate. He'd simply been in the main
office for an early meeting; he'd run into David Lomax
in the lobby on his way in; and he had badge-level clearance to the security back offices where the archive CDs
were stored.

David Lomax, of course, had been unavailable for
comment.

The team had yet to discover the person who had seen
Gregor Tavlin between the dates of July 31 and August 2.
By the time they'd obtained search warrants for David
Lomax's office and Silver Lake bungalow, the heir appar-
ent—the last person known to have seen Gregor Tavlin
alive—was officially 84 hours MIA.

On the morning of August 6, the day of Gregor
Tavlin's public memorial service, Team Two and SID
techs had searched David Lomax's office and his house
in Silver Lake. Doren Lomax had attended both searches
with lawyers.

It had been a delicate operation. Foul-ups were not an
option. They didn't make a move without consultation

from the district attorney's office, and they followed the book like an instruction manual.

Three days later, SID returned expedited forensic analyses of items collected during the search. The showpiece had come from the cushions of David Lomax's living room couch: his company security badge.

The blood smears on the clear plastic card carrier had been typed against the samples collected from the trunk of Gregor Tavlin's car. Both came up AB-negative, with an antigen profile shared by one person in 10,000. DNA cross was still in the works, but the likelihood of a match didn't get much higher.

They didn't have a murder weapon, and they didn't have a motive, and they weren't any closer to a case they could hand over to the D.A. than they'd been on day one. But they hadn't found David Lomax yet, either.

"Okay," Timms said. He nodded at Keene. "That's good work, Aaron. See if you can get the paper together for the tap and tech support on Corbin. Home landline only."

"Already working on it," Keene said.

"You've got something cooking," Drea said.

Timms looked at everybody. Everybody looked back at him.

"I've got a thought," he said. "But it'd have to be a group vote kind of thing. A vote we never had, because I never brought it up."

Drea shrugged. "We're not getting any younger."

Timms kept one eye on Keene while he laid it out.

"Today we get our ducks in a row. This afternoon, I'll leak the security badge to Melanie Roth at the *Times.* Give her enough room to make deadline for tomorrow's edition. Then we stick on Corbin close as we can for the next 48, see if anything shakes loose."

He looked around the table again. Aaron Keene wore a smirk. Everybody else just sat with it for a minute or two.

Carvajal spoke first. "Don't have much up our sleeves if that badge gets thrown out of court down the road."

"Nope," Timms agreed. "Not yet. But if Lomax turns out to be our boy, we need a hell of a lot more than the badge anyway."

"Good luck getting Graham to sign off," Drea said.

"I think we can rule that out. Once more for clarity: This discussion never took place."

Timms waited. Keene looked at a fingernail, still smirking. Drea, Reese, and Carvajal sat by.

"Any vote cast is a vote no," Timms said. "No pressure, no blame. We move on."

Silence.

"Okay," Timms said. "Joe, Ruben, go home until your pagers go off, or your alarm clocks, whichever comes first. The rest of us can hold down the fort until then. Meeting adjourned, unless anybody's got anything else."

Nobody did.

As the group rose from their chairs, Timms added, "Aaron. Hang back a minute."

Keene looked over his shoulder. Drea glanced at Timms, eyebrows raised. Timms shook his head slightly, cueing her to go on ahead.

She did.

Parker Center had a nickname in other divisions of the LAPD: the glass house. The tag had more to do with culture than architecture.

Timms had been recruited from outside the department on the sponsorship of a retiring Robbery-Homicide vet named Hart, an old friend and long-ago

mentor with whom he'd shared a squad car during his
patrol days as a rookie with the Santa Monica Police
Department. He'd finally traded his tenure as a Detective Supervisor with SMPD for a Detective-2 position
in the Homicide Special Section of the notoriously elite
RHD bullpen five years ago. In that time, he'd come
across two kinds of detectives: those who worked the job,
and those like Aaron Keene.

Since his recent promotion to Detective-3 Supervisor, Timms swore he'd been running into Keene more
and more.

"You look like you've got something on your mind,"
he said when they were alone. "You on board with this,
Aaron?"

"Why not?" Keene still hadn't lost the smirk. "It's
your funeral."

"Funny you say that," Timms said. "I was watching
you at your desk earlier. You must have gone through
today's paper three times. Looking for something in
particular?"

"Getting at something in particular?"

Timms shrugged.

Keene waited.

"Melanie Roth," Timms finally said. "Good reporter. She started working the crime beat right about
the same time I came on LAPD."

"Fascinating," Keene said.

"What fascinates me," Timms said, "is how few really
good reporters you find these days. Most of these young
kids out of school, you know these hacks, they'll run
with anything that comes their way. Not Mel Roth. She
double, triple-checks her leads." Timms grinned a little.
"Real bulldog that way, long as I've known her. We go
back a few years. I don't know if you knew that."

Keene was starting to look bored.

"So Mel Roth calls me this morning," Timms went on. "Just to get my okay before she went to print with the evidence on David Lomax. Seems she already got a tip from somebody on the investigation. Don't think I probably need to tell you whose name came up."

Now Keene stiffened his shoulders. He still said nothing.

"Don't get me wrong," Timms said. "I was ten years younger and had better luck with women, I might be trying to get in her pants, too." He sat back in his chair. "I mean, I figure it's gotta be something like that. Because I know you wouldn't be trying to cowboy this investigation. Only an asshole would buck for D-3 that way."

Keene worked a muscle in his jaw. After a long moment, he said, "I'll do us both a favor and pretend we never had this conversation."

"So you're saying I'm barking up the wrong tree on this. I just want to be clear."

"You can bark up any tree you feel like," Keene said. "You're King Shit on this case. I get it."

"I know you think chasing down that letter was a bullshit waste of time. Maybe it was. Maybe not. Call 'em how you see 'em, Aaron. You're part of this investigation, you've got a right." Timms folded his hands in his lap. "What you don't have is the right to backdoor the rest of the team. That shit ends up getting people hurt."

"Thanks for the words of wisdom."

"Anytime." Timms took his boot off his knee but did not stand. "As long as I'm giving 'em out, here's a few more. You don't have to like me, Keene. You don't even have to respect me. But don't fuck with me."

Keene looked at him for a long, silent moment.

He finally said, "Is that all you had to get off your chest?"

"I feel much better."

"You know," Keene said, "I'm going to enjoy watching you take the heat that's coming your way on this thing."

Timms offered him a friendly parting smile. "I'd be careful not to hold the match too long, if I were you."

14

ANDREW didn't know what kind of car he'd expected a guy like Travis Plum to drive.

An ailing beater, maybe. Something the guy couldn't afford to fix or get rid of because he spent all his income on expensive camera equipment and laughable disguises. Or maybe just the opposite: something sporty and ridiculous that made him feel like Magnum P.I. tooling around town.

When Plum finally pulled into the parking lot of the Chevron station in a garden-variety beige Toyota Camry, Andrew felt his confidence rise. Here was the sort of car he imagined a good private snoop ought to drive: reliable, common as a parking meter, inconspicuous. Maybe there was hope after all.

As Andrew let himself in the passenger side, Plum looked over and asked, "Is there a reason why you couldn't just come by my office like a regular person?"

Gone, Andrew noted, were the goofy shorts and nightmarish luau shirt from yesterday. Today, Plum seemed to favor basic Gap wear. Khakis. A short-sleeved plaid button-down. Brown leather sandals.

"I could have met you at your office," Andrew told him. "But I figured it wasn't apt to do either of us any good if the cops followed me to your place of business."

Plum had the windows up and the air-conditioning blasting. It felt glorious. Briefly. As soon as Andrew pulled the passenger door shut, Plum switched off the ignition, removed his sunglasses, and turned in the driver's seat.

"About that," he said.

"Long story."

"I've got time."

"That makes one of us," Andrew said. He held up the envelope he'd brought along. "I'd just as soon start the meter."

Plum seemed to recognize the envelope. He looked at Andrew.

"Working for hire is one thing," he said. "Aiding and abetting is another. Maybe it's a fine line sometimes. But I'm not in the business of crossing it."

"Then you can relax," Andrew told him. "This is strictly an aiding type of deal."

"I presume you won't take offense," Plum said, "if I'm not entirely comfortable taking your word on that."

"That's up to you." Andrew placed the bundle on the fat padded armrest between them. "So. What's it going to be?"

Plum ignored the cash and spent a minute on Andrew's face. He drummed the steering wheel with his fingers. He checked his mirrors.

"One question," he said. "One time only."

"Go for it."

"David Lomax." Plum watched Andrew closely. "Do you know anything about it, or don't you?"

Andrew took two fingers and made an X over his heart. "If David Lomax came up to this car right now with a rag and a squeegee, I wouldn't know to look twice."

Plum clamped his sunglasses in his teeth and picked up the bundle. "For this kind of money, something tells me you protest too much."

"Now *that's* what I should have told your man Benjy yesterday," Andrew said.

"Maybe instead of being a wiseass you should try harder to convince me why I'm worth five grand to you."

"Maybe you're not," Andrew said. "Maybe I just don't happen to have anything better to do with it."

Plum seemed to think about that.

Without another glance, he squeezed a latch, lifted the armrest, and dropped the bundle into the storage well beneath.

"That makes one of us," he said, and started the car.

———————

Whatever else could be said for Travis Plum, a quarter pound of cash did wonders for his demeanor. By the time he'd pulled to a shady curb on a quiet street in a gated residential pocket of Beverly Hills, he'd grown downright chatty.

"Chez Lomax," he said, nodding toward a tall wrought-iron fence grown high with bougainvillea. "The girl's got her own place in Los Feliz. She's been living at home with Daddy and the hired help since her brother went Hoffa."

"Heather Lomax. What's she like?"

"Rich," Plum said.

"See, the way I was hoping this might work was, you'd be able to tell me things I don't already know."

"Never met her in person," Plum told him. "I dealt strictly through Corbin. If I had to make a guess, I'd guess the girl's not playing with a full bag of marbles."

"What makes you say that?"

"Would *you* have hired me to follow a cop?"

It wasn't a bad point. Andrew resisted the urge to ask Plum about his own marbles for taking the job in the first place. After all, he'd taken this one.

"So does she work the family farm? Same as her brother?"

Plum seemed amused.

"What?"

"The family fat farm. That's good."

Andrew tried to be patient.

"I don't expect Princess Lomax is especially intimate with the 40-hour workweek," Plum said. "She did have fifteen minutes a few years ago, played a role on a TV show. One of those sexy-wexy prime-time things. *Malibu Sunsets,* I think it was called. *Melrose Place* meets *Baywatch* is the way I remembered it. Not that anybody remembers it."

Andrew made a mental note to ask Caroline. His cousin was an unrepentant sucker for trashy television. She'd know.

"As I recall, Miss Lomax went on to do the whole flavor of the month, actresses-with-eating-disorders cover story thing," Plum said. "Showed up in the gossip columns for a while, dated a few movie stars, whatever. 'Seen on the arm of' stuff. At that point, I guess she still rated as an appendage. Now she's hardly a footnote."

"Is she older or younger?"

"Older or younger than what?"

"Than her brother."

"They're twins, actually," Plum said. "Couldn't tell you who came out first."

"I was only looking for a ballpark estimate," Andrew said. Twins. Of everything Plum had just told him, this was the only thing that struck him as particularly interesting. "So, thirty. Little old to be moving back home."

At this comment, Plum seemed to take pause. He removed his sunglasses again and looked at Andrew carefully.

"That's a pretty tight ballpark, Kreskin. How would you know that? If you don't know David?"

"They gave his age in the newspaper."

"Oh. Right."

"Seriously, we're not going to keep doing this all day, are we?"

"My apologies," Plum said. Then he sat up an inch. "Now isn't this lucky?"

Andrew followed the snoop's gaze. Down the street, between the twin bearded palm trees standing sentry, he saw the gates to the Lomax estate swinging open. A small, sporty yellow BMW convertible emerged, top folding back as the car rolled. As the driver hung an easy right and hummed away down the street, Andrew caught a glimpse of big black sunglasses, bare shoulders, and an ash-blond ponytail.

"Heather Lomax, I presume?"

Plum grinned. "Kinda cute, isn't she?"

"As a button. What are you waiting for?"

Plum had already put his shades back on and twisted

the ignition, but for some reason he now sat with his hands on the wheel.

"What?"

"Oh, come on," Plum said. "Let's hear you say it. You know you want to."

Hopeless. The guy was hopeless.

Andrew sighed and said, "Follow that car."

15

TODD Todman tried never to think in terms of problems: only challenges and opportunities.

As director of corporate identity for Lomax Enterprises, he'd converted his share of one to the other. But in all his years with the Lomax family, he'd never faced a challenge quite the likes of the one on its way through the door now.

"Sheri," he said, "I hate to run you out of your own house. But I'd like to speak with Rod alone for a few minutes. Would you mind?"

Todd spoke to Sheri Forman, general manager of Club Maximum's flagship location on Wilshire Boulevard. They'd been having a chat in her office above the club: Sheri in her chair, Todd holding down one corner of her desk. Behind him, a row of large windows overlooked the club's front lobby, where members in bright tight garb came in toting duffel bags, milled with nutrient drinks in the common area, bellied up to the courtesy counter for fresh towels.

He was speaking, of course, about the inimitable Rod Marvalis, who had just slouched in reeking of cigarettes.

Without a word, Sheri vacated her position, rounded the corner of the desk opposite Todd, and brushed by Marvalis without looking at him. She closed the door to the office firmly on the way out.

When she was gone, Marvalis smirked in Todd's direction. "This ought to be good."

"Hey, Rod. Take a load off."

As Marvalis plopped himself down, Todd assumed Sheri's still-warm chair.

"Sheri called," he said.

"I figured that much all by my lonesome. What's up her ass this time?"

Todd grinned. "Before we get into that, let me just ask. Are you okay? You're not having any kind of trouble, are you?"

"Trouble."

"I don't know, Rodney. You tell me. It's not anything . . . transmitted again, is it? I'm not judging, you ought to know that by now. It's just that I can see you haven't been sleeping well."

"I've been sleeping like a baby, thanks."

"I guess what I'm trying to say is that you're part of the Lomax Enterprises family, Rod. We take care of our family."

"That's nice to know." Rod propped a cross-trainer on the edge of Sheri's desk. He pushed back, balancing on the back legs of his chair as he dug into an open Doritos Big Grab with two fingers. He had orange nacho cheese dust at the corners of his mouth and crumbs all over his black Club Maximum tank top. "But I'm peachy."

Todd looked at him closely.

"What did you need, Todman? I have a massage in ten minutes."

"You're four and a half hours late to work. I think your daily back rub can spare a few minutes."

"It's not a back rub," Marvalis said. "It's physical therapy. I have a note from the doc. And Cinnamon doesn't like to be kept waiting." Rod referred to the club's in-house chiropractic specialist. He sucked cheese powder from the tips of his fingers and offered a grin full of innuendo.

"Cinnamon is skilled," Todd said.

"You don't need to tell me."

"But her first obligation during regular business hours is to the paying club membership." Todd leaned in. "Now, maybe I'm off base. But it occurs to me, Rod, that maybe I need to remind you that yours is, too."

"Christ," Rod said. "Here we go."

"Listen," Todd told him. "I didn't come all the way down here to bust your hump."

"Oh, no?"

"Try to look at things from my perspective." Todd opened his hands. "Never mind that I've got enough to worry about at the moment without taking time out for this nonsense. You're our marquee name now. As far as I'm concerned, you're entitled to some latitude. Sheri Forman is just going to have to learn to accept that."

"Couldn't have said it better myself."

"But."

"Christ, Todman, you're wearing me out already. What's the goddamned emergency? Next week's show is in the can. We don't tape again until the day after tomorrow. And we wrapped the stupid video yesterday."

"After I had to send Denny almost to Malibu in the

middle of the morning while a full production crew stood around charging us union rates by the hour," Todd reminded him.

Rod cocked back his head, opened his mouth wide, and upended the Doritos bag into it.

"The point I'm trying to make," Todd went on, "is that whether we're scheduled to tape the daily, or to shoot a special project, or whatever the case, the very least we need from you is a degree of professionalism. I mean come on, Rod. This morning. You couldn't have put in a call? Do you even know your own schedule anymore?"

"I'm sure you're about to refresh my memory."

"I certainly can if you need me to." Todd checked the weekly calendar Sheri had left open on the desk for him. "According to this, you have a low-impact, a high-impact, and an advanced Pilates class on Wednesdays. All before lunch. And every one of them has a waiting list as long as my arm." Todd closed the book. "We had to cancel your eight o'clock and scramble to cover the other two. And don't think there weren't complaints. These people pay top dollar for Rod Marvalis. They expect Rod Marvalis at the front of the room."

Marvalis seemed to soak up this information like a sponge. There was no limit to the man's powers of self-aggrandizement, no matter what the specifics of the situation.

Rodney Marvalis—now a decade and a half and counting past his Heisman-candidate glory days as the slipperiest scrambling quarterback in USC history—had come into the Lomax fold as part of a product acquisition a little over a year ago.

Despite solid numbers in the Tavlin line, overall growth in the company's retail division had flattened in recent quarters. In hopes of jump-starting the projections, Doren had put together the buyout of a promising start-up called LifeRite, Inc. LifeRite had been climbing the mail-order charts with a little product they called The Abdominator.

Said product's face man, of course, had been none other than Rod "The Bod" Marvalis, whose twinkling wink and movie-star grin was proven to keep callers—primarily middle-aged women with one to three children—on hold with credit cards in hand.

The whole thing seemed like an iffy move, in Todd's professional opinion. In the years following his college football career, Rodney Marvalis had added little to his résumé beyond washing out of the NFL after a single injury-riddled season; costarring in one straight-to-video, now out-of-print action flick opposite Arsenio Hall; and pissing away most of his earnings on a string of paternity suit settlements. The fact of the matter was that Rod Marvalis had only landed the LifeRite gig in the first place by dint of his connections with the USC alums who had founded the company. There just wasn't much to work with.

But Doren had seen things differently, and when Doren made up his mind, he made up his mind. He believed that when it came to leveraging a customer base, it paid to stick with the face the base already knew. No sense throwing out the Bod with the bathwater, as it were.

So Todd—as always—had rolled up his sleeves. He'd never complained. Not one time. Another challenge, another opportunity.

And until now, he'd always thought of Rodney Marvalis as a creative work-in-progress bordering masterpiece territory.

Because any common hack could sell a Gregor Tavlin.

A Rod the Bod? This took more than craftsmanship; it even took more than art. This took genuine wizardry.

Lately, Todd was beginning to imagine how Dr. Frankenstein must have felt.

"So who'd you find for a stand-in, anyway? Landon?"

Brad Landon, if Todd remembered correctly, was one of the regular staff instructors at the club. A hard-working, fatally uncharismatic fellow.

"Bet that made the little pissant's day," Marvalis said. "He's convinced he should have my job anyway. I'd like to see that mutant on camera."

"Actually," Todd said, "I convinced Sheri to go another way. A little trial run I've had in mind."

Rod raised an eyebrow. "Yeah? Who else? Don't tell me you stuck that bull dyke Sawyer in front of my room. I'll be undoing that damage for a week."

"No, Rod. Not Sawyer." Todd had no idea who Sawyer was. "We gave Luther your classes this morning."

"Who?"

"Luther. Luther Vines."

Rod's eyes widened at this. "You jest."

Todd folded his hands and waited.

"Vines?" Rod's laugh came out like a belch. "Seriously. You're yanking my chain."

"I wouldn't dream of it."

Marvalis shook his bottle-bleached mass of hair and looked at the ceiling: delighted, disbelieving. "Luther Vines? You really put that animal in a soundproof room full of Beverly Hills housewives? Oh, *Christ,* but how I'd love to have seen that. I love it! Luther Vines."

"From what I'm told," Todd said, "Luther handled himself quite well."

"Shut up."

"And I'll let you in on something else. Brad Landon isn't the only one who likes the look of your job. Just so you know, Luther has approached me more than once along those lines."

Marvalis pretended he hadn't just sat up a notch. "Has he, now?"

"I know," Todd said. "He's plenty rough around the edges. But believe it or not, for a security man, Luther actually has some interesting ideas about strength and cardio."

"What are you trying to pull, Todman?"

"Excuse me?"

"Don't insult my intelligence," Rod said. "What. I'm supposed to get all worried and start high-stepping my ass off just because you let some low-rent Billy Blanks wannabe sub in for *me* for a day? You really think I'm too stupid to see the game you're playing?"

"Game?" Todd raised his palms. "Rod, all I'm trying to do is keep the offense running around here."

"Wow, Coach. Great metaphor." Rod yawned. "Very inspiring."

"I'm glad you enjoyed it," Todd said.

"Tell you what. If that's the end of the pep talk, I'll be off to enjoy my back rub now." Marvalis removed his foot from the desk and stood. "But do me a favor and keep one thing in mind. You're not dealing with a gum-drop like Gregor Tavlin anymore. We've got all kinds of time before *my* contract comes up, so you can go ahead and get off my ass. In the meantime, you'd better make sure your big, bad security man knows what's what and who's who around here. I'm beginning to think he might not be completely clear on that."

"Don't worry, Rodney." Todd smiled. "I try to go

out of my way to make sure everybody knows exactly where they stand."

Marvalis gave a dismissive snort as he brushed Dorito crumbs from his person and tugged his tank top smooth over his waist.

"As long as you bring up your contract," Todd said, "maybe now is a good time to revisit one small point."

Marvalis looked back over his shoulder. "Oh, pray fucking tell, Todd."

"Maybe 'small' isn't a fitting choice of words."

"Do you ever just go ahead and say *anything* without dicking around?"

"Fine, Rodney. I'm talking about the Personal Maintenance clause you agreed to when you signed on here. It's on page six, if memory serves. Items 9.2a and b. If I could make a friendly suggestion, you might want to take a look. Just as a review."

Marvalis narrowed his eyes. "What are you getting at, pal?"

"I know it's a sensitive area. There's really no easy way to bring it up." Todd leaned forward and used his most gentle tone. "But I can't help but notice you've put on a few pounds lately."

Rod's bed-tanned hide creased like cured leather when he squared his shoulders.

"Bullshit," he said.

"It's okay, Rodney. We're speaking privately. And believe me, I can understand the difficulties. We're both getting up there." He shrugged. "But you know the occupational hazards as well as I do. I don't need to tell you the camera can be cruel."

"Fuck you."

"There's no need to be abusive," Todd counseled. "I'm only looking out for you."

"You've got a hell of a lot of nerve."

"Tell you what," Todd said. "If it makes you feel better, I'll have the pro shop order you up the next size tank top for the taping on Friday. It'll probably be baggy on you." He made a point of nodding toward Rodney's belt line. "But at least that . . . um . . . back brace you've been wearing won't play so much on camera when you twist and reach."

Marvalis set his jaw so tightly that a vein began to jitter near his left eye. He didn't utter another word.

Todd was not above admitting it: a small, childish part of him genuinely enjoyed watching Rod the Bod jerk open the office door and stalk through, stung and seething.

He supposed he hadn't done Sheri Forman any favors today.

On the other hand, if poor Rodney happened to cross paths with Luther Vines on the club floor in such a state, the inevitable result of *that* confrontation could only make everybody's job easier in the long run.

Gazing out the window over the lobby, Todd found himself daydreaming about the evening ahead. He wondered what the birthday girl was doing right now. He really was having trouble keeping his mind on the job today.

Todd practically had to force himself to get up from Sheri Forman's desk and move on to the next opportunity.

16

HEATHER Lomax drove like a soccer mom.

On the city streets, she observed traffic laws and practiced thoughtful road etiquette. She let people in, yielded to pedestrians, and braked sensibly. She didn't so much as run a yellow light. Plum seemed to have no trouble maintaining the tail.

Princess Lomax opened up a bit on the freeways, but she only took to the passing lane when respectable traffic flow required. Plum kept a couple of cars between them whenever possible.

She led them north on the 405, to the 5, past San Fernando. They followed, racking miles on the odometer as they climbed gradually out of the basin, through the foothills, and into the San Gabriel Mountains. Soon they'd left the shimmering sprawl of Los Angeles proper behind and below.

Andrew could smell the smoke up here even with

the windows closed. Just to the west of them, great dark whorls hung over the landscape. He looked at his watch and realized that it was just about time for the noon Hot Spot. He reached toward the car radio and asked Plum if he minded.

"Knock yourself out," Plum said. "Personally, I don't know why they waste the airtime. These fires always go away when they run out of stuff to burn."

"Folks who live up there probably see it a little differently," Andrew said.

"I'm sure they do."

"You don't sound very sympathetic."

"Hey. You're dumb enough to live in a tinderbox, what the hell do you expect?" Plum smirked and dismissed the smoke banks with a wave. "Get enough money to live anywhere in the world, and what do these geniuses do? Head straight to an area known for its fires, mudslides, and earthquakes. Find a place right in the middle, and put a house on stilts. How can you not root for Mother Nature?"

"You make an interesting argument."

Plum wasn't finished with it, either. "That's setting aside the fact that it's tax dollars from working schlubs like yours truly that pay to protect these idiots from the inevitable."

"They say this one was probably caused by an illegal campfire," Andrew said. "Probably started by some taxpaying schlub. What about that?"

"What about it?" Plum faded into the left lane, passed a rumbling eighteen-wheeler, and merged right again three cars back from the Lomax girl. "That's supposed to make me feel sorry for these people? Some hiker flicks a cigarette. Somebody's riding horseback, horse shoes a rock and throws a spark. Lightning hits a dead tree. What's the difference? This one was just due."

"You should get a job writing real estate brochures."

"It's a fire ecology," Plum said. "Hello. If you need a brochure to tell you that, sorry, Charlie. You're beyond my help. Hope the view was worth it."

Andrew opted to listen to the fire report on the radio anyway. He let the conversation ebb for a while. He was beginning to wonder where Heather Lomax could possibly be going, and when she was going to get there. It seemed as if they'd been driving all day.

Eventually, the little Beemer exited the 5 at a junction for State Highway 14. Northeast they traveled. Andrew saw a sign that said Antelope Valley Freeway. Plum had started to spool out more distance between them and the convertible, hanging farther back with each mile.

"What's the matter?"

"Don't worry," Plum said. "I know where she's going. Not so much traffic up here. Best to drop a little before our cover gets any thinner."

"Where's she going?"

"Just kick back and enjoy the scenery. I don't want to spoil the suspense."

Andrew considered reminding Travis Plum that he was being paid to spoil the suspense. But at some point along the long winding ride, the past thirty hours had caught up with him. Andrew felt like he had bags of sand on his shoulders; his eyelids kept sagging to half-mast, and he was rapidly losing the battle with gravity. Banter was suddenly beyond him.

He didn't know when he nodded off, or for how many miles. He only knew that when his head snapped up again, they'd left the main road and arrived at what appeared to be a long driveway lined with cedars and pines. A broad wooden arch across the stone-walled entrance read WELCOME TO MOUNTAIN VIEW.

"Where are we?"

"Mountain View," Plum said as they passed under the arch. "Welcome."

The driveway opened up into what appeared to be some kind of hillside resort. Andrew could see a sprawling ranch-level main building with big windows and a wood shake roof. Beyond this building, groupings of what looked like A-frame lodges surrounded an open garden plaza. Wildflowers bloomed all about. Through a small orchard of almond trees, Andrew could see glints of lake blue.

"I don't suppose it's possible," he said, "that David Lomax is hiding out in an off-season ski lodge."

"Those aren't ski lodges," Plum said.

"Do I have to keep guessing?"

Plum grinned. "Remember when I said Heather Lomax might not be shooting all her marbles?"

"I remember."

"Let's just say maybe the nut didn't fall far from the tree."

Andrew looked at him. Plum said nothing for the moment, maneuvering the Camry into a space between two other cars in the lot off the main building. He nodded at the windshield as he killed the engine.

Up ahead, Heather Lomax took a flagstone path toward the garden square on foot. She wore flat sandals, jean shorts, and a pale yellow halter top. In her arms, she carried what looked to Andrew like a big bunch of cut daisies tied with a ribbon.

"What say we scooch down in the seat, just in case?"

"In case of what? She can't see us this far."

"I like to be cautious," Plum said.

Andrew exhaled and did as Plum requested. After they'd settled, he braced his knees against the dashboard and looked at Plum again. He felt ridiculous.

"I give up. Where are we?"

"Mountain View," Plum told him, "is sort of an assisted-living facility."

"What, like an old folks home?"

"Not exactly, no." Plum shifted in the seat to a more conversational angle. "I only use the phrase 'assisted-living facility' because I don't know what the politically correct term for nuthouse is. Whatever you call it, Mountain View is one. An expensive one."

Andrew absorbed this information.

"Who does the girl come here to visit?"

"Her mother," Plum said. "Barbara Lomax."

Andrew cocked his head.

"I tell you true," Plum said. "Don't know the story, but as I understand it, she's been here a few years now."

"Her mom."

"Her mom." Plum peered up over the steering wheel, saw that the coast had cleared, and sat up in the seat. "This was the first place I followed that cop Timms and his partner. I figure they came up here thinking a good boy might have said good-bye to his mother before skipping town. That hunch must have struck out, though, so I don't know. Maybe David Lomax isn't such a good boy."

Plum put his hands on the wheel.

"So. What do you want to do?"

Andrew looked through the windshield, off toward the A-frame unit into which Heather Lomax had disappeared.

"Wait," he said.

———————————

Heather Lomax didn't reappear for nearly two hours. Andrew slept in the passenger seat half the time, fidgeted the other half. He didn't know how those cops in the park managed to sit and watch the same house all day long without shooting themselves in the brain out of boredom.

Every so often, Plum started the car, ran up the windows, and punched on the air-conditioning for a few minutes. In between, Andrew sat and tried to ignore the heat as his armpits grew slick with sweat, and his clothes wilted into his skin. Plum tried to make conversation, but Andrew wasn't in the mood.

He was dozing again when things finally began happening. First, Andrew felt motion. He sat up in the seat and saw they were on the move again, traveling back down the long driveway in the direction they'd come. Up ahead, he saw Heather Lomax's little Z3 at the stone gates. Brake lights pulsed briefly as the car took a rolling left and disappeared from view.

"Better step on it," Andrew said.

"I'm stepping," said Plum. "Ease up, Sleeping Beauty. There's kind of an art to this, you know."

Plum's greatest artistic challenge, Andrew observed, now seemed to be keeping the BMW within range. Lomax had become a different driver since her visit to Mountain View. On the return trip, she hugged the mountain turns like a racetrack.

By the time they finally made it back to the 5, she'd kicked out the jams. Even with the needle anchored at 85, Plum still struggled to keep up.

"I think we're losing her," Andrew said.

"If you'd rather do the driving, I can pull over."

"Don't be so sensitive." Andrew pointed. "She's changing lanes again."

Through the miles they zigzagged. When the time came, instead of taking the junction back to Beverly Hills, Lomax sailed past and took the 5 down into Glendale.

They followed her off the freeway at the Colorado exit. Back in city traffic, Plum fared better, though he seemed to have dispensed with the notion of surveillance as an art form in favor of good old-fashioned bumper riding.

Heather led them east. The next time she stopped, Andrew looked at his watch. It was almost three-thirty in the afternoon. The Lomax girl turned right off Columbus Avenue, into the maw of a parking structure.

"Glendale Galleria," Andrew said. "What's Glendale Galleria?"

"Shopping mall," Plum said. He sounded a touch frazzled by now. "I'm guessing David Lomax isn't hiding here, either. What say we hit the food court? I'm about starved."

"She's parking."

"So I see. Strange thing to do in a parking garage. Very fishy. Can we go eat now?"

"Just find us a space. I want to try and see where she goes."

Plum sighed.

He rolled past Heather Lomax's parking stall and steered the Camry onward. "It's your dime."

They found a slot on the next level, a corner space freshly vacated by a Suzuki Sidekick bristling with teenagers. Plum pulled into the vacuum the fun wagon's thudding stereo system left behind. Then he killed the engine and rubbed his eyeballs with the heels of his hands.

"Nicely done," Andrew told him. "Have a good lunch. I'll meet you back here in an hour."

"What are you going to do?"

"Stretch my legs. See you in an hour."

He left Plum kneading his temples with his fingertips.

———————

Glendale Galleria was hopping. Andrew realized he'd walked smack-dab into the middle of the back-to-school shopping season. Not to mention one of the hottest days of the summer, the kind of day when young and old flooded indoor shopping malls in seething waves, all seeking respite from the heat outside.

He hadn't seen where Heather Lomax had entered the inner complex, and he estimated the odds of marking her again in this bright, soaring, climate-controlled mess to be just short of astronomical. Which left him with approximately 55 minutes to kill before reconnoitering with Travis Plum, P.I.

Andrew wound up doing exactly what he'd said he was going to do: He stretched his legs, working out the kinks that had set in over the course of nearly five car-bound hours.

Only blind luck put him next to Heather Lomax again inside the mall.

He'd been taking a spin around the second level when he happened to catch a glimpse of yellow out of the corner of his eye. Andrew glanced across the way and saw her emerging from a Godiva Chocolatier with a small white sack clutched in hand. He kept on in the direction he'd been walking, then hung a casual U-turn and followed the bobbing ponytail.

Whenever she stopped to browse a storefront window,

he did the same. When she paused at a directory kiosk, he looked down at his watch and veered toward the rail. Soon he'd lost sight of her altogether.

He thought: *Forget it.* His hour was almost up, this was ridiculous, and he was beyond ready to pack it in. He stopped at a drinking fountain and stooped to gulp from the cool anemic stream.

When he straightened, wiped his mouth, and turned, his heart leapt into his throat.

Heather Lomax stood directly behind him. Before he could shake off the surprise, he saw her thrust her hand forward. He heard keys jingling just as he felt something hard jam up against his left nostril.

"This is pepper gas," she informed him. "Had any experience with it?"

Andrew looked down a slender bare wrist into a pair of steady brown eyes. He said, "Not really."

Passersby began to glance over. Heather Lomax ignored them. She looked directly at Andrew. Through his unblocked nostril, he caught a light whiff of clean-smelling perfume.

"It's no picnic," she said. "Helpless coughing, weeping, choking, eyes swelling shut, and according to the label that's at five to fifteen feet." She grinned sweetly and nudged her hand forward another inch, forcing him to breathe through his mouth. "Make a move, and I'll napalm your brain."

Very slowly, Andrew showed his palms. "I wouldn't want that."

Just as quickly as she'd raised it, Heather Lomax dropped her hand and folded her arms. She stood with one hip cocked: Godiva sack in one hand, keyring with the pepper-gas attachment in the other, finger still poised on the trigger button of the black-plastic spray canister.

"I thought I lost you jerks on the freeway," she said. "Still having fun, are you?"

Andrew just lowered his hands. What could he say? He'd felt this pathetic before, but not often. It was entirely possible he'd misjudged her.

She looked him once up and once down.

"So it *is* you," she said. "I thought you didn't want to meet me until tonight. Did I get the wrong message?"

Andrew said, "How do you know who I am?"

Thinking: *Plum. You dirty little snitch.*

But the answer was far less devious than that. He knew the moment her eyes flickered over his face.

"Benjy described you."

"Ah." He nodded. "I see."

Andrew realized that even despite the awkward circumstances, she was being polite about his scars. For some reason, this small bit of grace impressed him.

"So."

"So."

She shrugged. "So what's the story, Ace? There must be some reason why you're following me all over creation."

"With all due respect," he said, "you started it."

First, her brown eyes glinted. Then the paper sack rustled in her hand as she shifted hips. She said, "Touché."

For the first time, Andrew really looked at her. She was pretty but not overdone. She didn't even wear makeup. Andrew didn't know why he noticed that.

"I have an idea," he said.

"I can't wait to hear it."

"How would it be if you and I just called it even and started over from scratch?"

"I seem to recall giving you a bunch of money," she pointed out. "I'd say one of us is starting out ahead."

"Actually, I used that to hire Plum back, so basically, you just gave him what you originally promised," he told her. "It's kind of a push, if you think about it."

"What do you want?"

"Look," he said. "I don't have any reason to bullshit you. I know that you're looking for your brother. The way it turns out, I guess I am, too. I don't know if we can help each other or not. But I think we need to talk."

The light in Heather Lomax's eyes could have been optimism. "Let's talk."

"Not here."

"Fine, we can go somewhere else. You name a place and I'll follow you there."

"Keegan's," Andrew said. "Tonight, ten P.M. Just like we originally planned."

"*We* didn't originally plan anything," Heather Lomax said. "You called Benjy and told him the way it had to be."

"Fair enough."

She stood for a moment. She uncrossed her arms.

"No," she said. "I don't think it is. If we're going to start over from scratch, why should you be the one to call the shots?"

It wasn't an unreasonable question. He didn't offer an answer. After a short stretch of silence, she asked another. This one surprised him.

"Do you know what today is?"

"Besides Wednesday?"

She smirked. "You might find this funny. Today happens to be my birthday."

"Hey, no kidding." He didn't know what was so funny about it. "Happy birthday."

"It's been a real laugh riot so far," she said. "But I'll tell you one thing: if you think I'm going to cap it off by driving all the way to some beer joint in the sticks, think again."

It took effort not to smile. Andrew could see he was going to have to try harder not to like this girl.

"I guess I can be flexible."

"Good. I'm in the mood for food. Think you're flexible enough to talk and eat at the same time?"

"I'll do my best."

"Do you have a car of your very own?"

"I have a car of my very own."

"Pick me up at the house, then," she said. "Six o'clock. And don't ring at the gate; I'll meet you on the street."

"I don't know about that."

"What's the matter? Forget the directions already?"

Andrew took a moment to ponder the scenario. He looked her in her clear brown eyes but found he still couldn't read them.

"I think we should keep this simple."

"Relax," she told him. "This is a business appointment, not a date. I'll pay for my own dinner and everything."

Andrew looked at her.

"See you at six," she said.

Before he could say a word, she pivoted on a sandal and left him standing there.

Andrew watched Heather Lomax move off through the crowd. Even after she was long gone, he still tingled with strange energy.

He turned his attention to Travis Plum, whom he'd spied in the near distance. Plum relaxed on an iron bench with a food court soda cup in his hand. He had a smile on his face. Andrew walked over.

"How long have you been sitting there?"

"Long enough," Plum said.

Andrew sighed. "Go ahead and say it."

"Say what?" Plum sucked on his soda straw, chuckling to himself.

"You're like a child," Andrew said. "I swear."

"Oh, don't feel so bad," Plum told him. "This isn't as easy as it looks. I told you there was an art to it."

He smiled around his soda straw all the way back to the parking garage.

17

THOUGH the sun had already begun its long hanging arc toward the waterline, daylight wouldn't begin to fade for some time. Andrew parked in the shade of a squat avocado tree to cut late-afternoon glare. From this position, he had a partial view through the gates to the Lomax spread. He could see rows of hedges, the first curve of what appeared to be a large circle driveway, and the wide stone lip of an outdoor fountain surrounded by manicured green.

At 5:57, the gates opened. Andrew undid his seat belt and got out of the car.

Heather Lomax saw him, looked both ways, and crossed the street. She twisted as she walked, reaching back with one hand to aim some type of key fob in the direction of the fence. A red eye winked from the center of a small box nestled in the bougainvillea, and the gates closed again behind her.

This girl didn't need a keyring, Andrew thought. She needed a utility belt.

For this appointment, she wore a simple sleeveless blouse and a knee-length skirt with some Spanish-looking embroidery around the hem. She'd pulled out her ponytail; let down this way, her hair just touched the strap of the small purse Heather Lomax carried from one shoulder.

Andrew walked around the front bumper and waited for her at the passenger side. When she stepped up onto the curb, he opened the door.

"You showed up," she said.

"I have this new thing about starting over on the right foot." He stuck out his hand. "Andrew Kindler. Pleased to meet you."

The twitch at the corner of her mouth might or might not have been a grin. Either way, she shook his hand.

"Heather," she said. "Likewise, I'm sure."

While Andrew held the door, she bent at the waist and eased herself into the car, smoothing her skirt as she pulled her leg in after her. When he saw that she was in, Andrew shut the door. He waited for a car on the street to pass, then walked back around and got in his own side again.

Heather Lomax waited calmly in the passenger seat, hands folded in her lap. In the confines of the car, he could smell some kind of lotion on her skin. The silence in the space seemed gelid; Andrew started the engine just to put a ripple in it.

While the car idled, he turned in the seat.

"This isn't going to work until we get one thing out of the way," he said.

Heather Lomax shrugged. "Then let's get it out of the way."

"You seem like an intelligent person."

"Thank you."

"Don't thank me. Just tell me why you're sitting here."

She looked at him. "Why are you?"

"This isn't a game," he said. "So let's agree to phrase our answers in the form of an answer. Deal?"

Her brown eyes flashed.

"If you think this is a game to me, you're wrong," she said. "And if you want an answer, ask a real question. How about we agree on that?"

She was either a better actress than Plum seemed to take her for, or the anger in her voice was genuine. Either way, Andrew saw no reason not to oblige.

First, he stated the obvious.

"We could have met at the restaurant, or wherever it is we're going. A familiar, public place—that makes sense. If I were you, that's exactly the way I'd want it to be." He looked at her. "But you have me pick you up at your house."

"This isn't my house. This is my father's house."

"And if you really aren't playing games, then you're way more trusting than you should be. Either that, or you're not as smart as I thought."

"Maybe I just like to trust my first impressions about people."

"Am I supposed to take that as a compliment?"

"If it seems like a compliment," she said, "then by all means do."

Andrew cut to the point instead.

"Yesterday morning, I traded introductions with the first three new people I've met since I moved to this town," he said. "One was a cop. One was a private investigator. And one was your friend Benjamin. All three of them were looking for your brother. Him I haven't met."

"Then why are *you* looking for him?"

"I'll explain what I can about that. But only if you can explain to me why you sent your friend Benjy to pay me off," he said. "And don't tell me you figured I must know something about your brother because Plum followed some cop to the place where I'm staying. That doesn't wash."

"That didn't stop you from taking my money."

"I didn't take your money. Benjy left your money. There's a difference."

Heather opened her mouth, but she closed it again without saying anything.

"He didn't tell you that, did he?"

"He said he gave you the money," Heather said. "I didn't ask him for a play-by-play."

"Oh, he gave it to me. All five thousand dollars of it. Damage control, right? Isn't that what he was supposed to say?" Andrew shook his head. "Come on."

She said nothing.

"You were making an investment," he said. "And you had some reason to think it might pay off. I want to know why."

This time, Heather Lomax didn't quip. She didn't even wait for him to finish speaking. She simply opened up her purse, reached inside, and pulled out a folded piece of paper. She unfolded the paper, ran a finger along the crease, and handed it to him.

"I got that yesterday morning. About an hour before Benjy called to tell me we had a problem."

The sheet was a photocopy of a typed note. Andrew read it twice while she spoke.

Detective Timms,

The man you need to speak with is named Andrew Kindler. He's staying at the enclosed address. He will not be expecting you.

> *Yours,*
> *David Lomax*

"I don't know who wrote it," Heather said, "but that's not my brother's signature. That is *not* my brother's handwriting."

Andrew read the note again, shaking his head. He folded the paper and handed it back to her.

"I know who wrote it," he said.

It would have taken a colder soul than his not to feel the look that came to her eyes. Andrew reminded himself whose neck was on the line.

"Please," she said. "There's more money. However much you want. If you know something . . . please."

"First, tell me where you got that."

"Right here," she said. "It came by courier around ten o'clock. Not to me, to my father. The delivery guy wouldn't even let me sign for it at first." She shook her head quickly. "I knew right then something was rotten. I practically had to stick my tongue in his ear to get him to leave it with me."

"Who was the sender?"

"Blind," she said. "At least on the manifest. Inside the envelope, there was a cover note clipped to this one. All it said was 'FYI.' No name. But that number on the top of the sheet? That's an LAPD evidence tag."

Andrew thought about that for a moment.

He said, "I take it your father has a friend on the force."

"My father helped start the largest officer-assistance fund in that police department," Heather said. "He's on the board of commissioners, and when he votes, he votes blue. He's got all kinds of friends on the force."

"Then I guess I should probably be thanking you for intercepting your daddy's mail."

"Don't thank me," she said. "Just tell me why you're sitting here."

Andrew smiled. She was something.

Instead of answering her question, he fastened his seat belt, let down the parking brake, and put the car in gear.

"It's your birthday," he said. "Dinner's on me."

———————

Todd Todman left the office early enough for an oatmeal facial and a long soak in the whirlpool tub. He buffed his elbows with a loofah sponge and moisturized from his forehead to his toes. He tweezed his eyebrows, trimmed the sprouts from his nostrils, and used a dab of product on his hair.

Todd brushed his teeth and gargled with sea salt. He shaved and spritzed a little Rocabar under his jaw.

Then he dressed, collected his cell phone and keys, grabbed the vase of greenery and fresh yellow blooms he'd picked up from the florist on the way home, and chewed two breath mints on his way out the door.

Traffic was monstrous, but Todd tried to think of it as an opportunity. He kept a finger on the cue button of the CD player while he idled in the clogs, scanning through the "best of" disc the kid at the Tower on Sunset had recommended as required prep for tonight's concert at Royce Hall. Todd had never heard of the performer before Heather had mentioned her in casual conversation a month or two ago, even though he'd pretended to be a huge fan. In truth, he hadn't even known that "Sam Phillips" was a woman until the kid at the record store clued him in.

The good news was that he'd actually gotten to the point where he could hum along to most of the tracks for a few bars at a time. It wasn't until he turned onto Heather's street that the melodies hitched in his throat and died.

From a block away, Todd saw something up ahead that registered only peripherally at first glance. At first, he saw only a man holding a car door. A man awkwardly shaking a young woman's hand. He saw a first date in progress. The scene actually made him smile; buoyed by a sense of kinship, inspired by the prospect of romance in bud, he wished the two of them all the goodwill in the world.

As he neared Doren's front gates, however, Todd felt a sudden sizzle in his heart. He looked twice and touched the brake pedal, almost certain that his eyes were playing tricks on him.

Because surely that hadn't been *Heather* getting into that car.

The man shut the woman's door for her and waited for Todd to pass by. Todd didn't get a good look at him; he maintained his speed, keeping his eyes forward, his hands on the wheel.

As soon as he passed, he began to scour the rearview mirror for details. He saw the man walk around the front of the car, check the street both ways, and get in.

Todd realized that his knuckles had gone white from gripping the steering wheel. The time was 5:59 P.M.

Todd hung the first available right and pulled his Acura to the curb. Eyes still fixed on the rearview, he scooped up his phone and called Heather's line at the house. The answering machine picked up after two rings. He punched off and sat for a moment. Then he scrolled through his presets to Heather's cell number.

When the service spat back its unavailable customer announcement and bounced him to Heather's voicemail, Todd hung up again and closed his phone.

He thought: *Heather. You're not really doing this to me.*

He thought: *Who IS that guy?*

Todd caught a glimpse of motion. In the rearview, he saw the mystery car drive past, carrying away the evening he'd been planning for weeks. Todd forced himself to consider reasonable explanations for this shocking disappointment.

He only wished that he'd taken it easier on the gas pedal as he pulled away from the curb.

The vase of flowers he'd brought for Heather toppled as he swung the car around, and by the time he'd caught up with the other vehicle, the empty passenger seat was soaked to the springs.

18

IN the summer of 1950, the 1st Provisional Marine Brigade of Camp Pendleton, California, sailed from San Diego to the port of Pusan, Korea.

That August, in the hills to the east of Chinju, North Korean troops scattered and pinned a U.S. Army rifle company belonging to the 25th Infantry Division. A support team of 5th Marines from the 1st Brigade attacked from flanking positions, sustaining numerous casualties but eventually routing the enemy force.

Days later, while recovering in adjacent beds of a MASH unit in Taejon, a young Marine and an infantryman from the 25th became friends. Before their respective discharges—the infantryman to Tripler Army Hospital in Honolulu, the Marine back to his unit at the Pusan Perimeter—the two men promised each other two things: to not get shot again for as long as they lived, and to keep contact stateside after they'd found their way home from the war.

The wounded Marine's name was Doren Lomax. After completing his military service, Lomax would return to his native southern California to establish himself in the private sector, most notably as the founder and CEO of the multimillion-dollar corporation known as Lomax Enterprises.

But apparently he'd also kept his word.

At least that was the way Larry Tomiczek had told Andrew the story. When he'd finished, he'd swirled his drink in hand, grinned a little, and said, "Is that some crazy shit, or what?"

Andrew still hadn't interpreted the personal ramifications of the history lesson. But he couldn't help but marvel at the cosmic scope of the odds that seemed to be organizing against him.

"Who was that guy used to be on the radio when we were kids?" Larry had dipped a finger in his bourbon and licked it. "Your ma always played him on that clock radio you guys had on top of the fridge. What was his name?"

"I don't know who you're talking about."

"Used to always say, 'And now you know . . .'"

Larry had intoned the words with tenor gravity.

"'. . . the rest of the story.'"

"Paul Harvey."

"Riiight." Larry had nodded fondly, riding the memory. "Paul Harvey, right, right. That guy still on the radio? He even alive anymore?"

"I have no idea," Andrew had said.

He truly hadn't. But since Larry had planted the cue, Andrew couldn't help but hear Paul Harvey's avuncular cadence delivering the inevitable kicker that tied every tale with a trademark twist.

The man in the other bed of that Taejon Army field hospital: Private First Class Zaganos, Cedric A.

Good old Cedric. Andrew's former boss. The man who sent Eyebrow Larry Tomiczek to California.

And now you know . . .

It was a story best retold over dinner, Andrew decided. As it turned out, he never quite had the chance.

They didn't drive far. Heather Lomax directed him to a little steak and seafood place five minutes away. Andrew didn't know the restaurant, but the restaurant seemed to know Heather Lomax.

It began the moment they walked in together. The slender man greeting and seating clearly recognized Heather, and he came forward to meet her with open arms. The two embraced; when the man finally broke the clinch and leaned back to look at her, Andrew noted that he'd traded the smile for tear-brimmed eyes.

When Heather touched Andrew's elbow and introduced him as a friend of the family, the man smiled earnestly and shook Andrew's hand with the most heartfelt grip Andrew had received all week.

It went on like this. They were seated at an out-of-the way table, but they might as well have been the center of the room. Every few minutes, somebody new appeared. Their waitress pulled up a chair and sat with them at the table for ten minutes, squeezing Heather's hand while the two of them talked. The chef came out from the kitchen. Even the bar staff took their turns. Andrew sat by quietly, smiling the way he imagined a friend of the family might, as each new visitor wished Heather a happy birthday.

You hang in there, they said. *David's fine. Keep the faith, sweetie, he'll turn up. Any day now. He'll be milking this for weeks. . . .*

When he finally found an uninterrupted moment, Andrew looked up from his whiskey rib eye and said, "You're a popular person around here."

Heather dipped the tip of her fork into the little tin of salad dressing next to her plate. She then speared a small bite from her only entrée, a half portion of turkey Cobb salad.

"David and I always come here on our birthday," she said. "It's his favorite place in town. I know it was stupid dragging you here, of all people. But I . . . I just needed this today."

That, Andrew thought, *and you wanted to show me how nobody who knows your brother thinks he did what he probably did.*

He felt snide for thinking it, but that didn't change the situation he seemed to be in. All because of the rich kid of some rich guy who happened to have indirectly saved the skin of Cedric Zaganos on some other continent, some other lifetime ago.

Andrew had never considered himself a philosophical person, but he was beginning to wonder if this was what people meant when they worried about their karma.

Heather Lomax seemed preoccupied throughout the rest of the meal. When the traffic to and from their table finally thinned, Andrew tried asking a question about her brother. Heather didn't even seem to hear it.

While they ate, he noticed three things.

He noticed the way she ingested her salad deliberately, in layers, from the top down, one ingredient at a time: bean sprouts, turkey strips, blue cheese crumbles, and so on down the line until only the lettuce remained.

He noticed that she put her fork down after each bite and didn't pick it up again until the next.

And he noticed that she'd raved about the cheesecake for almost a full minute on the car ride over. But when dessert came, she didn't touch a bite.

No check arrived for the meal. The busboy asked Heather for her autograph. She rose, kissed him on the cheek, and refused. After the kid scooted back to the kitchen—embarrassed, but seemingly unwounded—Heather took up her purse from the seat and looked at Andrew.

"Thank you," she said. "I feel better. Let's go."

Andrew said, "Where now?"

"Someplace where we can talk," she said.

Andrew followed her out of the restaurant, back to the car.

19

ROD had grown to despise the sound of marimbas. Every bouncy, tropical note of the scale. He was starting to wish he'd never had the silly goddamned doorbell installed in the first place.

A few months ago, it had seemed quirky and fun, announcing his visitors to the opening few notes of *To the Max with Rod Marvalis*. Why the hell not? He'd never had a theme song before.

But the novelty had long worn off. Lately, Rod longed for a simple ding, a standard dong. Better yet, sweet silence. He vowed to have somebody out to disconnect the wires one of these days.

In the meantime, he called out, "Christ, Denny, the door's open. You can come on in."

The front door burst wide before the last lilting marimba beat trailed away. Denny Hoyle skidded into the house, carried by the force of his own momentum. He stopped and stood, panting, in a Padres T-shirt with the sleeves cut off. He wore a black Club Maximum ball cap pulled low over his eyes. The eyes darted about, scanning every corner. Hoyle gripped a tire iron in his left hand.

"Rod!"

"Denny. Take it easy. I'm right over here."

Rod raised a hand from behind the Ikea buffet module he'd picked up a couple of months ago to use as a dry bar for the living room.

"Rod. Shit. You okay?"

"I'm fine, Denny. Take a breath."

"What's happening?"

"I'm fixing drinks."

Denny Hoyle blinked. "I mean . . ." He looked over his shoulder. He turned in a circle.

"Ice?"

"Huh?"

"Do you want ice? For the gin, Denny. Bombay Sapphire. We've got ten botanicals here. I'll drink 'em all myself if I have to, but I was planning to share."

"I thought there was some emergency. You said . . . I came quick as I could."

"Yes, you did," Rod said. "You damn well did."

"Huh?"

"I may have exaggerated on the phone." Rod grinned. "Sorry about that. I just wanted to be sure I had your attention."

Denny just stood, vibrating in place.

"But, Denny," Rod said, holding the cocktail tongs over the ice bucket. "Let me just get this straight. It's one in the morning. I call you and tell you I need you right away. You jump in your car, make it all the way up here in fifteen flat, grab that thing out of your trunk ready for trouble . . . and then you ring the doorbell?"

Denny blinked back at Rod from beneath the barn-roof crease of the ball cap's bill. "Didn't feel right just busting in."

Rod laughed. "My friend, you are a piece of work. I swear."

Denny Hoyle released a long breath and bent to a resting position, tire iron across his knees.

Just then—speaking of ding and dong—Rod's other guests appeared from the hallway, each with a drink already in hand. The two had gone off to powder their noses together a few minutes before. From behind the buffet, Rod could see that the tall one still had a faint white streak of dust above her top lip.

"Ladies," Rod said. "Denny. You remember Cammie and Vivian?"

Denny looked more confused than ever. "Um . . . hi."

"We were just getting ready to have a hot tub," Rod said. "I hope you brought your trunks."

"My what?"

Vivian took her cue. She looked at her taller friend, took a deep breath, and drained her drink in one gulp. Then she sashayed over to Denny in her stretchy one-piece sport dress with the sexy white strips down each side.

"Don't worry," she told him, swiping his cap and planting it backward on her own head. She hooked an arm around his neck and beeped his nose. "I didn't bring mine either."

The look on Denny Hoyle's face was priceless. "Rod?"

Rod came around and handed Denny a tumbler of gin. Then he went to Cammie, who beckoned with a slow curling finger. Rod licked his pinky, wiped off her leftover coke mustache, and rubbed it into his gums.

Cammie made a purring sound, leaned in, and tried to lick it back.

"So," Rod said, smacking his lips. "Who's ready to party?"

———————————————

Andrew made Heather Lomax a deal.

Her argument: *You met me on my court. Now I meet you on yours. Fair is fair.*

He didn't understand her insistence, but frankly, he liked her idea. He was exhausted to the point of meltdown; if they went somewhere else and one more person recognized her, he was afraid he might send them away with their teeth in their hands. So he agreed, on one condition. Heather Lomax couldn't have surprised him more than by accepting it.

She rode all the way to the beach house curled up in the backseat of the car, underneath the emergency blanket he'd pulled from the trunk, out of view of whatever friends of her father happened to be working tonight's shift in the park on behalf of the LAPD.

While he made coffee, Heather wandered, looking around. She complimented his taste. He told her it wasn't his. She didn't ask what he meant by that, and he didn't elaborate.

She finally sat down to wait on the same couch upon which he'd bound Travis Plum the day before. Andrew asked her about her friend Benjamin over the buzz of the bean grinder.

"What about him?"

"He strikes me as the protective type," Andrew said. "I expected to see him tonight."

"You told him not to come, didn't you?"

"That's what I told him. That doesn't mean I thought he wouldn't."

"My guess," she said, "is that he's parked outside your little pub down in Torrance. Waiting for me to show up."

Andrew poured a pot of water into the coffeemaker. "So you didn't fill him in on the change of plans."

"No."

"Just like you didn't tell him about that letter in your purse before sending him to pay me off yesterday."

"How do you know I didn't tell him about the letter?"

"Call it a hunch."

"I didn't want him to worry."

"Considerate," Andrew said.

"Don't get high and mighty with me," she said. "You don't know a thing. I love Benjy. And he's risking a lot, looking out for me. But I don't need a chaperone."

Andrew let it drop. He brought down a pair of heavy ceramic mugs from the cupboard and leaned against the counter, waiting for the coffee to brew.

She took hers with milk. He topped off her mug, put the jug back in the fridge, and poured his own cup black. When he brought the mugs out to the living room, he saw that she'd slipped off her sandals and turned on the television. She sat with her legs pulled up on the couch. She'd helped herself to the remote control.

Andrew sat in one of the rattan chairs with his coffee, saying nothing. He watched Heather flip through the muted channels as she took a careful taste from her mug. She snorted and rolled her eyes.

"Something wrong with the coffee?"

Heather glanced at him, then shook her head. "No, nothing. Never mind. I just get cranky every time I see this stupid thing."

Andrew looked at the television. On the screen, he saw one of those late-night infomercials.

"What's that?"

"You mean besides a good way to put yourself in traction?" Heather snorted again. "That's probably the dumbest idea my father ever had."

Andrew squinted at the screen. "The what?"

"The Abdominator, good God. I don't know what he could have been thinking. We lost Greg over this, you know. I don't blame him, either. I wouldn't have let anybody use *my* name to help sell that piece of garbage."

Andrew said, "Who's Greg?"

Heather frowned at him over her coffee mug. Suddenly, she seemed to remember that Andrew wasn't, in fact, a friend of the family after all.

"Gregor," she said. "Gregor Tavlin."

Andrew nodded. "Ah." He thought: *You mean the guy your brother smeared.* He didn't say it.

"I'm starting to believe that you don't know my brother," she said, "because if you did, you'd know that there's no way on earth he could hurt anybody."

"You're right," Andrew said. "I don't know your brother."

Heather brushed quickly at an eye with the back of one hand. She blinked and set her jaw.

"David and Greg may not have seen eye-to-eye on everything. They may have butted heads a time or two. But David respected him. I think they basically even liked each other. Business is business, fine. But I knew Greg. And I know my brother. He didn't kill a human being."

"Then where is he?" Andrew could see that she was having a rough moment, and he didn't particularly enjoy

making it rougher, but he was too tired to continue danc-
ing around the topic. "Look, I said I didn't have any reason to bullshit you. The fact is, I don't care what your
brother did. But let's say you're right. If he's innocent,
why disappear?"

He didn't verbalize the obvious flip side to the question, that wherever her brother went, perhaps it wasn't
by choice. That perhaps he wasn't coming back at all.

Heather rummaged in her purse and took out a cellular phone. She turned it on, punched a couple of but-
tons, leaned forward, and handed the phone to him.

"What do you want me to do with this?"

"Just listen."

Andrew did. He heard a generic recorded voice an-
nounce a message received today, early this morning. He
waited. When the message finally played, Andrew immediately recognized what he was hearing.

You say it's your birthday. The Beatles, right off *The
White Album. My birthday too, yeah.*

Andrew turned off the phone and handed it back to
Heather.

"Ever since we were teenagers," Heather said, "David
would wake me up playing that song. Even after we
moved out of the house. Every year, bright and early, I'd
start my day by answering the telephone and hearing
that on the other end of the line."

Her eyes glistened, but her voice didn't falter.

"My brother didn't disappear. He's right here in
town, or somewhere near. Don't bother asking me how
I know that. I just know. He doesn't want me to know
where. He blocked the number when he called; he's
trying to protect me, the idiot, but he wants me to know
he's okay." She made a quick fist in her lap and released

it. "But he's not okay. And I'm going to find him if I have to . . . dammit, I don't even know what. But I'm going to find him."

Andrew sat quietly for a moment. He sipped his coffee, watched her take her own mug up in her hands again. After a minute, she leaned forward, picked up the remote control, and turned off the television.

Then she looked at him and waited.

He told her a war story.

It only took a few minutes; now that he finally found himself telling it, Andrew was surprised at how quickly it all went. After he'd edited the tale to its pertinent points, there really wasn't much to it. Simple.

Heather sat for a long while after he'd finished. Andrew expected her to begin with a question, but he didn't expect the question she chose.

"You worked for Uncle Cedric?"

Andrew laughed before he could check himself. It was a reflexive response, involuntary, the first thing that came out of his mouth.

"*Uncle* Cedric?"

"Yeah," she said. "That's what we always called him. He used to come visit every couple of years. This was before Mom . . . it's been a while. He'd spend a week or so in the summer. He and Dad would play golf, stay up talking all night long."

Andrew couldn't think of a single thing to say. The image of Cedric Zaganos in golf cleats overloaded every mental circuit.

"What did you do for him, anyway? No offense, but you don't seem like the corporate type." He must have been looking at her strangely, because she leaned back and said, "What?"

"How much do you really know about your uncle

Cedric? I mean, what exactly is it that you think he does?"

"What? For a living?" Heather shrugged. "Business-man, same as my father. I guess we never really asked. We were kids, what did we care? He was fun. But I haven't seen him in years. How is he?"

"Uncle Cedric?" Andrew couldn't stop shaking his head. "Oh, he's just dandy."

Last night, as he'd sat with Larry Tomiczek drinking bourbon at the counter just a few feet away, there had come a point when Andrew had finally recognized that his old friend hadn't come to collect on a favor at all. Larry had put himself in the shithouse with Cedric Zaganos; he'd been given a chance to work his way out again. All of that may have been true.

But the job didn't require a face-to-face. Larry hadn't been asking a favor, he'd been performing an-other one. He'd been delivering a warning.

Suddenly, so many things began to make sense that Andrew found himself unable to absorb them all at once.

"Listen," he said. "I hate to be the one to tell you this, but . . . *shit!*"

Heather jumped at the sudden bleat of his voice. She started to say something, but Andrew was already on the move.

Coffee flew as he launched himself out of the chair and charged across the hardwood, heading for the slid-ing glass door to the deck. The face he'd just glimpsed there pulled back and disappeared.

Andrew nearly hauled the door off its track as he bar-reled through. He could hear fast footsteps beating a re-treat around the side of the house, loud on the planks.

He went after them.

Just as he rounded the corner, Andrew heard a bright,

splintering crack. He ducked and sat tight out of reflex.
A male voice cried out in the darkness, then faded away
in a sudden thudding tumble that began at the top of
the stairs and descended all the way to the bottom.
From where he crouched, Andrew could feel the vibra-
tions through the soles of his shoes.

By the time he identified what he was hearing, he'd
figured out exactly what must have happened.

The intruder had hit the cracked top step full speed
ahead, and the weakened tread had finally given way.
Andrew sprang up and poured it on.

He reached the stairs to find the front half of the
fractured step hanging like a broken hinge; the intruder
had already made the gate down below. Andrew's eyes
still hadn't adjusted to the night. He couldn't make out
more than a silhouette.

"Hey!"

The intruder left the gate swinging open behind
him. Andrew took the steps down three at a time. He
heard a car door, an engine, the squeal of tires. As he hit
ground level, he heard another long screech of rubber
and a bawling horn blast from the southbound lane of
the highway.

He didn't even hear Heather come up behind him.
When she spoke at his shoulder, he jumped.

"Who *was* that?"

Andrew looked at her. He looked across the highway,
at the taillights in the distance, speeding north. He
cursed under his breath. Then he turned and stormed
back up the stairs.

He was pacing the floor when Heather joined him
inside again. Without a word, she walked past and into
the kitchen. She took the liberty of rummaging through
drawers until she found a towel. Andrew watched her

take the towel back into the living room, kneel down, and sop up the puddle of spilled coffee from the wood floor.

Heather returned to the kitchen with her purse, his empty mug, and the sodden, brown-stained towel. She put the mug in the sink and rinsed out the towel under the tap. She wrung out the towel and draped it over the edge of the countertop.

Then she grabbed his keys from where he'd left them on the breakfast bar and walked directly toward him.

"Here," she said. "Let's go."

"Go where?"

"To see my father," she said, and pressed the car keys into his palm hard enough to make his fingers close around them.

When he just stood there, Heather took the keys back.

"Snap out of it," she said, already heading for the stairs down to the garage.

20

"I'M dead." Denny spoke over the murmuring water jets. These were the first words he'd managed in more than two hours. "I'm dead, and this is heaven."

On the other side of the tub, Rod leaned back and forced a grin.

He was not comfortable being naked in the Jacuzzi with Denny Hoyle. But they were alone for the moment; the girls had gone off to freshen up, freshen their drinks, no doubt snort up again. Rod didn't see how he could rightly blame them. Lord only knew, after the hour they'd just put in, they surely needed it.

"I'm glad you're having a good time."

"A good time. I'm in love."

Rod chuckled. "They're something, all right. I'll give you that."

"I didn't even know a person could hold their breath that long."

Rod closed his eyes. There: one more image he'd have to find a way to purge from his memory.

"Damn." Denny rested his head back against the edge of the tub and smiled at the ceiling. "You sure know how to live."

"Hey. They say life is short? I say it's way too god-damned long if you don't know how to have a little fun."

"Amen to that one," Denny said. "So, okay. Don't take me wrong, man, I ain't complaining. But what's all this about?"

"How do you mean?"

"Rod, no offense, but you never exactly invited me to your place before. Didn't think you really even liked me all that much, tell you the truth."

"Listen, Denny, the crazy shit that's been going on . . . what can I tell you? I've been a little rough on you lately. I know that. But the fact is, you might just be the one guy I know I can count on in a pinch. Don't think I don't appreciate it."

Denny seemed to take this load of crap to heart. "Well, hey. I mean, no sweat. I guess I don't know what to say."

"You don't have to say anything," Rod told him. "I take care of the people who take care of me."

"Luthe ain't *even* gonna believe this."

Rod figured this was as good an opening as any. He took it.

"What?" Denny said. "What'd I say?"

"Forget it."

"No, seriously. What? You want me to, like, not mention this or something?" Hoyle brought his hand to the corner of his mouth, made a twisting motion, and threw away an imaginary key. "Say no more, boss. That's totally cool."

"Denny, I'm not your boss. You can say whatever you want to whoever you want. I just . . . nah. Never mind. Help me finish this bottle."

But Hoyle's brow had creased. He reached across the water and took the half-empty bottle of Cuervo that Rod had just found tucked behind the outboard filtration unit.

"Denny. Forget it, okay? This is a party. Bottoms up."

"Yeah," said Denny. "Sure."

"Okay, okay, look," Rod said. "I hate to lay this on you when you're feeling so good, but I'd be a son of a bitch if I didn't. Man to man, I don't think Luther Vines is the friend you think he is."

Denny sat up straighter on his side of the tub.

"Personally, I'd just as soon you never knew how close you came to losing your job this afternoon," Rod lied. This was too easy. It wasn't even fun. "But the way it's going around that snake pit lately, I figure you deserve a heads-up. A guy can watch his back better that way."

Denny let the tequila bottle loll in the foamy water, but he didn't seem to notice. Rod leaned across and took the booze off his hands before it submerged entirely.

Denny said, "The crap you talking about?"

"Todman let me know about it this morning," Rod said. "Don't worry, I straightened that shithead out but quick. But there you have it. That's the real reason I wanted you to come up here tonight. Like I said, you deserve to know."

"You say they were gonna fire me?" Denny couldn't seem to comprehend it. "How come?"

"Bad moon rising, good buddy. This whole thing with the big guy's kid? Cops and reporters crawling all over the place? Don't kid yourself, this is putting the hurt on. Investors are shitting their pants."

"So they're gonna start cuttin' people loose already? Just like that?"

"Every department manager has slash-and-burn orders," Rod said. "That's straight from Todman himself."

"No."

"The way I hear it, your good buddy Luther stretched you out on the chopping block without shedding too many tears. Not that he'd admit it if you asked."

Denny took the entire preposterous fabrication as if absorbing a blow.

"Luther? Nah."

"Just the way these bastards do business, Denny. Better get used to it."

"I don't buy it," Denny said. "I mean, Luthe's an asshole and all, but we're buds. He wouldn't do me like that."

"Hey, I'm sure it's nothing personal. But think about it. You've got a full salary with benefits. They can keep five or six jerk-off college part-timers for the price of a Denny Hoyle. But tell me any one of those cro mags would get in their car in the middle of the night and come in here ready to tee off on some nutcase stalker or burglar or whatever the case with an iron bar if it came down to it."

"You said there was trouble."

"And you passed the test," Rod said. "Not that I had any doubts. You make me glad I fought for you. Where do you think old Luther is right now while you're here, off the clock, helping me fend off two sex-crazed airheads who obviously are prepared to do just about anything to get their pretty mugs on TV?"

Denny grinned a little, though he didn't lift his eyes. "I guess somebody's gotta do it."

Rod laughed. "Atta boy. There's no faith in this world, Denny. There's no such thing as fair. That's why loyalty counts for something. With me? Denny? It god-damn counts for something."

Denny Hoyle said nothing to that. He just kept staring at the bubbling foam in front of him, his grin slowly fading. Rod passed him back the bottle. This time, Hoyle guzzled long and hard.

Rod said, "Sorry to be the one to tell you."

"Hey, Rod," Denny said. "About all this. Maybe you just got some bad info or something. I mean maybe Luther didn't know nothing about it."

"Sure, Denny. Could be." Rod looked at him gently. "I guess the next thing you'll tell me is the big bald bastard isn't angling for my job, either."

Denny glanced up. His eyes clouded, and he looked down again quickly.

"That's okay," Rod said. "I'm not asking you to rat out your so-called pal. I know all about it. How he's been going around to Todman behind my back, trying to make me look bad, the whole song and dance. That's the thing about these muscle freaks, Denny. Balls like little peanuts."

"That's just Luthe. He ain't nothin' for you to worry about."

"Don't be so sure," Rod said. "Listen, you might think I've got it made. But the fact is, we're in the same boat, you and me."

"Come on," Denny said. "You're the man, man. You're Rod Marvalis. Besides, you got contracts and shit, right? What you got to worry about?"

"Ask the last guy if a contract with Lomax Enterprises means anything. Go ahead. Go ask Gregor Tavlin if there's any love and tell me what he says." Rod snapped his fingers. "Oh, wait. I forgot. He's dead."

Denny pressed his knuckles into his eyes.

"I didn't just get off the bus in this town," Rod said. "I know the score. Tell me something. Do you think they pay me what they paid Gregor Tavlin? That arrogant jag-off?"

"Guess I never wondered."

"Well, don't bother, because I'll clue you in on a little something. It ain't even close. I'm a joke to them. They know it and I know it."

"Nah."

"It's time you woke up to reality, my man. All that matters is bottom dollar. These pricks know they can have Rod Marvalis for half what they had to fork over to keep Gregor Tavlin around. And they know they can get somebody young and hungry for pocket change compared to what they need to keep me. Forget about style. Forget about talent. Forget about everything you think matters in this life. And don't ever bend over to pick up your paycheck."

"Damn, Rod. You're startin' to kill my buzz over here."

"Then I'm doing you a favor," Rod said. "Believe it or not, I lost my buzz a long time ago."

"Dude."

"Listen up, Denny. I'm going to tell you something. And this is something I've never told anybody. But I feel like we understand each other."

Denny finally looked at him.

"I hate this gig," Rod said. "I truly do. But I'm smart enough to realize that this is as good as it's going to get for me now. I'm probably lucky it ever got this good at all."

"Don't talk like that."

"It's true. Before this, Denny, it was getting to the point where I couldn't even get arrested in this town anymore." Rod reached and took the bottle back. "People forget, Denny. It doesn't matter what you did yesterday. There's no love. Ten years ago, if anybody had told me this is where I'd be right now? Prancing around in a pair of tights in front of a roomful of huffing heifers every day? I would have laughed in their face. Right in their face. Then banged their girlfriend just to make my point."

"But you're on television, man."

"Cable."

"Still."

"You don't need to try and cheer me up," Rod said. "It *is* a joke. My life hasn't worked out the way I thought it would, hey, fine. I'm not crying about it. There comes a point a guy takes what he can get." Rod tipped the bottle high. "But I'll be goddamned if I'm going to let some nutless nobody like Luther Vines try and take it away."

Denny stared at the water.

"We're the last of a breed, you and me." Rod didn't know what that was supposed to mean, but he liked the sound of it. It sounded like just the sort of bullshit a guy like Denny Hoyle could sink his teeth into. "We've got to look out for each other."

"I gotta tell you this is kinda fuckin' with my head," Denny said. "I'm totally hammered, for one thing."

"Sobriety is highly overrated," Rod said. "But for what it's worth, I know how you feel. I just wanted you to know that we're on the same side. You keep looking out for me? I'll keep looking out for you. The way things are right now, that might be the only thing guys like you and me have going for us."

A husky voice said, "Not the *only* thing, hon."

Together, Rod and Denny looked to see that Cammie and Vivian had returned. They'd left their towels somewhere else.

It was a sight to behold. As Rod and Denny watched, the girls crisscrossed paths as they moved. This time, Cammie slipped back into the water on Denny's side of the tub, Vivian on Rod's.

"Hi," Cammie said.

Denny looked at her with glimmering, intoxicated eyes. "Hey."

Cammie giggled and swung a leg over him like she was mounting a Harley. Her tight smooth skin glistened like a wet seal's.

Lord, was she high.

"Last of a breed," Rod called over to Denny. "You and me."

"You're a couple talking animals, all right."

Rod leaned back and looked at Vivian. "Excuse me? Did you say something?"

He couldn't be sure in the dark, but he thought he saw her roll her eyes.

"I said talk to me, you animal."

Before he could, she took a deep breath and went underwater again.

The clock on the dresser read 1:00 A.M. when Adrian Timms finally peeled himself out of bed.

The clock was last year's Father's Day present, one of those that kept time by a signal from the U.S. atomic clock in Colorado. Rachel said she'd ordered it out of one of those pricey men's gadget catalogs. Besides the time, the clock featured a temperature display that hadn't dipped below 84 degrees since the overworked window A/C unit had fried itself the day before yesterday.

A warm breeze circulated through the open windows, but it only pushed the rest of the hot air around. Convection ovens operated on a similar principle.

Drea Munoz had offered to put him up, but so far Timms had held out. Frankly, he hadn't expected the situation to go on this long. But each day this week, when he finally dragged himself home for the night, he'd found another apology note from the building manager taped to his door. Each day, the note claimed the service tech would be out the next. But each day the heat wave broke a new record, and everybody in town was booked tight with emergency calls.

Timms left his own note behind each morning, instructing the manager to make sure he sent the repair guys to the elderly couple across the quad first.

Air, no air. He hadn't been sleeping lately anyway.

At 1:03 A.M., 88.4 degrees, Timms shambled into the kitchen. He wet down his hair at the sink, grabbed a cold beer from the refrigerator, and took the beer with him to the living room.

On his way to the couch, Timms stooped to slip out a magazine from the case file he'd left strewn across the coffee table. This was a back issue of *Health & Fitness* from last December. Timms turned back to the spot where he'd tented the magazine, right in the middle of the cover piece.

They'd titled the segment "The Bold Behind the Beautiful." It was the annual compilation of profiles and interviews with the men and women the editors had selected as the ten most influential people in the industry.

Down two slots from the previous year's ranking, but still holding strong at number eight: Gregor Tavlin, Club Maximum, Los Angeles.

Mostly it was fluff, nothing about Tavlin they didn't already know. But something about the article had been nagging Timms. The publication date, for one thing.

According to Lomax Enterprises, Gregor Tavlin had left "the family"—this was how the PR man, Todman, seemed to prefer phrasing it—after nearly a decade of filial love and loyalty because the man disagreed with new directions the company had begun to explore.

Timms knew canned corporate babble when he heard it. Which was exactly what he'd told Doren Lomax the morning they'd searched his office building. Without blinking twice, the CEO had sent his attorneys out of earshot and provided interpretation.

"Disagreed with new directions" was just the official explanation for the ugly truth: the company's resident alpha male had gotten territorial. According to Lomax, Gregor Tavlin had snorted and stamped his feet at the first sight of Rod Marvalis. When he hadn't gotten his way, he'd packed up his jockstrap and abandoned the herd.

Yet the magazine's lead time for the issue had obviously overlapped Tavlin's sudden departure from the same company for which he expressed such commitment in print.

If the interviews they'd conducted so far gave any indication, the Maximum Health family was a tight-knit bunch. It wasn't easy finding the employee who readily dissed the franchise. But Timms had to believe he wasn't the first person to think sacrificing Gregor Tavlin for Rodney Marvalis had to be the dumbest trade since the Dodgers gave up Martinez for DeShields.

He could remember mixing up baby formula on this same couch as he'd watched the Trojans ramble over Michigan State in the Rose Bowl the year his teenage daughter had been born. Marvelous Rod Marvalis had run for three touchdowns and thrown for another in that game. An overrated arm, but he could always find the pocket. And the guy ran the short-side option like a man possessed.

Even back then, Marvalis had been an undisciplined glory hound, and Timms hadn't been all that surprised when the guy crapped out in the pros. Still: from All-American to infomercial huckster in a double-handful of inglorious years?

Rod the Bod, they called him now.

It was sad.

And something about the whole acquisition of LifeRite, Incorporated just didn't play. These get-buff-quick scams like The Abdominator were a dime a dozen. Especially in L.A., this land where impossible silicon-based life-forms roamed free among the flabby. But it didn't take an MBA to recognize that The Abdominator was aimed at a Denominator. As in Lowest Common.

Timms still couldn't factor it. Rod Marvalis shilling spring-loaded plastic just didn't jibe with the corporate image Lomax Enterprises projected.

He sat in the heat and stared at the fitness magazine. After a while, he began flipping pages.

When he noticed that he'd begun to pat his own midsection absently, he made himself stop and fetched another beer.

21

ANDREW did the math in the car.

The way he figured it, the man must have been in his
seventies at least, even if he'd been only draft age when
he and Cedric had been busy fighting for the country
that would later make each of them wealthy men. Andrew didn't know Cedric's age. He guessed the old
crook had to be pushing eighty by now.

By appearances alone, Doren Lomax could have been
a hale fifty-five. His hair had gone silver but stayed
thick. He had a strong face, lined with character but un-
withered by age. The square shoulders had yet to sag,
the waistline yet to give way. Lomax's eyes were still full
of steel, the smile he turned on his daughter still vibrant.
Even at midnight, half in the bag.

Which was how they found him, camped in a big
leather armchair deep inside the big dark house, in what
Andrew took to be the man's study. Built-in bookcases

spanned the height and length of the two nearest walls. A large plasma-screen television pumped flickering blue light into the room, but Lomax didn't seem to be watching.

"Sweetie," he said, reaching to set a drink on the side table near his hand. Next to the glass, facedown, he placed the picture frame he'd been holding. Lomax pointed a remote control, muted the television, and rose to meet Heather. He leaned to kiss her forehead.

"I was hoping you'd be getting home soon. I haven't even had a chance to wish you a happy birthday."

"Daddy." She raised on her tiptoes and pecked his cheek. "I need to talk to you."

Lomax looked over her shoulder to Andrew. Andrew turned his attention from the silenced television. He'd recognized the program on the screen the moment they'd come in. It was the same program that had gotten Heather's blood up back at the beach house. Something about the worst idea her dad ever had.

"Hello," Lomax said, offering his hand. "I'm Doren Lomax, Heather's father. How do you do?"

"I've done better," Andrew said.

Lomax looked at him. He looked at his daughter.

"You've been drinking," Heather said.

"I've been reminiscing," he told her. "Sit down and tell me what's wrong."

Heather didn't sit. She stood and told what she had to tell, handing over the letter from her purse as she spoke. She kept talking as Lomax returned to the chair and read over the paper in his hands. He started out looking like a man scanning a business agreement; he ended up looking like a man rereading positive test results, as if the act of doing so might change the horrible news.

Heather started with Travis Plum and ended with the unidentified intruder at the beach house a half hour ago.

By the time she'd finished, Doren Lomax's face had drawn in on itself. But the steely glint hadn't faded from his eyes. He turned the blade of it on Andrew for a long moment. Then he looked at Heather.

"What were you thinking?" he said quietly. "Heather." He held up the note she'd handed him. "You should have given this to me the minute you . . . what on earth were you thinking?"

"Daddy."

"And Benjy! Going along with *any* of this. What were you two *thinking?*"

"Leave Benjy out. He's got nothing to do with it."

"Like hell he doesn't. He's going to answer for himself, too."

Heather folded her arms and waited. Andrew stood by. Doren Lomax glanced at him once. Briefly.

"Thank God," he finally murmured, as though exhaling two days of worry concentrated into one unexpected five-minute dose. "Sweetheart. Thank God you're okay."

"I'm not okay," Heather told him. "I'm not okay at all."

"You should have come to me."

"Explain this," she said, pointing to the letter. "Explain this."

Lomax just looked at the letter again. After a moment, he reached for his drink and finished it off. He glanced at the television. Folded the paper. Rose out of the chair.

"Excuse us, Mr. Kindler."

Andrew assumed the man meant for him to leave. He didn't want to make this ugly, but he planned to stand his ground until he had some answers. He meant to let Lomax know it.

But Doren Lomax just belted his robe and said, "Make yourself comfortable if you like."

Without looking at Andrew, Heather followed her father out of the room.

Comfortable.

Andrew didn't go that far. But while he waited, alone in the low light of Doren Lomax's sanctuary, he did help himself to a look around.

The bookcase had books in it. Books and books. From floor to ceiling, Andrew found a lending library's worth of volumes shelved according to no particular system he could discern. Classic literature rubbed covers with business and finance, health and fitness, art and architecture. He came across a wide band of psychology texts in a row; heavy stuff, by the look of it, not the fluffy learn-to-love-yourself crap Caroline kept trying to get him to read. He spotted biographies of Winston Churchill, Raymond Chandler, Frank Zappa, and Sally Ride. He found a copy of Sun Tzu's *The Art of War* leaning against Betty Friedan's *The Feminine Mystique*. History, philosophy, law, science. Social this and cultural that, all over the map. The only things most of these books had in common were the creases in their spines.

Lomax was either a true lover of knowledge or a true lover of feeling like one. Either way, the guy must have been hell on wheels at a cocktail party.

But his books didn't interest Andrew nearly so much as his photographs, which he found all over the room—on the walls, the tables, the shelves, crowded at the corners of an enormous oak desk hulking in a windowed alcove.

A few of the photos depicted Doren Lomax standing or sitting or shaking hands with somebody who looked like they must have been important. One faded black-and-white print in a flimsy tin frame showed a group of five hard young men gathered in front of a pile of large knobby tires. Two of the men were shirtless; two held rifles; the last, Andrew recognized as a younger edition of the man who had just left the room. All wore dog tags and military fatigues.

But the greatest number of photos by far were simple, candid snapshots, often layers on layers of them tucked into a single frame. Days at the beach, graduations. Christmas mornings. Random moments that had no obvious context.

Family pictures.

Andrew paused over one in particular: a shot of Heather as a little girl, no more than nine or ten years old. She had freckles and a missing front tooth, and he could see where she'd gotten her eyes. The composition of the shot provided a telltale comparison; it could only have been Heather's mother there in soft focus in the background, smiling from a yellow blanket spread out over green grass.

The room was a walk-in scrapbook, and Andrew finally gave up browsing it. He went directly to one last frame: the one Lomax had left turned over by his chair.

The picture beneath the glass was obviously of a more recent vintage than most of the others. Not taken yesterday, but not more than a handful of years past. It was yet another photo of what Andrew could now identify as the Lomax nuclear family: Doren, Barbara, Heather . . . and none other than the fugitive son himself, giving his sister a set of bunny ears. They were dressed for evening, all sitting together around a table in a restaurant, everybody smiling for the lens. David Lomax had his dad's square chin and shoulders, but he shared the same eyes as Heather.

One more person sat at this family table, in the chair to David's left. Andrew only recognized this face because he'd seen it going through the newspapers yesterday. The head shot in the paper hadn't quite caught whatever it was that made this guy such big news, but you could see a little of it here.

This snapshot captured Barbara and Heather's uncomplicated beauty, Doren Lomax's character, David's confidence. But you could have charged your camera's flash pack with the charisma in Gregor Tavlin's grin. Studying the photo by the light of the television, Andrew thought, *pal, you were bound to get killed by somebody.*

"A moment from a happier time."

Andrew looked up to find that Doren Lomax had returned. He hadn't heard so much as a whisper of movement. He placed the frame back the way he'd found it.

"Nice-looking family," he said. "Cedric must be one proud uncle."

Lomax stood with his hands in the pockets of his robe. He regarded Andrew thoughtfully. He looked older than when he'd left the room.

"I wouldn't pretend to have any idea what a person does to earn a vendetta from Cedric Zaganos," he finally said. "I wouldn't pretend I was interested to know. But I don't suppose I'd want to be wearing that person's skin."

"If I were you," Andrew said, "I wouldn't want that person's skin in my den. Not unless it was tacked to the wall."

"I'm not sure if that's supposed to sound threatening," Lomax said. "If it is, don't bother. I don't know you, and I make no assumptions. But whoever you are, from what my daughter has told me, you must have some sense of nobility."

"My shining armor is at the cleaners," Andrew said.

"Well. Another man might have behaved differently, under the circumstances. You have my gratitude."

"You might want to save it until we're finished."

"As far as I'm concerned, we are."

Lomax walked to a keypad on the wall. At the touch of a button, the television went dead, and the lights in the room came up to a slightly less romantic level. Andrew tensed, suddenly considering the fact that Heather hadn't returned to the room.

Larry was right, he thought. He really could be dumb when he tried.

But when Lomax's right hand came out of its pocket, it held only a small slip of paper, folded in half. Lomax seemed to ponder the paper a moment before handing it to Andrew.

"Cedric has his own sense of nobility, I suppose. But his contribution to the conversation you and I find ourselves having now was unsolicited. I won't insult you with an apology, but I'm not sure what else to say." He put the hand back into the pocket at his waist again. "I'm sorry to have made each other's acquaintance, Mr. Kindler."

On the slip of paper, Lomax had written a name and an address. Andrew recognized neither. He assumed by the name—Digman Self Storage—that the address belonged to some kind of rental facility somewhere in town. At the bottom of the paper, Lomax had printed: *601D.* Below that, a six-digit number.

"What is this?"

"I wouldn't know. I only made a long-distance phone call and wrote down what you see there." Lomax paused, then added, "For what it's worth, the man I called didn't hang up happy. When I described the person my daughter brought home to meet me tonight, I got the impression the information . . . well. I got the impression the information contradicted Cedric's expectations."

"I'll bet it did."

Andrew thought about Larry Tomiczek. A sick, cold feeling settled in his gut. He wondered where Larry was at this moment. He wondered what he was doing. He hoped he was packing to go somewhere else.

"He wasn't very happy with my request, either," Lomax said. "But the prerogative here isn't his, it's mine. So that piece of paper is yours."

"Sounds like quite an understanding you and Uncle Cedric have."

"I don't ask Ced to understand my choices in life, and he returns the favor. That's the only way it can be sometimes with very old friends."

Andrew said nothing to that.

"My house," Lomax said, "is in disarray. I hold myself accountable for that. But my family carries its own burdens. From here on, whatever unsettled business you have with Cedric is yours again."

My house is in disarray. Somehow, the guy managed to talk like this without sounding like an asshole or a fool. Andrew wondered how long it had been since anybody had intimidated Doren Lomax.

"Swell," he said. "Think you can give me a note along those lines? Something I can give to your cop friends when I go home?"

"That's a regrettable situation. I'm not going to tell you I can undo what's already been done. I can tell you that tomorrow I'll be speaking to the police about a few things I should have volunteered when all of this started. I don't know what the result of that will be. Hopefully you'll have your privacy back sooner rather than later." Lomax seemed to consider his next statement before he made it. "In the meantime, if it eases your mind, you can use one of our guest rooms for the rest of tonight. I'll tell Rosa to have breakfast for you in the morning. You can leave here with a night's rest and a full stomach. And if we're both very fortunate, neither of us will see the other ever again."

"Thanks," Andrew said. "But I'll just cut to the 'ever again' part."

"Whatever you like."

"Where's the birthday girl?"

Lomax looked at him. In a quick sharp flash, the steel returned to his eyes for the first time since he'd returned to the room.

"Heather," he said, "is accepting some news I wish I didn't have to give her. What concern is it of yours?"

"She drove my car here," Andrew told him. "She still has my keys."

Lomax seemed to grow older by the moment. Or maybe just wearier. He exhaled.

"I'll tell her you're leaving," he said.

"That'd be fantastic."

"Good night, Mr. Kindler."

With that, Lomax left the room again.

When he was gone, Andrew looked at the slip of paper one more time. He put it in his pocket. The last of his energy seemed to run out of his body like water through an unplugged drain. He'd lost track of how long it had been now since he'd last slept. He tried to process everything that had happened this past hour, but he couldn't seem to get any traction. The gears in his brain had begun to slip and grind.

He took a step and dumped himself into Lomax's big leather chair to wait for Heather—or whoever—to show up with his keys.

Andrew couldn't remember ever sitting in a chair so comfortable.

He couldn't remember deciding to rest his head back, or closing his eyes.

22

HE still sometimes woke up disoriented.

Andrew sat tight until he could get his bearings. He forced his eyes open wide, straining to collect the available light. Slowly, he regained a sense of his surroundings. Shapes emerged from the shadows. He remembered where he was and what he was doing there.

Somehow, his feet had found their way up to the footstool in front of Doren Lomax's reading chair. Somebody had taken off his shoes and draped an afghan over his legs.

Beautiful. One day, Andrew thought, people just might stop taking him seriously.

He looked at his watch, saw that it was almost four in the morning. *Long* past time to be out of here. Which was exactly where he planned to get, just as soon as he found his keys.

Andrew pulled on his shoes and set off on the dumbest

scavenger hunt he could imagine, feeling his way through the deep-night silence of the Lomax household.

He followed the hallway off the study into a larger room, which became a larger room still. The ceiling soared somewhere over his head, and silver light leaked in through clerestory windows all around. Thick carpet muffled his steps, and the darkness seemed to amplify the tidal rush of his own blood in his ears. He came upon a low glow somewhere near the end of another short hallway and headed toward the light.

Andrew found himself in a kitchen no larger than an airplane hangar. The glow he'd followed, he now discovered, emanated from within the open cavity of a Sub-Zero refrigerator large enough to hold other refrigerators. The door of the fridge stood open, propped that way by a rail-backed chair.

In the bright light, Andrew could see a collection of empty containers littering a central island surrounded by tall stools: a Chinese takeout carton, some empty Tupperware. A couple pint tubs of Ben and Jerry's, both down to runny remnants. He picked up an empty white sack with the words *Godiva Chocolatier* printed in gold. He recognized the sack at about the same time he recognized the sound he'd been hearing. Soft, but unmistakable.

The sound of retching.

Before he could decide whether to stand there listening or retreat back down the hall, Andrew heard a toilet lid drop. A flush.

Soft footsteps padded across the tile of the kitchen floor. Heather appeared in a tank top and panties, hair disheveled, tangled strands hanging in her eyes.

She saw him and stopped. Andrew put the candy sack back where he'd found it. She brushed the hair out of her face. They looked at each other.

Then Heather continued on to the refrigerator, pulled the chair away, and closed the door.

"If you're looking for a late-night snack," she said, "we're out."

Her voice sounded flat. Andrew wasn't quite sure what to say. He felt awkward.

"I need my car keys."

Heather nodded without looking at him. "They're still in my purse."

Andrew waited for her to say more, but she didn't. She bent down, opened a door by her knee, and retrieved a thin plastic garbage bag. She began collecting the empty containers and putting them into the bag.

"Look," he finally said, "I can find my way back to your dad's study and wait there for you. Unless you want me to wait here."

"I'll bring them to you," she said.

Andrew nodded. He watched her a moment.

"Please don't stare at me."

He didn't have anything to say to that. So he turned and left her be.

Back in her father's room of memories, he waited for a long time.

Thursday, August 16

EVIDENCE LINKS LOMAX EXECUTIVE

By MELANIE ROTH

TIMES staff writer

A soiled photo identification card may link local businessman David Lomax to the suspected murder of former employee Gregor Tavlin, police said late Wednesday afternoon.

"An ID badge belonging to Mr. Lomax was discovered during an authorized search," LAPD investigator Detective Adrian Timms confirmed. "Lab analysis revealed evidence that makes [the badge] potentially relevant to our investigation. That's the only determination we've made about it at this time."

Detective Timms declined to comment about the nature of the evidence. Despite findings related to the security badge, authorities have not issued an arrest warrant for Lomax, a junior vice-president of the Los Angeles corporation Lomax Enterprises. Investigators have been unable to locate the 30-year-old Lomax.

Lomax's father, Doren Lomax, is the founder and CEO of Lomax Enterprises and an appointed member of the LAPD Board of Police Commissioners.

Neither corporate officials nor legal representatives for Lomax Enterprises could be reached for comment Wednesday.

23

HE wouldn't have thought himself capable of dozing again. He must have managed, because someone woke him up.

Andrew opened his eyes to a middle-aged woman with hard features and laugh lines around her eyes and mouth. She roused him by patting the back of his hand. He sat up in the armchair. Sunlight streamed into the room.

"You must be Rosa," he said. His tongue stuck to the roof of his mouth.

Rosa smiled. "Time for breakfast, Mister Andrew. How do you drink your coffee?"

Andrew looked at his watch. It was 7:30 in the morning. He glanced to his left and saw that his car keys had been returned. They waited for him on the side table by the chair.

"Thank you," he said. "But I need to be going."

Rosa didn't try to convince him to stay. Andrew left

her folding the afghan he'd been loaned. By following the housekeeper's directions, he found his own way to the front door.

Outside, the world was already on slow bake. Andrew walked out into the bright fragrant morning and into a wall of heat. The air outside wrapped him like a lead quilt, parched his sinuses when he breathed.

Crushed oyster shells crunched underfoot as he walked toward his car, which sat in the nearest bend of the circular driveway where Heather had parked it last night.

Andrew stopped at the driver's-side door and took one last look over his shoulder. By daylight, the grounds and the house seemed less palatial than the image Andrew had developed in his mind.

He couldn't wait to be gone.

Andrew got in the car, started the engine, and dropped into gear. He'd just started to pull away when the passenger door opened. Andrew hit the brakes reflexively.

Heather Lomax got in beside him and shut the door. She had her purse with her, hair pulled back in a ponytail. She was wearing what looked like the same tank top he'd seen her using for pajamas a couple of hours ago. She'd pulled on a pair of cutoff jeans and jogging shoes.

"I'm ready," she said. "Let's go."

"Excuse me?"

"My father gave you an address. I heard the two of you talking last night. I'm going with you."

"Sorry," Andrew said. "But I don't think so."

"No?" Heather tilted her head at him. "How do you plan to drive out of here? Going to ram through the gates, are you? Like the movies?"

Andrew kept looking at her. The gates. He hadn't even thought about it.

Heather held up her keyring, the one with the pepper spray and the little doodad that opened sesame.

Andrew sighed. He looked ahead, through the windshield.

Then he shot out his hand and grabbed the dangling keys.

He wasn't sure what happened in the meantime, but the pain shot up his arm like a bolt of electricity. His arm twisted, and he didn't have the keys in his grip anymore. His foot slipped off the brake momentarily, and the car lurched. The next thing he knew, he was biting the steering wheel.

"Not a terrible move," she said, holding him in a thumb lock, bracing his elbow with her other hand. "But you telegraphed it."

"Thanks for the pointer."

She applied more pressure.

"Ouch," Andrew said.

Heather gave one final twist and let him go. He sat up rubbing his thumb.

"Where'd you learn that?" he said. "Ninja summer camp?"

"Gregor taught self-defense courses at the club," she told him. "He designed this whole system, works for anybody. If you're big, it makes you quicker; if you're small, it makes you bigger—that kind of idea."

"Neat."

"Tell you what: next time, grab my shoulders. I'll show you another little thing. Works great on dates."

"It's a little early in the morning," Andrew said, still massaging his throbbing thumb.

"Some other time," Heather said. "So what's the deal? Are we sitting here, or are we going?"

Andrew shook his head. This girl. He didn't have the energy.

"You're the gatekeeper," he said.

———————————

Beyond the high fence between the Lomax estate and the rest of the world, the quiet street wasn't so quiet this morning.

At first, Andrew didn't know what had gotten into Heather. As the gates opened, she launched herself up over the console between the seats and disappeared into the backseat so quickly he thought she might be having some kind of fit. When he looked over his shoulder, he saw only a lumpy, vaguely human-shaped pile of emergency blanket on the floor.

He saw the news vans parked out on the street as they rounded the final bend of the driveway. As they reached the gates, he saw miscellaneous crew hands hanging time along the curbs.

He guessed there must be news. He put on his sunglasses and rolled on through.

A slim blond woman with a microphone scurried in front of the car as a belabored camera guy trailed cables behind her. Andrew braked. The reporter hustled over, smiling with all her teeth. He rolled down the window and breathed in a lungful of hair spray.

"Carla Sheppard, Channel 5," she said, trying to peer inside the car. "Would you tell us your name, sir?"

"Plum," Andrew said. "Travis Plum. I'm a private investigator. You can call me at my office. Gotta go."

He raised the window and punched the gas.

From the floor behind him, Andrew heard a muffled beep. He looked in the rearview mirror and saw the gates closing again.

Heather looked at the Thomas Guide he kept under the passenger seat while Andrew turned where she told him to turn. Between the two of them, they managed to find their way onto a side street where a city crew was shaving old bark off the palm trees.

Curled strips of wood the size of boogie boards fell to the pavement up ahead, blocking their lane. He couldn't turn around because of the traffic behind him. So they waited while the guys on the ground signaled to the guys up above. Then they waited some more as the workers waved the oncoming lane through first.

While they sat there, idling, Andrew could feel Heather studying the Guide in the passenger seat. Besides feeding him directions, she hadn't said a word since they'd left the snarl of reporters back at her father's house. He'd responded in kind.

But for some reason, now that they'd stopped moving forward, the silence began to grate on Andrew's nerves. Part of him was curious to know what the old man had told her to set her off last night. Another part of him didn't want to get into it.

So he said, "That was something back there."

"That was nothing. It was worse last week." She didn't look up from the map.

"I take it you must be feeling better."

"I'm feeling fine," she said. "Why?"

"You just seemed a little under the weather," he said. "When we bumped into each other earlier. That's all."

Now she looked up for a moment. Straight ahead, out the windshield. She didn't look at him.

"Under the weather," she mused. "Tactful."

"I'm just making conversation."

"You're chatty all of a sudden."

She turned a page and folded the Guide back on it-self, rested the thick oblong book against her bare thigh. Andrew assumed the conversation was over until she finally spoke again.

"I've been under the weather since I was fifteen," she said. "So there you go. It's been under control for years now, but when I get stressed enough, sometimes the old habits still . . . flare up."

Andrew didn't say anything.

"For the record, last night wasn't the first time I've broken down and binged since I got myself together. But it's the first time I've purged anything since my twentieth birthday. Hell of a way to kick off my thirties, don't you think?

Andrew didn't think anything. The guy in the or-ange vest up ahead started waving at him, so he pressed on the gas, eased around the worksite, and rolled on.

"That quieted you down," she said. "More than you needed to know?"

"It's really not any of my business."

"You asked."

"So I did."

"If it makes you feel any better, you're right. It *isn't* any of your business. But it just so happens you caught me in a need-to-talk-about-it kind of mood. Normally I'd call my brother on a morning like this. Under the circumstances, I guess you'll have to do."

Andrew thought: *lucky me.*

"I saw you watching me eat last night at the restaurant. You saw me in all my glory in the kitchen this morning. So go ahead. Take your best shot. You've earned it."

He took his best shot. "Why?"

"Usually it helps keep me honest," she said. "It's a

trick Greg came up with, actually. A way of holding myself accountable." She smoothed the map again, making the thin paper crinkle beneath her hand. "I eat my meals slowly. And every time I pick up my fork, I've made a conscious decision to do it. I take ownership of every bite."

"I mean," he said, checking his side mirror and changing lanes, "why? You're rich. Who cares what you look like?"

"My father is rich," she said. "And haven't you ever heard that money isn't everything?"

"Spoken like somebody who's always had it," he said.

"Don't think I don't know that I'm privileged," she said. "If this is your way of making small talk, you could use some work."

"Just stating an observation."

"Have you ever observed your own ass on camera?"

Andrew was forced to confess that he had not.

Heather sighed and waved at the air with a hand.

"Forget I even said that, it doesn't matter. That's just an excuse. It doesn't really have anything to do with looks. At least it never did for me."

"Then what?"

"What. You want the definitive explanation?" She looked out the window. "I don't know what you're hoping to hear. You were in my father's den, you must have seen some of his pictures. So you've seen me when I was younger. You know I was one fat little kid."

"I guess I didn't notice."

She nodded up ahead. "That car's snaking you."

Andrew saw it. He touched the brake and let the other driver in.

"Kids can be sinister. It's not easy being the daughter

of a man who owns health clubs when you weigh a hundred and sixty pounds in the seventh grade."

The comment reminded Andrew of his conversation with Caroline yesterday. He thought about Lane Borland, what Caroline had said about the old neighborhood. He said, "I don't suppose it is."

"But I never liked easy," Heather said. "Food was sort of my personal revolution when I was that age. Screw 'em, right? You want fat? I'll show you fat."

In the visor mirror, he saw her smiling to herself. It really was a nice smile.

"The ironic part is that when I got into my teens, my body rebelled against *me,*" she said. "I slimmed up and got curvy without even trying. You don't have to be thin to be healthy. Greg believed that, and so do I. But once I felt what it was like to be skinny, I decided I liked it. I didn't stop liking my Twinkies and Fruit Pies, though."

"Old habits die hard," Andrew said.

"The term my nutritionist uses is 'self-destructive pattern behavior.' All I can tell you is, I don't care how many health clubs your daddy owns, a girl can only burn so many calories the old-fashioned way. By the time I graduated high school, I had holes in my throat and my teeth from the constant puking. All the gastric acid. When I was nineteen, I broke three fingers catching a Frisbee because my bones had gotten so brittle."

"Jesus."

"I'm sure it seems pathetic to you. It seems pathetic to me."

Andrew shook his head. "Only the fact that you're still doing it to yourself."

The fact that he cared enough to pass judgment surprised him. Maybe Heather Lomax just reminded him too much of Caroline. Maybe it wasn't that at all. He had to get away from this girl.

"Hey," she said. She sounded neither angry nor offended. "You've got to work pretty hard to change yourself. I'm starting to wonder if it's even possible."

Andrew said nothing to that. He kept his eyes on the road. He could feel her watching him.

"Do you?"

"Do I what?"

"Do you think it's possible?"

Andrew said, "I think you're asking the wrong guy."

"Take a left at the next light," she told him. "I think we're almost there."

24

DIGMAN Self Storage consisted of several squat, square cinder-block buildings on a large dusty lot surrounded by a high chain-link fence. They found it in the heart of a weedy, sun-blasted neighborhood of dusty lots and high fences.

A rust-streaked gate arm regulated access to the grounds. Andrew pulled up to the touch-tone key box and played a hunch. He ran down his window and punched in the six-digit number printed on the scrap of paper Lomax had given him.

Bingo. The arm shuddered and then lifted with a grinding sound, granting them passage inside.

Building number 6 crouched at the back corner of the property at the end of a trash-littered frontage road. Andrew parked in front.

"I'll be back," he said. "Hang tight."

"Sure thing, dude." Heather opened her door and got

out, waited for him to join her on the other side of the car.

He didn't waste time arguing about it. They went inside together.

The first thing Andrew noticed was the musty heat. The concrete floor shone with sweat, and you could smell the iron stairwell railings. If the building was air-conditioned, this outfit wasn't paying much in electric bills.

The access code for the gate didn't help them at unit 601D, the last gray door on the ground level. Andrew saw a regular lock on the knob, plus a Schlage dead bolt up top, both basic pin-and-tumbler jobs. Easy enough to bypass if you knew your way around with a pick and a tension wrench, which he did.

But on their way in, Heather had pointed out what she figured to be the main office building. Andrew headed back outside, and she followed. They walked across the compound.

The air-conditioning in the office seemed to be running fine. A jingle bell above the front door announced their entrance, and in a few moments, a bearded man wearing leather wristbands emerged from somewhere in the back. From where they stood, Andrew could see tooled lettering on the wristbands. The guy's right wrist said: PISS. The left: OFF. He took position behind the grimy, cluttered service counter and looked at them.

"Howdy," Andrew said. "I'm 601D. Lost my key. You got a spare back there somewhere?"

"You got ID?"

"Sure thing," Andrew said, handing over his wallet.

The guy took it without looking up, turned his back, and stepped to a large metal file cabinet. Andrew watched

him open the wallet, find the driver's license, and pause.
The guy kept his back to them.

"What unit you say again?"

"601D," Andrew repeated. "Andrew Kindler."

The guy tipped a look over his shoulder. Something
passed over his face. He turned around. He took another
look at Andrew's license, took another look at Andrew.
Licked his lips.

"Problem?"

The guy just stood. He moved his mouth but he
didn't say anything.

"Oh, come on," Andrew said. "You just rented me the
place a couple days ago. You forget me already?"

That was all it took. Without a word, the guy flung
the wallet back at them and went for something beneath
the counter.

Andrew beat him there.

Not a terrible move, he thought as he vaulted over the
countertop, *but you telegraphed it.* He planted both feet in
the center of the guy's chest and shoved him back hard
against the file cabinet. When Andrew landed on the
other side of the counter, he stepped quickly, took the
guy's Adam's apple in his fingers.

He squeezed just enough to make the guy gurgle, then
used his other hand to pop the guy's head back against
the handle of a file drawer. Twice for good measure.

Behind him, he heard Heather say, "Jesus!"

"Go on outside," he said over his shoulder. "And
wait for me."

"What are you *doing?*"

"Stay if you want, then."

He heard a long silence.

When he heard the bell jingle, Andrew turned his

full attention back to the guy. He looked him in his wide, jittery eyes.

———————

Ten minutes later, Andrew emerged from the office with a key in one hand and a set of carbon forms in the other. He found Heather waiting around the corner of the building. She held her arms tight across her waist. She looked at him with an expression that seemed equal parts scathing and fearful.

"What did you *do* in there?" she said. "What the hell did you do in there? I heard that man scream."

"Your friend Gregor had his self-defense tactics," he told her. "I have mine."

Based on the look she gave him, he almost didn't expect her to follow him back to number 6 again.

But she did.

25

"I don't understand." Heather turned in a slow circle. "I definitely don't understand this at all."

Andrew thought he understood even before he started reading the stack of pages he'd just found. He turned and looked all around, thinking, *Larry, you crazy punk. You really outdid yourself.*

The storage unit looked to be about eight feet by ten. Cramped, but big enough to pass for what it had been decorated to look like: a hideaway.

The walls had been papered with clippings, obsessive as the bedroom walls of a teenage girl. Or, in this case, the lair of your standard-issue psycho lunatic straight out of central casting. The whole thing was so over-the-top that it almost defied skepticism. Somehow, it just looked too implausible not to be real.

There were photocopies of magazine covers and articles, a few pinup posters. A year's worth of glossy photo pages torn from what Heather identified as last year's Club Maximum wall calendar. All featured the dead aerobics man, Gregor Tavlin. Andrew tried to imagine the legwork it must have taken to assemble the display.

A scrapbook on a small table in the corner contained every newspaper story from the past two weeks that dealt with the man's death and the murder investigation. In the later stories, each occurrence of David Lomax's name had earned a mark with a highlighter pen.

Larry obviously had wanted electrical outlets, but the storage unit offered none. He'd cleared this obstacle to his artistic vision with a small emergency generator, the kind powered by a car battery. The backup gennie served a small television/VCR combo unit on a roll-around cart. Next to the television: a stack of Gregor Tavlin workout videos. Next to the videos: a crinkled tube of Astroglide. There was a beanbag chair in front of the cart.

Larry had even found an inflatable male sex doll. He would have inflated it with some type of pump, Andrew assumed, leaving no pesky saliva residue around the plug. He'd dressed the doll in a track suit and taped an enlarged photocopy of Tavlin's face over the doll's. He'd slashed out the eyes of the photocopy, first with a black marker, then with something sharp, one thick ragged X over each.

The clincher sat in the center of the space: a chair, another table. Andrew had found the pages he now held in his hand neatly stacked on the table next to an old portable manual typewriter. He handed the top sheet to Heather, still marveling. Larry must have been a busy fellow.

Andrew took his time absorbing it all.

"Check out the typeface," he finally said. "Notice anything?"

Heather stared at the page.

"See how the tail is broken on the lowercase a's? And the ink blot in the e's. Ever seen that before?"

"The letter," she said. "The letter I showed you."

"Yep." He would have laughed if he could have stopped thinking about what this aborted mission no doubt meant for Larry Tomiczek back home. "The letter. You know who really wrote it now, don't you?"

"Your friend," Heather said. "I was there when my father called Cedric."

"No. That letter was composed by a guilty head case who really wants to get caught, deep down." He held up the rest of the pages. "Same guy who wrote this."

He handed her each sheet as he finished reading it. She devoured them faster than he did and waited impatiently for him to hand her the next page. By the time he handed her the last, her eyes had gone slightly manic.

"This is ridiculous," she said. "What is this supposed to be?"

"My confession, apparently. I never knew I was such an emotionally troubled individual."

The manuscript was five single-spaced pages in length. Larry's spelling was atrocious, but considering the fact that he'd dropped out of school the day he'd turned sixteen, Andrew thought he'd done a pretty fair job overall. The whole thing had a nice feverish tone to it. Larry was no writer, and that worked in his favor.

They'd met earlier in the summer, Andrew and Gregor had, at some bar down in Long Beach. Gregor Tavlin was the first person Andrew had met since he'd moved to town. And even though they'd spent just that one sizzling night together, they'd connected like Andrew had never connected with another man. It had been more than just a physical encounter.

But not for Gregor Tavlin, apparently. All summer, he'd rejected Andrew's attempts to make contact. Andrew had become depressed, despondent. Finally desperate. Et cetera, et cetera.

The narrative became increasingly disjointed the longer it ran on, bouncing around, derailing into wandering tangents, finding its way back to the confessional thread again. Larry, wisely, had kept the details vague enough to remain flexible under scrutiny, specific enough for the idea to emerge.

There came the night when Andrew had followed Gregor to the Lomax office building. He'd confronted Tavlin in the parking lot. They'd exchanged words, hurtful words. Andrew hadn't meant to lose control.

After, while Andrew slipped away to retrieve Gregor's car, another man had emerged from the building to find Tavlin's body still warm on the ground. David Lomax.

Lomax had fled when Andrew returned with Gregor's car. Andrew would have given chase, if he hadn't had so much work to do. And quickly.

He'd remembered how the news had predicted that the fires would take Mandeville Canyon by week's end. . . .

"This is ridiculous," Heather said again.

"Actually, given what the old goat had to work with, it's reasonably clever," Andrew said. "I can't imagine whether it would have worked or not. But you've got to hand it to your uncle Cedric. Framing somebody for a stranger's murder? After the fact? With no firsthand evidence to plant? *And* clearing your brother at the same time? It's a hell of a try."

"What are you talking about?" Heather shook the pages. "None of this makes *sense*."

"It doesn't have to make sense. I was disturbed."

"I mean it doesn't make sense," Heather said. "It doesn't make any sense."

He handed her the carbon copy of the rental agreement for the space. "Take a look. It's in my name, but it's been backdated to July 3."

"I can read."

"Our friend with the dislocated shoulder in the office back there tells me Larry offered two grand, but he talked him up to four. I didn't have the heart to tell him you gave me five for doing nothing."

She didn't smile. "Four thousand dollars for what?"

"A thousand to tweak the papers, three to call the cops later in the week. After he opened this place up with his manager's key because of the smell." Andrew looked around. "Hot as it is in here, I'm guessing it wouldn't have taken more than two or three days, tops."

"Two or three days for what?"

"You don't see it, yet?" Andrew held out his hand. "Pleased to meet you. I'm the evidence."

Heather just stared at him.

"I wasn't supposed to find this place. They were supposed to find me in here. It would have looked like a suicide." Andrew shook his head. "But he couldn't go through with it. He couldn't do it. The crazy shit took it this far, then warned me away."

"That's insane."

"That doesn't mean it isn't the setup," he said. "Look, your uncle Cedric and me . . . there's a thing that goes back a few years. I'm not going to go into it."

"Stop calling him my uncle Cedric," she said. "It's good and rubbed in. You can give it a rest."

"The point is, there's history," Andrew said. "History that doesn't have anything to do with you or your family. But the minute Cedric heard about your brother, he knew he was sitting on the perfect opportunity. He knows I'm out here, he just hasn't bothered to do anything about it. But now here's his chance to get his satisfaction and help your dad at the same time. From where he's sitting, it's beautiful."

"It's *ridiculous*," she said again. "Let me tell you something. I once had a part on the worst television show ever created, and *they* would have rejected this pitch. No cop in the world with any sense would buy it for a minute."

"The cops," Andrew said, "don't want your brother to be guilty any more than you do. Believe me."

"Is that why they turned his house and his office inside out?"

"Why haven't they issued an arrest warrant? Why haven't they named him yet?" Andrew shook his head. "Whatever they've got on your brother, I guarantee they don't think it's strong enough for a conviction, or they wouldn't be stringing this along."

"I see. And you're a lawyer?"

"Close enough," Andrew said. "Listen. My guess is the cops are all over your brother because he's the only thing they've got. But if they had an alternative?"

He gestured around the room.

"Cedric aimed to give them an alternative. It's a little over the top, I'll give you that. But it's got a nice little bow on it. I'll bet they wouldn't have wasted much energy punching holes in the wrapping paper."

"Please."

"Think about it. Set aside the fact that your dad has personal friends on the duty rosters. He's a *commissioner.*

Talk about an embarrassment the LAPD does not need."
He shook his head. "The media would have loved this
story. Forget it. This would have been an easy sell. And
once I was all over the news, your brother wouldn't have
any reason not to come in from wherever he is. If he's
anywhere near as bright as his sister, I imagine he could
have improvised whatever Cedric and your dad couldn't
coach him on, story-wise."

"The media." She shook her head at him. "Boy, you
really haven't been in this town long, have you? Do you
honestly think the LAPD would come off better in the
press if they tried to close the case on *this*? I know reporters who would work overtime to prove the police
set you up themselves to protect the son of a commissioner. *That's* a story."

"But they wouldn't get anywhere." Andrew shrugged.
"Besides. Say the cops did end up dropping the hammer
on your brother one day down the road. Say he actually
went to trial. The kind of lawyers your father can afford?
I'd say Cedric's little diorama project here would have
bought them more than enough reasonable doubt to
work with. They got O. J. off with less."

Heather tossed the confession on the floor. The pages
scattered. She paced a few steps, then came back.

"Why would you send a letter to the cops and sign
my brother's name?"

"Who knows why crazy people do anything? The
guilt was eating me up inside, I guess. Doesn't really
matter. Forging your brother's name, though, that's
kind of brilliant."

"Explain why."

"Because it forced the cops to follow up," Andrew
said. "Do you know how many loser tips they must be

getting on a case like this? If I really had sent that letter, I would have needed some way to get their attention. Cedric was in the same position. By the time the cops verified the letter was a fraud, they would have already found Casa Cuckoo here, thanks to our friend in the front office."

"But that doesn't make *sense*," she said. "I mean, is 'Andrew Kindler' your real name, or what? You used to work for Cedric, right? Wouldn't the police be able to connect you with him, somehow? I don't care how long he and my father have been friends. If he's the man you say he is, surely he wouldn't go to all this trouble to fake your suicide just to trash his own business." She flung up her arms. "Besides! If the police connected you to Cedric's . . . what? Mob? Whatever it is? That would sink the whole thing! It'd make this all look like one big setup again."

"I came to California to disappear," Andrew said. "I'm a nonentity here. I don't use credit cards. I don't belong to anything. I don't even have my own telephone number. Until the day before yesterday, there were only two people in Los Angeles who even know who I am. One of them wouldn't defend my name if you poured acid in his eyes. And the other. . . ."

He looked at her, really thinking this through for the first time. As he did, something cold slithered around the base of his spine, curled up, and went to sleep there.

"The other is family. And she'd walk through fire." He was starting to run low on shrugs. "But she has a healthy mother who still lives in Baltimore. My aunt Judy. Cedric knows what to do with that."

Heather said nothing. She looked back to the pages scattered on the floor.

"My own mother passed away not long ago," he told her. "If the rat bastard she divorced when I was a kid is even alive, I'm sure he would have sent Cedric a thank-you note. That about covers family."

Heather raised her head.

"As for back home," he told her, "if I have any friends left, they wouldn't be dumb enough to take their chances with Cedric Zaganos. And even if the cops did put me there—which I'm sure they have by now—I'm clean. No convictions, no arrest record, not even a parking ticket. I assume you could have called me up on a 'known associates' list a couple weeks ago. But now. . . ."

"But now what?"

He gave her the best grin he could manage. "Suffice to say your dad isn't the only person who has friends inside a police department."

"I can't believe this," Heather said. "I can't believe what you're telling me."

"I know I've heard all *I* need to hear," a voice behind them said.

Andrew tensed, but he didn't turn.

He waited. He waited for the sudden spike in his pulse rate to equalize, for the voice to speak again. For any sound. He imagined the space behind him, the voice's position in it. He watched Heather's eyes widen.

"Benjy?"

"Come on," said the voice, now familiar. "We're out of here."

Andrew felt his entire body uncoil. He turned to see Lomax's driver standing just inside the doorway of the storage space. Benjamin Corbin either wore the same green polo he'd worn the other day, or he owned several.

Heather went straight to him. Benjy hugged her tight,

keeping his eyes on Andrew the whole time. She craned back her head and said, "What are you doing here?"

"Your dad sent me down," Benjy told her. "As soon as he found out you'd left this morning." He looked down into her eyes. "I'm a little bit pissed at you."

She mashed her face in his chest. "I know, I know. I know." Then she stepped away and swiped her arm viciously at the room. "Would you look at this? Would you *look* at this?"

Benjy only looked at Andrew. "I see it."

Andrew nodded to him. "I was wondering when we might run into each other again."

"You haven't run into me yet," Benjy told him.

"I get that feeling, Benjy."

Heather looked at both of them. "What do you two think you're doing?"

"Reaching an understanding," Andrew said.

Benjy said nothing.

"Well, put your dicks away and let's figure out what to do about all of this," Heather said. "Because I can't take it anymore. I swear to God, I can't last another day."

"I know," Benjy told her, finally taking his eyes off Andrew. He looked at her and sighed. "I know."

"Benjy," she said, and her voice had no weight.

"Come on," he told her.

"Gee," Andrew said. "You mean you guys aren't going to stick around and help me clean up?"

"Don't forget to untie your boy in the office," Benjy advised. "His hands were turning blue when I checked on him. Heather. Let's go."

"I'm not going anywhere," Heather said. "If you want to stay and help us, Benjy, I wish you would. But I'm not going anywhere."

"Not even to see your brother?"

Heather's eyes widened. Then they narrowed.

She said, *"Benjy?"*

"Enough's enough," he said, and took her by the hand.

26

HIS left ankle had taken the worst.

Todd didn't think he'd broken it, but he'd felt a pop when the joint had folded, and it looked to be a bad sprain. This morning, the bruising had settled into the bottom of his foot, turning his instep black.

The tub of ice water doled far greater punishment than the injury itself: twenty stabbing minutes of knitting needle through bone, rays of pain climbing all the way into his hip. But he wanted to keep the swelling under control, so he forced himself to endure the cure despite the jaw-clenching agony of the treatment. He followed the ice bath with a megadose of ibuprofen and a tightly wrapped Ace bandage.

Once he'd redressed the ankle, Todd hobbled to his golf bag in the closet and tested club lengths. He finally settled on his nine iron for a cane. He wasn't sure which he needed worse: a doctor or a caddy.

The rest seemed superficial enough. Abrasions on his right hip, his back, shoulders, left forearm, left cheekbone. He irrigated with Bactine, applied a triple-medicated ointment to everything he could reach, and covered the rawest areas with adhesive pads.

He'd sustained a deep cut across the bridge of his nose. But there wasn't much swelling, nothing knocked crooked. Bactine and salve, two butterfly closures, then a Breathe Right strip over the top to help his airflow.

Not much to be done about the faint bruise-shadows beneath his eyes except apply a little vanishing cream and wait for them to fade on their own.

All in all, Todd felt far worse than he looked. His spirit throbbed. It was going to be one hell of a long day.

It began the minute he limped into the building. Todd could sense an uneasy vibe in the office, a quiet tension, and it did nothing for his mood. But he'd woken in such a funk that he hadn't even thought about how he'd explain his condition if anybody asked. He wasn't on his game today at all.

The people whose paths he crossed on his way to the elevators either held their tongues in light of his appearance, or they went ahead and accosted him anyway, usually with the day's newspaper.

Have you seen?

Todd did the best he could.

Yes, I've seen it. But let's not go jumping to assumptions until David's had a chance to speak for himself. We're all in this together.

Somebody must have called upstairs, because Sharla, his assistant, intercepted him as soon as the elevator doors opened. Her eyes went wide.

"My God, look at you! Mr. Todman, are you okay?"

Todd forced a smile onto his face, leaned on the

nine iron, and patted her shoulder with his free hand. "I'm fine, Sharla. Had a little fender bender yesterday. Good morning."

"No wonder I couldn't reach you! I must have called twenty times after you left the office yesterday . . . that reporter from the *Times* called, and I tried to. . . ."

"I've seen the paper, Sharla. Don't worry, it's okay. You did fine." Todd hopped off the elevator and into the carpeted hallway, using the golf club for balance. "It's my fault. I forgot that I had my call forwarding set to the mailbox. But I got your messages. We'll need to set up a press conference for later this afternoon."

Sharla looked both ways and dropped her voice.

"The police are here," she said. "Detectives Timms and Munoz. I told them I'd have you call them back, but they wanted to wait."

Todd let out a long breath. He was in no mood for this. No mood at all.

"Where?"

"Right outside your office," she said.

"Stop *whispering,* Sharla," he told her. "Good grief, you'd think we were the criminals."

———————

"Nothing lamer than a hit and run," the detective said. Munoz. "Hope you got the slug's tag number."

"I wasn't much good by the time the smoke cleared." Todd shrugged. "It was the other guy's lucky day, I guess."

"Well, what comes around goes around," Munoz said. "At least some of the time."

Todd tried to make his wince look like a grin. "Here's hoping. Sorry to make you wait, Detectives. It's already been quite a morning."

Timms propped a boot on his knee. "Not at all."

"Yeah, don't worry about it," Munoz said. "Couple of things, won't take long. You've obviously got a lot going on."

"Nothing more important than whatever you need," Todd said. "How can I help?"

"We're hoping you can verify a few points on our timeline," Timms said. He took his boot down again and opened the file folder he held on his lap.

"I'll certainly do my best."

"Then I'll get right to it. We've got that Mr. Tavlin decided to leave the company last. . . ." Timms ran his finger down a page. "November. November?"

"November, that's correct."

"Right. So I'm wondering if we've been reading too much into some of our initial interviews," Timms said. "Going by what you and Mr. Lomax and others have stated so far, we've been operating under the impression that Mr. Tavlin's decision to buy out his contract came abruptly. Is that a fair way to characterize the circumstance as you remember it? Or do we have the wrong idea?"

"Well, there wasn't a great deal of warning," Todd said. "We knew that Gregor was unhappy with our decision to acquire LifeRite. But yes, given ten years with the family, I'd say 'abrupt' is a fair way to put it."

"And that was in October," Munoz said. "The acquisition."

Todd tried to breathe evenly. He was really starting to feel his pulse in his nose. "We announced in late October, as I recall. I'm sure Doren and David must have been speaking with the LifeRite people for some time before that, but I wasn't involved from the beginning." Todd grinned and held up his hands. "They build it. I just slap a coat of paint on it and put it in the window."

This rated a chuckle from the lady cop.

Timms merely studied his folder. "Do you know if Mr. Tavlin was involved in or aware of these discussions? Between your company and LifeRite? Previous to the October announcement, I mean."

"Well, we would have announced internally—to our own employees, that is—a week or so before the official public announcement. So that would have been mid-October. I know that we brought Gregor in before that. He was always extremely involved in programming." Todd squeezed out another grin. "I say 'we.' Actually, Gregor and I learned about the LifeRite buy at the same time. That was quite a memorable meeting. Unfortunate, but memorable."

"Do you remember when that meeting took place?"

"Not off the top of my head," Todd said. "But I can have Sharla pull it up if you'd like. Late September, early October?" He reached toward his phone and punched the intercom button. "Sharla?"

"The exact date isn't necessarily important. But no earlier than September, you'd say?"

"Thanks, Sharla, I'm sorry. Never mind." Todd leaned back. "Certainly no earlier than last September. Detective Timms, if you don't mind me asking . . . is there something off-kilter in anything somebody here has told you?"

"Not in anything anybody has told us," Munoz said. She gave Todd the first smile he'd found himself unable to read in a very long time.

He saw Timms throw her a glance.

"We don't believe we have any special reason to scrutinize anybody's statements per se," Timms said. "But like I said, sometimes we can read too much into what's been offered. This isn't a science. There's sort of what you might call an editorial process to it."

Todd nodded. "Of course."

"Which is what I'd like to ask you about. The editorial process."

"Yes? Please."

"Well, I had a thought yesterday. Way out of left field, but I didn't have anything better to do that particular minute so I poked it around a bit." Timms shuffled through the folder and held up a saddle-stitched booklet. "This is the Lomax Enterprises company backgrounder, right?"

Todd leaned forward, looked closer, and nodded. "That's right. We send them out in press kits, with our prospectus, what have you."

"Well, what I have me is a receipt for a job order and a set of page proofs," the detective said. He handed the stuff over. "This is from an outfit in town called Luna-Graphix."

"Yes," Todd said. He pretended to examine the material before he handed it back to the detective.

He wondered what Heather was doing. Did she wake up at that beach house this morning? Did she wake *up* with that animal?

He said, "We contract with them for all our print production."

"Yeah, that's what one of your staffers told me when I called in yesterday," Timms said. He held up the invoices in one hand, the bound backgrounder in the other. "Now, this job order is for this booklet here. Two thousand units."

"So I see."

"But according to these receipts, LunaGraphix completed the order on the tenth of last July. Drop-shipped it to your department on July twelve."

"I'll take their word for it," Todd said.

"What I notice," Timms said, "is the Company Profile section. You've got little bios here for all the first-stringers. And I see one for Mr. Marvalis, who didn't join on until late October, early November. But not for Mr. Tavlin, who didn't leave until approximately the same time."

Todd thought: *Shit.*

"Right. Sure. Well, July," he said, for the first time bringing his full attention to bear. "There's always a bit of a lead when it comes to big print stuff. With something like this, we like to build in an extra cushion. I can tell you from experience. My first year in this department, we sent out an entire run of banquet invites from Lomaz Enterprises."

This brought another chuckle from Munoz.

"But see," Timms said, "what I'm wondering is, why Mr. Tavlin—if he didn't even know about the buyout the company was planning until September—had already been written out of the company material as early as July?"

"That's some lead time," Munoz said.

Todd scrambled, buying time. He really wasn't on top of his game this morning.

"You're absolutely right," he said. He pretended to think about it, pretended to chuckle at his own thick-headedness. "I'm sorry. I see. I see. Yes. That'd be prognostication, wouldn't it?"

"Yeah," Munoz said, matching his laugh a little too closely. "Or, like, predicting the future."

Todd noticed that she'd earned another glance from Timms.

Her cell phone rang. Detective Munoz answered, then excused herself and stepped out. When she was gone, the big detective nodded at Todd.

"Like I said, this isn't a science. But it would help if we could nail down as much as we can."

"Absolutely. I must be misremembering when we. . . ." He punched the intercom again. "Sharla?"

"It's probably not important," Timms said. "We'll need to speak with Mr. Lomax again anyway. He may be able to shed some light. Like I said, we're just trying to nail things down."

"Maybe it was in the spring," Todd said, lifting his finger off the button and shrugging an apology. "I really am sorry about this. I feel silly. But we keep things a little busy around here. Sometimes one project sort of blends into another."

"I imagine so."

Detective Munoz stuck her head back in. Detective Timms looked over. They didn't speak, but something was up. Todd could feel the change in the energy of the room.

"We'll get out of your hair for now," Timms said, and extended a hand. "Thanks for your time, Mr. Todman. As always."

"My pleasure," Todd said. He shook the detective's hand and nodded toward Munoz, who waved pleasantly as she ducked out of the room again. "Again, I apologize. I'm not quite a hundred percent this morning."

"No apology necessary. Feel better, now." At the door, Timms paused and looked back. "By the way, how did your car come out?"

"My car?"

"Your fender bender," Timms said.

"Oh. Right." Todd smiled wearily, shook his head. "A little better than I did, but not by much."

Timms seemed to think that was a shame. "You drive that white Acura, right?"

"Diamond Pearl, yes."

Timms smiled back, nodding. "I've been looking at those myself. They seem nice. You've got, what, the TL?"

"The Type-S. Right."

"Mind if I ask how you like it?"

"Hm? Oh. Yes, great. No complaints."

Todd thought: *Heather.*

Who *was* that guy? And what could she possibly see in him? Was it those ridiculous scars on his face? Did she think it made him mysterious?

Did she even know she'd missed their date? Todd couldn't decide which would be worse: forgetting, or standing him up intentionally. She *had* been half asleep when he'd called. Of course she'd only forgotten.

But who was that *guy?*

"I'll have to go give one a test drive," Timms said. "Thanks again for your time. I may give you another call later in the week."

"Absolutely."

Todd smiled.

Timms left.

Todd shut the door.

———————————

"What's up?"

"This ought to cheer you up." Drea waited until they'd walked out of earshot of Todman's receptionist. "The old man's down at the shop."

"Who?"

"Lomax."

Timms looked at her. "Right now?"

"He wants to talk to us."

"Guess he must have seen the papers."

"That's what I figured. But Ruben said Lomax had no

idea about the story yet. Even asked about all the reporters."

"No shit," he said.

"Graham briefed him, so he knows now."

"Is the driver with him?"

"Ruben says he and Reese followed Corbin to the
house in Beverly Hills this morning. Then they tailed the
Lincoln from there to Parker Center, same as the news
crews. But Lomax was driving himself. No Corbin."

The elevator doors opened. Timms thought he heard
the sound of chains rattling. He looked up just as a muscular, bald black man stepped out.

The man wore some kind of brace on his head. It
looked like a . . . Timms didn't know what the hell
it looked like. But he recognized the man right away.

"Hey there," he said.

"Mornin'."

"Vines, right?" Timms nodded at him. "Luther
Vines?"

"You got it."

Timms glanced at Drea. She was staring at the security man with a wide grin. Vines didn't seem to notice.

"Say," Timms said. "That's quite a . . . what is that
you've got on there, exactly?"

Luther Vines turned to face him. He swiveled his entire upper body at the waist, not moving his head.

"Little somethin' I been workin' on. You like it?"

"It's an attention grabber," Timms said.

"I'll check you later on," Vines told him. "Get you in
on a discount while supplies last."

With that, he walked on down the hall toward Todman's office, head high, spine ramrod straight, chains
jingling faintly.

Timms looked at Drea again.

She just shook her head. "I wouldn't know where to start."

They got on the elevator and took it all the way down.

━━━━━━━━━━

In the parking lot, under the blazing sun, Timms walked all the way around the car, front bumper to back, before he looked at Drea.

"You know," he said, "this makes the second guy this week who fed me some bullshit story about being in a car accident. Is it just me?"

Drea looked bored. "I know what we could do. As long as it's so nice and cool out, and we're not in a hurry or anything, we could walk around the parking lot counting up white Acuras. Can't be more than thirty, forty of 'em."

Timms took one last look at the vehicle's pristine front end. The paint was buffed to a high gleam, spotless chrome glinting in the sun.

"It isn't white," he told her. "It's Diamond Pearl. And the vanity tag says TODMAN, Detective."

Drea shrugged. "Maybe his old lady beat him up. That's how he got the bruises."

"No wedding band."

"Oooh! You think that means he's on the market?"

"Smart-ass."

They headed for her car.

27

"LUTHER," Todd said, "I can't do this today. I really can't."

Vines didn't put up an argument. He merely shut Todd's office door in Sharla's worried face.

Todd sighed and pushed his chair back from the desk. He really needed to get his ankle elevated. While Vines waited silently in the middle of the room, Todd swung his leg up. He eased the ankle onto the cushion he'd had Sharla bring over from the couch. He was starting to think the ibuprofen alone wasn't going to cut it after all.

"Okay, Luther. Fine, I'll play." He winced across the desk. "What in God's holy name *is* that thing on your head?"

"Ain't settled on a name for it yet," Luther said. His deep voice rumbled with something that almost sounded, Todd thought, like pride. "But check this shit out."

Todd had little choice. Vines wore some type of home-grown harness on his shaven head. From the harness hung lengths of chain that met several inches beneath Luther's chin in a tight descending Y. Pulling the chain taut: a ten-pound iron dumbbell plate.

Todd recognized the free weight immediately as Luther's commemorative disc. Doren had given them as gifts to all the department heads last spring in celebration of *To the Max with Gregor Tavlin* reaching its tenth year on the air. Todd had outdone himself with the idea, even if he did say so. Each plate had the words TO THE MAX custom-cast on one side, the individual manager's name on the flip. Vines hadn't really earned his; he'd only lucked into it by virtue of a slim two-month employment overlap.

The savage irony was not lost on Todd.

At present, Luther wore the anniversary token approximately sternum level. He'd threaded the chain through the hole in the center and attached it back to itself with . . . Todd leaned forward for a closer look . . . indeed. A dog's collar clip.

The man had a ten-pound weight hanging from his head on a dog leash. This had to be what Todd had heard about yesterday when he'd instructed Sheri Forman to let Vines take over Rodney's classes at the club. He wondered if Vines had actually worn the contraption during class. He could only imagine.

While Todd watched, Vines began to narrate his own demonstration.

"You got your basic position," he said, standing as he'd been since he walked in: shoulders back, arms at his sides, chin level. "That's posture maintenance."

He began to nod slowly: chin to chest, back up again. He completed five repetitions. Then he repeated the motion to each side, ear to shoulder. "You got your anterior, your posterior, your upper trapezius."

Todd struggled mightily to appear intrigued.

Next, Luther rotated his head in wide, slow circles. "You got your range of motion. And if you wanna talk abs. . . ."

Moving gracefully, Luther cleared Todd's credenza with a swipe of his arm and a mad flurry of press kits. He climbed up and reclined slowly, arms crossed over his broad chest. When he'd settled into position, his head hung just over the edge of the credenza, the weighted chain swaying over the floor behind him like a pendulum. He began doing stomach crunches.

"Lower back!" Luther called, flipping onto his stomach and lacing his fingers behind his head. He released a pneumatic hiss, raised his chest a few inches off the credenza top, held this position for a few seconds, and lowered himself again. Repeated.

It was unlike anything Todd had ever witnessed, at least in his office. Luther's uncharacteristic enthusiasm was almost enough to make Todd stop wondering what Heather and her mystery man had done together after he'd escaped the rabid dog's attack last night.

Almost.

Todd began to grow urgent. He had to get back down to the parking lot, get the Acura out of there. He could call the company account at Hertz and see about a rental for the next few days.

A fender bender! It had just come out of his mouth to the first person who'd asked. Todd knew he should have planned a better story. He should have given it some *thought*. But he'd just limped into the office in a funky haze. How could he have been so addle-headed?

He wasn't on his game. He just wasn't himself this morning at all.

"Luther," he said, "I'm speechless. Let me absorb what you've showed me, and we'll meet again. I really do want to hear more."

"This here's just a prototype," Luther said, ignoring the glaring motion to adjourn. "I'm thinking you'd want to make the real thing out of something . . . Kevlar, maybe. Lots of padding around here and here. Maybe some Velcro."

"Tell you what," Todd said. "Why don't you draw up a proposal. Like I said, I'd like to hear more."

Luther's eyes darkened. "This is the proposal."

Todd thought: *Oh, no. No no no.* He tried to calm his nerves. This was going to take finesse. The look on Luther's face began to make Todd feel like a hostage in his own office. He needed to get out of here.

"I'm just having a little trouble visualizing the practical demographic, that's all." Todd made a scribbling motion with his hand. "It'd help me if I could see something on paper. A few 'for examples.' In the meantime, I've got to run out of here and. . . ."

"You want a for example? I got a for example." Luther nodded at him. "Check you out. For example. Got in a car wreck I heard."

"Just a fender bender," Todd said. It would be all over the office by now. But if he could get to the car before the lunch-hour exodus, he thought, there was still a chance he'd be able to contain the stupid lie before anybody noticed. "That's all."

"Sore today though, right?"

"I'm a little banged up, Luther. You can see that."

"Got a headache?"

"Yes," Todd said, "I do. And I can't say it's getting any better just at the moment."

"Ears ringing?"

Todd opened his mouth, then paused to consider the question.

"Actually," he said, "yes. A little bit, to tell you the truth. When I first woke up this morning. Not so bad now."

"Shoulders hurt? Right on top, maybe a little down the back?"

"Both."

"Congratulations," Luther said. "That'd be whiplash. Stronger neck muscles, you'da come out better."

"Hmm," Todd said. "I see where you're going. Maybe you're on to something here. If you could just sit down and sketch out a few. . . ."

"Ain't no maybe about it," Luther said. "Neck's an important motherfucker, but nobody pays any attention. Why bother, right? It just holds your head up is all. But look here. What you got is basically an eight-pound bowling ball on top of a flexible tube. You got all kinds of major nerves runnin' through there. All kinds of pressure points. Plus a little somethin' called your spinal cord. You got all kinds of injuries can happen, fuck your shit up good."

"I suppose I never thought about it."

"Exactly what I'm talkin' about. So you get some statistics, right? Some shit about how many Americans suffer from neck problems, whatever. You get some quad case who has to blow through a straw to run his wheelchair around. Find us a doc to say how important it is to Neckercise."

"Neckercise?"

"Name I been tossin' around," Luther said. He lifted the dumbbell plate by the chain. "The Neckerciser."

"The Neckerciser," Todd said. He smiled broadly,

thinking, *Lord, help me.* "That's great, Luther. I like that. Tell you what: If you're really serious about this, let's take it seriously. We'll need to find out if there are any similar products on the market. If not, we'll need to look into the patent-pending end, see if anybody else is working on this. We'll need to explore the marketing angles. Determine how The Neckerciser stacks up to our existing products. Right now I've got to. . . ."

"You wanna see how it stacks up?"

Before Todd could interrupt, Luther tore the harness from his head. He stormed over to a stack of promotional Abdominators sitting in their boxes in the corner of the office. Vines grabbed a box off the top of the stack and brought it back to the center of the room. He tore the box open and dumped the preassembled product out onto the floor with a clatter.

"Let's stack it up," he said.

Luther swung the iron plate around on its chain like some kind of medieval battle flail. Once. Twice. Then he brought it down with a whistle.

Todd jumped at the splintering crunch of the impact. The Abdominator hopped on the carpet and settled again, cracked and mangled. Luther swung the plate down once more; a bit of plastic shrapnel whizzed past Todd's ear like an angry insect. Gears came undone. A tension spring flew. As Todd watched, flinching with every strike, Luther continued to pulverize the Abdominator until only a shattered pile of rubble remained.

When he was finished, Luther looked up. He wasn't even breathing hard. "Any questions?"

Todd had reached the end of his patience. "You've made your point, Vines. I told you we'd talk more later, and we'll talk more later. Right now, I don't have time for this."

"You got more time than you think."

"Luther, I don't like your tone."

"Yeah? What you gonna do, call security?"

"That's not very funny."

"So you still want a proposal."

"I think it would help."

"Here's a proposal."

Luther dropped the weight to the carpet with a heavy thud. He unzipped the hip sack slung around his waist and plunged his hand inside. When he pulled his hand out, he held up something that didn't make sense to Todd: a clear plastic CD jewel case with an unlabeled disc inside.

"You asked for it," Luther said. "I came in here, I was all about doin' business the civilized way. But hey. You want to make it hard, we can make it hard."

Todd sighed and gave up. "What are you talking about? Am I supposed to know what that is?"

"You don't know what it is?"

"I'm sure I don't."

"Me either," Vines said. "I don't know shit about computers."

"Luther, I'm not following you."

"Bet them cops just left could tell us what's on here, though." Luther waggled the jewel case. "This is the one they been lookin' for, ain't it?"

Todd blinked.

"Guess you didn't figure you'd see this again, huh?"

As Luther spoke, Todd began to feel disconnected from his surroundings. A sudden floating sensation rose in his chest.

"Luther," he said quietly. "What are you trying to tell me?"

"You're a smart guy. You can probably figure it out if you think real hard."

"I think you're playing games," Todd said evenly. "That's what I think. And I still don't have time."

"Let's pop it in yours," Luther said, nodding toward the PC on Todd's desk. "We'll see what time it is."

Todd took his throbbing ankle down from the desk. He sat up straight in his chair. He placed his hands flat on the desk in front of him. He found a spot on the desktop just past his fingertips and focused on it. He sat this way for a while.

Finally, he looked back at Luther. He chose his words carefully.

"If that's what you'd like me to believe it is," he said, "where did you get it?"

"Got this from a guy down in IT," Luther said. "Darrold Franklin. You know him?"

"I don't know everybody in the building."

"Yeah, well, my man Darrold ain't hard to miss. He's the only brother down there in the egghead ward." Luther kicked Abdominator fragments out of his way and plopped down in one of the chairs facing Todd's desk. "I bring him in a few CDs now and then, few blank discs, he'll dupe copies for me. Did up a pyramid workout for him. We got a back-and-forth kinda thing."

"Is that so?"

"Thing to know about Darrold Franklin is, this is one uptight black man. Single dude, spends all day on computers. Then he goes home, and what's he do? Stays up all night makin' up his own programs and playin' these crazy games, all that shit. I've seen his place, it's like somebody dropped a nerd bomb in there." Luther shook his head. "Always thought that shit was for skinny whiteboys who couldn't get laid, but there you go. My man D benches 290 since I been helpin' him out. That don't make him less paranoid, though. Strange cat. You still listenin'?"

"I'm listening."

"So Darrold gets to work early one day couple weeks back. And he sees your ass comin' out the back office with one of them discs they keep up in there. Now, somethin' like that, that just kicks Darrold's inner geek into high gear, you know what I'm sayin'? He goes and takes himself a look. Figures out pretty quick which disc is missing. And what do you know? It's one they just did up. Building log for July."

Luther folded his bulging arms.

"Now, my boy tells me how after they back it up end of the month, that shit gets erased off the system automatically. But he knows a couple tricks, right? Just 'cause you erase something off a computer, it ain't necessarily gone. And it's only been a day, so he figures he can probably get it back. Which he does. And once he's got it, he burns himself a copy, just in case." Luther shrugged his shoulders. "In case of what? Who knows, man. That's just Darrold. Like I told you, the cat can be paranoid."

Todd said nothing. He could barely hear Luther over the roar in his ears.

"Now when the po-lice come around, looking for that missing disc, Darrold's already thinkin'. He's thinkin' there must be *somethin'* on this bad boy you don't want the cops to find. Somebody musta been in the building who said they weren't. Or somebody wasn't in the building who said they were. See, he knows you used *my* badge to get in that room, 'cause he looked up the record for that day. So he calls me up and tells me he's got somethin' for me. Figures a brother might want to have it. You know. Just in case. That's why they call it backup, right?"

Luther waggled the jewel case again.

"Then what Darrold does is, he goes back and makes sure that shit is gone off the system for good. Some program he wrote himself. Way he explained it, it's like writin' down a word and then writin' different words over the top of it like a million times. Point is, he goes back and nukes that file for real, covers his tracks. Just in case there's anything there might mess me up with the cops."

It was the most Todd Todman had ever heard Luther Vines speak at one time. It was possibly more than Todd had heard Luther Vines say ever. He found that it was more than he could process. He thought of Heather.

"So." Luther put the disc back into his hip sack and zipped up. "Here's what I'm sayin'. And you best listen up. You listening?"

"I'm listening. I told you, I'm listening."

"My time is here. That's all it is. It's my turn."

"Luther, let's talk about this."

"Oh, we gonna do more than talk about it. You're gonna make it *happen*. Just like you said you would. Dig?"

"Luther," Todd said. His own voice sounded strange in his ears. "It isn't that easy! This kind of thing takes time. We've got to lay groundwork. We've got to develop strategies. We've got to—"

"Bullshit," Luther said. "This is easy as you wanna make it. Deal's a deal."

"Be reasonable," Todd said. "I know we have a deal. And I don't go back on my word. But with everything that's going on around here now . . . this company is under siege, Luther. We've got to batten down the hatches or we'll all go down."

"Nah," Luther said. "Me, I'm movin' up. You can decide for yourself which way your ass is headed."

Todd just looked at him.

"And by the way, I saw y'all drive in," Luther said. He shook his head slowly. "Fender bender my hard black ass."

As Todd sat there behind his desk, he forgot about his injuries. He forgot about his throbbing nose, his throbbing ankle. He forgot about the many bruises and scrapes. He even forgot about the fender bender lie. A warm tide washed over him.

He thought about everything Luther Vines had just said.

He thought about Heather.

He thought about the eerie calm with which Luther had unleashed his violence upon the defenseless Abdominator. He thought about how the man's eyes had looked as he swung down his battering iron: cool, untroubled. Unbound.

He thought about Heather.

He looked at Luther.

He said, "How do I know that disc you have there is the only copy left? That your paranoid friend downstairs didn't make others?"

"You know 'cause I'm tellin' you," Luther said. "And that's all you got."

Todd nodded.

"My schedule seems to have opened up," he said. "I wonder if you'd consider renegotiating our deal."

28

YOU knew there had to be something in the air when you found grown homicide detectives with caseloads standing around the bullpen shooting the shit in the middle of a weekday morning. The squad room had taken on the air of a coffee klatch.

Captain Graham's door stood open. The captain saw Timms and Drea as soon as they hit the floor. He pointed at Timms from behind his desk. Timms detoured in that direction.

Drea followed him. They stuck their heads in.

"Looks busy around here," Timms said. "Did we miss the Krispy Kremes?"

Graham raised a finger without looking up. He had the morning *Times* on the desk in front of him. He put his finger down, used it to hold a spot in the middle of the page. He looked up at Timms, looked at Drea. Looked back at his finger and began to read.

" ' " . . . belonging to Mr. Lomax was discovered during an authorized search," LAPD investigator Detective Adrian Timms confirmed.' " Graham looked up again. "An *authorized* search, even."

"Yeah, that kid PIO you sent to coach me on my quotes is really paying off. I think I'm finally getting the hang of this. Especially with the big words."

"I have a couple words for you."

Timms had prepared for the moment, sort of. "Somebody leaked the badge, Captain. Mel Roth called me out on it. I didn't know what she had, and I didn't want to get caught denying anything."

"Gee, how nice it would have been to know that *before* getting a microphone shoved in my face bright and early this morning. Shut the door."

Timms and Drea stepped into the office. Drea pulled the door closed behind her.

"And you can cut the shit, Detective," Graham said. "Because I already know you leaked the badge yourself."

"Ah." Timms glanced at Drea, who wore a hard smirk. He looked back at Captain Graham. "So who ratted me out?"

Beside him, Drea muttered, "There's a big mystery."

Graham ignored both the question and the commentary. "So as long as the chief, the rest of the board, and the DA's office seem to be taking a short break from taking turns crawling up my ass this morning, would you like to offer an explanation as to why a bright detective like yourself would even think about jeopardizing future prosecution with a bullshit, bush-league play like this? Without clearing it with me?"

"I guess I was thinking," Timms said carefully, "that since you wouldn't have been able to approve it anyway, under the circumstances, you might appreciate the gift that keeps on giving."

"Which is?"

"Plausible denial."

"I'm touched."

"Yeah, well, I never got you anything for Boss's Day."

Graham didn't seem amused. "At least tell me you kept your mouth shut around those *Inside L.A.* idiots downstairs."

"We took the fifth," Drea said.

Timms elbowed her. "Stop helping."

"You two chuckleheads can save it." Graham stood up and came around the desk. "This discussion isn't finished, just so you know. But you don't have time at the moment."

"So we heard," Timms said. "Where is he?"

"Interview room. Waiting for you."

"He say what he wants to talk about?"

"Nope."

"All lawyered up?"

"He's in there by himself."

"So we're waiting for how many attorneys to show up before he talks to us?"

"He's not waiting for his attorneys," Graham said. "He's here by himself."

"You're kidding," Drea said.

Graham shook his head. "Mr. Lomax is asking to speak with our endlessly quotable LAPD investigator Detective Adrian Timms here. And he's made it clear that he wants to do so . . . how did he put it . . . 'without the impediment of legal counsel.'"

Timms shook his head. It was refreshing, sometimes. Discovering that you hadn't yet seen it all.

"I guess I oughtn't keep Commissioner Lomax waiting."

"Make a stop down the hall first," Graham said. "Joe and Ruben have a live one. She beat you two here by five minutes, waving that newspaper article."

"Who?" Timms said.

"Says her name is Iris Warner," Graham said. "Works as a private nurse practitioner. Want to guess where?"

Drea said, "The name rings a bell."

Timms thought so, too, but he couldn't think why.

"You already talked to her," Graham told them.

Timms snapped his fingers.

Drea said, "Okay, I give up, clue me in."

"Mountain View," Timms said.

"That's right," said Graham. "She's Barbara Lomax's caregiver."

29

DOREN Lomax sat alone at the table in the interview room, gazing at the backs of his hands. He raised his head when Timms opened the door.

"Commissioner," Timms said, pulling the door closed behind him. "Sorry to keep you waiting. We're kind of hopping around here this morning."

Lomax didn't seem the least bit impatient or perturbed. "I got that impression. About the time I saw the reporters waiting outside my house again this morning."

"You've seen the *Times*, then."

Lomax nodded.

"It's a bitch," Timms said. "I know Mel Roth. Don't know who her sources are, but she claims they're solid, and I know her well enough that I wasn't ready to call her bluff. Tried to talk her into holding off, but she's not in her usual quid pro quo kind of mood on this one."

"I thought you handled it as well as anybody could

be expected," Lomax said. "And you don't need to explain yourself to me. I didn't come in to talk about the story in today's paper."

"I see." Timms turned a chair around backward and took a seat. "What can I do for you, then? Do you want some coffee? Water?"

"I'm fine," Lomax said. "I have a statement to make, Detective, so I'd like to get to it."

"A statement, sir?"

"I've withheld information from your investigation."

Timms looked at the man for some time.

He said, "In that case, sir, I'd like to suggest we stop here. Until you have legal representation present."

"That won't be necessary."

"With all due respect, sir, I disagree. I'm thinking about your best interests here. Also the best interests of the investigation. We need to do this right."

"I thank you for your concern, but I'm old enough to look after my own best interests," Lomax said. "As for your investigation . . . that I understand. I'm prepared to do this again for the record. In the meantime, you can stop 'sir'-ing me, Detective. It's not impressing anybody."

Timms sat for a moment. He tapped his thumbs on the back of the chair. He and Lomax looked at each other.

"Listen," Timms said. "Since this isn't an interview, there's no reason to do it in an interview room. Let's go downstairs and get a cup of coffee. We can have a conversation if that's what you want."

"I think I've dodged enough reporters for today," Lomax said. "But I suppose a cup of coffee would be fine."

Timms nodded and rose from the table. "I'll go scare us up a couple. Be back in a minute."

"I'll be here."

Lomax didn't seem quite so impatient to get to his statement as he'd made out.

"Humans are strange animals," he said.

Timms sipped his coffee from a Styrofoam cup. "Agreed."

"In the wild, most animals spend their energy finding the next meal. Or trying not to become one. We humans are the only creatures I can think of who spend energy trying to burn off whatever we ate last. Why do you suppose that is?"

"I don't know," Timms said.

"Say you had to speculate. It's not a trick question, I'm interested in your opinion."

Timms began to feel like the guy who was supposed to be answering the questions instead of the guy who was supposed to be asking them. But he wanted the man to feel comfortable, wanted to preserve the conversational vibe. So he took a shot.

"Vanity, I guess."

Lomax gazed into his coffee cup as though pondering his reflection.

"You forgot procreation, though."

"Beg your pardon?"

"One of the other ways nature spends energy. Perpetuation of the species. Right?"

Lomax chuckled a little at that. "Detective, you're talking to a man who, at forty-five, married a woman less than half his age and decided he wanted offspring. I think you could argue that procreation can be a form of vanity, too."

Timms let that ride.

"I need to show you something," Lomax said.

He reached into his shirt pocket and pulled out a piece of paper. He unfolded the paper, looked it over, and handed it to Timms.

Timms took one look and didn't like what he saw. It was only a photocopy, but it still was what it was. DR tag and all.

"That isn't David's signature, of course," Lomax said. "I'm sure you've ascertained that by now. I'm only giving this back to you for your own information."

"With all due respect," Timms said, "how do you happen to be in possession of this, Commissioner?"

"It was delivered to my home."

"Delivered by who?"

"A private courier," Lomax said. "I can't be positive of the sending party. And I'm not prepared to suggest names in any case, lawyers or no lawyers. But I think we can assume by the fact that this letter has been assigned a Division of Records number that . . ."

". . . somebody around here is trying to keep you up to speed."

"It would seem."

They sat with their coffees, each studying the other's eyes.

"You were saying something about procreation," Lomax finally said. "But I think you really mean to talk about fornication. Why do I get the feeling you already know what I came here to tell you today?"

Lomax never did touch his coffee. He spoke long and candidly while it grew cold beside his hand.

"I don't know if you remember, Detective, but you met my wife once. Years ago."

Timms nodded. "I remember."

He'd still been with the Santa Monica force, rolling patrol. One night in November, late, he and his partner had responded to a call not far from the address contained in the bogus David Lomax letter. Several motorists had reported an apparently disoriented woman wandering the west shoulder of PCH. Timms and his partner had finally found the woman huddled in wet sand beneath Santa Monica Pier, unclothed and without ID. At the station, she'd said her name was Barbara Lomax. It had turned out that she was right.

"I remember your discretion," Lomax said. "And your kindness. Then as well as now."

Timms didn't know how to take that, so he took a pass.

"But you didn't really meet my wife," Lomax said. "You didn't meet Barbara. You only met her illness. At that time, the two weren't inseparable. Early on, when she was still diligent about her medication . . . well. Barbara is quite a human being."

"I have no doubt."

"Over the years, as her condition . . . evolved, as different prescriptions lost their usefulness, her doctors tried different combinations. Some were more effective than others. Though it's my way of thinking that 'effective' is too polite a way to describe a scorched-earth campaign."

"I've had some exposure," Timms said.

"Firsthand?"

"Close enough."

"Then you understand what I mean when I say that eventually even I found it difficult to discern which was worse for her: the drugs or the illness itself. I can't say I blame her for choosing the illness. After a point, she refused the medication altogether."

Timms nodded again.

Lomax waited a moment before continuing.

"I expect Gregor and Barbara must have become intimate before she moved out of the house," he said. "Looking back over the years, I can see now that they must have been. In photos of the three of us together, for example. It seems to me now almost as if the photographs themselves have changed. There's another symptom of vanity, Detective. The inability to see beyond your own viewpoint."

"Or a symptom of being human."

Lomax smiled gently. "In any case, I do love my wife. But loving my wife didn't make me a good husband. I was inattentive in many ways."

"I've had some experience there, too."

"I think Gregor wanted to believe that I knew about the two of them," Lomax said. "Even though her doctors eventually recommended institutional care for Barbara's own safety, I think on some level he must have wanted to believe I'd sent her away purely out of pettiness. I expect it would have eased his conscience to villainize me at least a little."

Timms listened.

"The fact is, I had no idea. Not until a year or so ago."

"About the time Mr. Tavlin left your company."

Lomax nodded. "That's correct."

"What happened?"

"One afternoon I went to Mountain View to sign some renewals, releases, things I'd been putting off. I rarely visit my wife. It tends to upset her, for many years' worth of reasons that aren't worth going into. But since I'd made the trip I thought I'd see if she needed anything. On my way to her unit, I noticed Gregor's SUV parked around back. I went back to my car and waited there until I saw him leave. Around dawn the next morning."

"Ah."

"I reacted strongly at first."

"I don't blame you."

"After giving myself a few days. . . ." He raised his hands. "The truth is, my wife is happy in the mountains. Or she's found peace, which may be the same thing. In any case, I'm not vain enough to claim it's a state I've had any real part in restoring. Outside funding her care and residency fees, that is."

"You're saying you decided to turn a blind eye to Mr. Tavlin's affair with your wife."

"I'm saying that I brought myself *not* to stand in the way of what happiness my wife could find for herself," Lomax said. "Her new home. Her children. Even her lover. But her lover was right: I *can* be petty when it suits my mood. Possessive, too."

"I take it there was never a divorce in the works, then."

"You take it correctly. As for Gregor, I wasn't about to *pay* the son of a bitch to leave."

"Sir?"

"I have friends in enterprise who would laugh me out of the room if they knew how I do business with those I trust. But until Gregor, I'd never seen that trust betrayed." Lomax shrugged. "He and I had another kind of marriage, really. It turned out to be a bitter divorce."

"I'm still not sure I'm following," Timms said.

"I think you're following well enough. You're just having trouble believing that any man would mock his own professional reputation just to prove a point. But I did. I liked the idea of using Gregor's so-called integrity against him. Funny how integrity can be so selective."

"I assume you're speaking about—"

"Our acquisition of LifeRite, Incorporated, yes. I knew Gregor would never stand for it, and he didn't. It would have been cheaper to sack the son of a bitch, but money wasn't the point. When I told you Gregor left the company because of a territorial squabble, Detective, I was telling you the truth." Lomax patted the tabletop with his palms. "What I didn't tell you is that Gregor Tavlin wasn't the alpha male. I was. And I would have spent millions if that's what it took, as long as I never put another dime in that man's pocket."

He grinned a sad grin.

"Maybe that's the final truth about vanity," he said. "Eventually, it always undermines itself."

Timms finished his coffee. He turned the empty cup in his hand, rolling the Styrofoam out of true. After a bit, he put the cup down on the table.

"Commissioner," he said, "why did Mr. Tavlin come to see you on thirty July?"

"I honestly don't know. I only know that's the day my son learned about Gregor and his mother."

"So neither of your kids ever . . ."

"Heather . . . my daughter . . . I think she may have known. I'm really not certain. We've never spoken about it. But I'm sure David had no idea. And it was David I worried most about. He's got far too much of me in him."

"I see."

"He came to me," Lomax said. "David did. After he'd seen Gregor. He'd suffered quite a blow, and I'm afraid it put him on the ropes."

Timms didn't interrupt.

"My children have great reservoirs of spirit. They get

that from their mother. I know you have a daughter yourself, so I'm guessing you can imagine how you might feel if she comes to you one day with a broken spirit."

"I try not to."

"Wise. If it happens, there won't be much you can do anyway. There wasn't much I could do for David. Except what he requested, and I wasn't willing to do that."

Timms nodded. "What did he request?"

"A meeting," Lomax said. "David wanted the three of us to meet. Gregor, and myself, and him. I don't know what he thought it might accomplish. He was . . . he was troubled that day. I suppose he wanted to interrogate us in some way, and I can't say I blame him, even though the idea would have been ridiculous. I don't think David was so idealistic as to think we might have resolved anything." Lomax sighed. "So I refused. I wish now that I hadn't."

Timms nodded. He pondered his next words before he chose them. "David didn't just find out about the affair between his mother and Mr. Tavlin. Did he?"

Lomax tilted his head. "I'm sorry?"

"He found out about the pregnancy," he said. "And the . . . termination. So had Mr. Tavlin. That's why he came to see you that day. Isn't it, sir?"

Lomax sat so quietly for so long that Timms began to wonder if the man had lost his capacity to speak. His tired eyes changed during this silence.

"Detective Timms," he finally said. "Please explain the question you're asking me."

Timms reached across the table and squeezed the man's hand. He didn't know why he did it. But he did it anyway.

"We're going to stop here, Commissioner," he said.

"I'm going to leave you alone now. When your attorneys arrive, we'll speak again. It's only fair to let you know that under the circumstances we'll need to approach our discussions a bit more formally from here on."

"Detective Timms."

He really doesn't know, Timms thought. The man had no idea.

It was going to be one hell of a long day.

"I'm going to give you some time alone," Timms said, and rose. "We'll speak again when your attorneys arrive."

He left Lomax sitting at the table the same way he'd found him, gazing at the backs of his hands.

———————————

On his way into the head, Timms bumped into another detective on his way out.

Aaron Keene clapped him on the shoulder.

"Congrats, Top Cop. That thing in the newspaper's really bringing 'em out of the woodwork. Good thing you thought of it."

Timms looked at the spot on his shoulder Keene had touched. He looked at Keene.

"Better go back and wash," he said. "I think you've still got shit on your fingers."

Keene smirked and ignored the comment. "Lomax must really be a fan. So what does the old man have to say, anyway?"

Timms took a step back. He reached inside his jacket.

"Actually, he asked me to thank you." Timms took out the photocopy of the Lomax letter and unfolded it.

"No kidding. What for?"

Timms shook his head slowly. He held up the letter.

"You're really covering all your bases this week, aren't you, Aaron?"

"Not sure what you mean." Keene's eyes flickered briefly at the letter, then fogged into innocent blanks again. "What's that?"

"Need a closer look?"

Timms pushed the letter forward. He held it by the top edge, between his thumb and forefinger, right over Keene's smirk.

Then he punched the letter right in the center.

Keene's head rocked back. His eyes went wide, and he grunted. By the time Timms lowered the letter, Keene had already clamped his left hand over his mouth and nose. Blood oozed between his fingers.

Above his fingers, his eyes flared hot.

"You scum-eating prick," he said.

Or something like that. Timms couldn't be sure. Keene's words came across muffled.

"That one's gonna cost you."

Timms leaned forward. "Press charges, asshole."

Just then, the inner door to the bathroom opened. Vaughn Chester, one of the bulls on Team One, came out zipping his fly. He stopped and looked at Keene. He looked at Timms.

Timms looked back.

Something tugged at the corner of Chester's mouth.

"Hey, Keene. Shit, man. Did I get you with the door?" Chester glanced at Timms. Back to Keene. He reached out and touched Keene's elbow. "Sorry, guy. I didn't even see you there. I gotta be more careful."

Without a word, Keene jerked his arm away, shoved past Timms, and stalked down the hall toward the water fountain.

Timms and Chester stood for a moment, watching, neither of them saying a word.

"Detective Timms," Vaughn finally said.

Timms nodded. "Detective Chester."

They stepped around each other and went their ways.

30

ANDREW waited for dusk to settle before he packed up and walked down to the beach.

He picked a spot down toward the water, past the closed lifeguard station, just beyond the reach of the surf. The air was a few degrees cooler this close to the ocean, the breeze clean and salty. The sand was hot and dry on top, cool and moist underneath.

He dug his pit there, three feet deep and three across.

Andrew spent a few minutes collecting up driftwood beneath the darkening purple sky. A helicopter passed overhead, chopping toward the mountains, where the sky lightened again to a hazy orange glow.

Back at the pit, Andrew used the pages of Larry's masterpiece for starter. He crumpled the typed sheets into tight balls and dropped them into the hard-packed hole. Driftwood next, then the storage unit's patchwork wallpaper, followed by the scrapbook of newspaper clippings and the videotapes. He held back the sex shop effigy, now deflated to a shapeless blob.

Andrew stood and uncapped the lighter fluid, doused the pit until its contents were soaked. Then he popped the top of a kitchen match with his thumbnail. He dropped the match while it flared.

The flames leapt high.

Andrew sat and watched awhile, elbows on his knees. When the fire gained momentum, crackling and sparking and sending up black smoke, he tossed in the inflatable man. He watched the plastic melt, watched the flames change color.

He remembered the rental agreement for the storage space, still in his pants pocket. Andrew dug that out for the fire, too. As he unfolded the thin white sheet for one last look, the heavier black backing rubbed off onto his fingertips.

For some reason, the carbon on his skin got him thinking back to different jobs from over the years. He thought about all the various structures—all of them built by workingmen—that he'd reduced to insurance money, or warnings, or open lot space in his day. He thought about this fire in front of him. He thought about the one in the mountains up the coast.

It all reminded him of something the miserable prick his mother married had once told him. He'd been eight or nine years old at the time; this had been after the guy had finished putting his belt to Andrew for playing with Mom's cigarette lighter, after he'd finished putting his knuckles to her for leaving it around.

Fire doesn't give a shit. Quite the sage, he was, after a twelve-pack and a shot or two. *It'll heat this dump or burn it down. You can sit there and cry about it if you want to, but*

I'm not going to catch you playing around ever again. You'd better believe it.

Andrew, too young and too scared, had let almost two more years pass before finally proving him right. Fire really would burn the dump down. And the son of a bitch didn't catch him. Mom had been in the emergency room again that night. It had been her third trip in six months.

Now here's what this dumb asshole did wrong, he'd say. These were his glory stories, the only ones he ever liked to tell. He'd make Andrew and Mom sit there on the couch while he tipped the bottle and recounted his latest triumph on the job. *If he'd wanted to do it right, not get caught, here's what he should have done.*

At least Andrew couldn't complain that the son of a bitch never taught him anything.

He sat and watched the fire.

The flames had just begun to die when white light flooded the sand all around.

Andrew looked over his shoulder, squinting against the glare. Twenty feet behind him, he saw a blue-and-white 4x4 parked on the sand. The truck had a winch mounted on the front and a light bar on the roof. The breezes blew down the beach, behind him, toward the distant lights and sounds rising up from the amusement park on Santa Monica Pier. He hadn't even heard the approaching engine.

Andrew got to his feet and held up a hand, shielding his eyes from the spotlight mounted on the driver's side of the truck. A door slammed. In a moment, he made out a young guy in a Harbor Patrol vest plodding toward him through the sand.

"Sir."

"Evening," Andrew said.

"This is a public beach. Campfires aren't allowed."
Officer Harbor Patrol pointed toward the silhouette of
the lifeguard station, a hulking body on skeletal legs.
"The regulations are posted."

"Oh," Andrew said. "Sorry about that. I'm not from
around here."

"Been doing a little drinking, sir?"

The kid couldn't have been much older than drinking age himself. Andrew said, "Not a drop."

"Right." The kid nodded slowly. "Well. Future, let's
pay a little more attention. Okay?"

"Absolutely."

"Wait right there. I'm going to get the extinguisher
out of the truck, we'll get this cleaned up."

Andrew didn't mean to smile. He wasn't laughing at
the kid, he really wasn't. He was just thinking: *All these
years, I get pinched for a bonfire.* He was just thinking that
it was probably a good thing he'd decided to retire.

"Something funny, sir?"

"No. No, not at all."

But apparently he'd gone and done it.

Without smiling, and without another word, the kid
from Harbor Patrol pulled out his ticket pad after all.

Andrew was still grinning to himself as he climbed the
stairs to the deck, citation in hand.

He'd rinsed off in the ocean, but he still had charcoal
smudges on his arms and clothes. He'd had to scoop up
his charred, warm mess and haul it to a nearby trash can
while the kid from Harbor Patrol stood by, extinguisher
in hand.

It had been one hell of a long day.

Andrew looked forward to a shower and a beer. He stepped over the broken tread at the top of the stairs and headed through the shadows around the corner of the house. He grabbed the handle of the sliding door and pulled it open.

Just then, an anvil dropped out of the sky and landed between his shoulder blades, driving him down.

31

ONE more thing to fix, Andrew thought, as he felt himself being hauled up from the deck. First the broken step, and now Caroline's sliding screen. The aluminum frame bent all to hell when he flew through it.

His weight tore the door out of its track. Andrew rode the screen across the tile on his stomach. He still didn't know what had hit him.

But it hadn't hurt as bad as the next blow, which landed on his outstretched forearm. Andrew felt the bone shudder. The arm went numb to the elbow.

He heard a whistle of air, and then a bomb went off in his hip. The force of it helped turn him over, and he got a look at his attacker for the first time.

Another stranger. Surprise. This time: a lean, muscular black man in a loose white tank top and baggy drawstring pants. The man had a chain wrapped around his fist, a flat round weight dangling a few inches below his grip. He wiped his bald head with his other hand.

"Yo. Goddamn hot out here, I'm workin' me up a sweat."

Andrew pulled his arm in tight to his body. When he looked down, he saw a gigantic purple goose egg just above his wrist. The numbness had begun to fade. He was already wishing it would come back.

He clenched his teeth and sucked in a breath and said, "Can I help you with something?"

"Best worry about helpin' yourself. You don't want me comin' back here."

Andrew probed his arm and wished he hadn't. On the bright side, the pain in his wrist did an excellent job of blotting out the deep aches in his hip and back.

"Here's the news," the guy said. "Heather Lomax ain't interested in your scarred-up, pasty white ass. And even if she was, she's off limits. Dig?"

Andrew worked his way up to a more comfortable position and leaned against the wall behind him. He couldn't believe what he was hearing.

Lomax.

He couldn't believe how gullible he'd been. He'd actually fallen for that honorable old warhorse routine. A night's rest and a full stomach. Oh, sure.

"I guess this means Daddy's hospitality only extends to within earshot of daughter dearest, huh?" Andrew adjusted his arm. He breathed in through the nose, out through the mouth. "So you must be the guy who does the heavy work. I had somebody else pegged for that job. Shows what I know, huh?"

"You know all you need to," the guy said. "Stay away from the girl. Or next time, you and me ain't gonna be talkin' all nice and friendly, way we are now."

"Gee," Andrew said. "And I was just starting to like

her. But don't worry. I'll be sure and tell her we're busted."

The guy grinned and shook his head.

Then he came forward fast, chain hand swinging around and across. Andrew barely had time to slip his head to the side.

The heavy plate knocked a divot in the drywall beside his ear. Andrew grabbed the chain with his good hand before the guy could draw back for another swing. He pulled down hard and used the leverage to swivel around on his hip. He raised his foot and pistoned it forward hard into the side of the guy's knee.

The leg buckled, but the guy was stubborn. Or maybe he was just as bad as he looked. Either way, he didn't go down. He grunted and cursed and pivoted around backward, stomping Andrew's injured arm with his other foot.

Andrew didn't know if he screamed out loud or only in his head. It sounded like a woman. He hoped he'd kept it to himself.

All in all, it was probably best that he passed out when he did. This was getting embarrassing.

———

He didn't go down very far, or for very long. He knew because he could smell the bright scorch of powder in the air. He could still hear the bang, echoing.

Andrew opened his eyes, and his vision swam back.

Caroline still stood where she'd stopped, just inside the screenless opening to the deck. She stood in a textbook shooter's stance: sneakers planted shoulder-width apart, shoulders square, head straight, Glock extended, palm cupped around her trigger hand.

The hired muscle lay on the floor beyond Andrew's feet, looking up at the ceiling, cursing as he struggled to breathe. He had a wide red stain growing wider on the right side of his white tank top.

Andrew scooted back against the wall and pushed himself to his feet. He said, "Care."

Slowly, Caroline lowered the gun to a 45-degree angle, muzzle toward the hardwood. Andrew noticed her purse upended at her feet, its contents spilled. She kept staring at the guy on the floor.

"I was coming from yoga," she said. "I wanted to see how you were doing. I was going-to make you take your gun back. I shot that man."

Holding his arm across his waist, Andrew crossed the distance between them as fast as he could hobble. He put his good hand to the side of her face. "Hey. Sweetie. Look at me."

She looked at him.

"You with me?"

"I think I'm going to be sick."

"Just breathe," he told her. "Breathe with me."

She closed her eyes, drew in a breath, let it out slow. She opened her eyes again. "I shot that man."

Andrew looked at her. He looked at the guy on the floor. He looked all around.

"No, you didn't," he said, and took the gun.

He found a towel in the kitchen, tucked the gun under his broken arm, and did his best to wipe down the frame. He was thinking about Caroline's prints. She would have powder residue on her hands, but he didn't see the point in worrying about that. He went to the guy on the floor.

While Caroline stood by, Andrew gritted his teeth and put both arms to work. He pressed the Glock into the guy's limp hand, curled the stranger's fingers around the grip and over the trigger. He slipped his own index finger through the trigger guard and over the stranger's. He took another look around, then raised the guy's arm and fired two rounds. He put one into the back of the couch, one into the ceiling. Then he took the gun with him to the telephone.

He dialed 911 and told the dispatcher he'd just shot an intruder. He gave the lady the address of the beach house.

Then he went back to Caroline.

"The neighbors have probably already seen your car in the driveway," he told her. "So you'd better stay until the cops get here. Here's the story. Care? You with me?"

She nodded, still staring at her handiwork on the floor.

"You came over after your yoga class. We were sitting here in the kitchen talking. This guy busted in. He never said anything, just waded in here and came after me with that chain. We struggled. He pulled a gun. The gun went off twice before I got it away from him. I put him down. Okay?" He looked into her eyes. "What's the story?"

"I came over after yoga class," she said, and repeated the rest in a distant tone.

He gave her the best squeeze around the shoulders he could manage.

Then he made his aching way to the nearest stool and sat down to wait.

32

THE emergency room at Santa Monica–UCLA Medical Center was bright and bustling. They gave Andrew Tylenol with codeine and left him in a private examination room. A robbery detective from the Santa Monica Police Department took turns between Andrew, the guy with the bullet in his chest being prepped for surgery, and Caroline, who stayed in the waiting area with Lane.

After an hour or so, X-rays.

An hour after that, a resident in scrubs and a long white coat came in to set Andrew's arm. It was almost as bad as answering questions.

Finally, at half past midnight, an E.R. nurse came in with a cart full of gear. She chatted Andrew up while she worked on casting his arm from elbow to knuckles. He wasn't much in the mood for conversation. But she was a nice kid with quick gentle hands, so he tried not to be an asshole. Jill, according to the name tag pinned to her smock. She said she was from the Midwest. He told her he'd driven through there recently but didn't see much; she told him you had to look hard. She was participating in an E.R. exchange program for the summer. She was pretty sure she'd spotted Billy Bob Thornton shopping at the grocery store near the apartment where they'd put her up. He told her that must have been exciting. She laughed.

Before he knew it, his arm had been cased in pale blue fiberglass.

The nurse packed up her cart and told him to avoid contact sports. As she left the room, Andrew glimpsed two men talking outside the slow-closing door. One, the SMPD detective, shook the hand of the other. The other clapped the SMPD man on the shoulder. The door closed on them.

Half a minute later, it opened again. Andrew nodded at the man who walked in.

"Detective Timms," he said. "Long time no see. What brings you to the beach?"

Timms chuckled and shook his head. Tonight, he wore his badge on his belt. The big cop looked like he hadn't closed his eyes in days. Andrew could empathize.

"My partner got a call from your cousin. Mr. Borland. He wanted to report an incident he believed we ought to know about."

"Cousin-in-law," Andrew said. Good old Lane.

Timms looked him over.

"I guess we're both having a week," he said. "Want to tell me about it?"

"Not much to tell that I didn't tell the other guys." Andrew shrugged. "This guy busts into the house."

"That's what your cousin tells me. Carol, is it?"

"Caroline."

"Right. Well, I'm just getting up to speed on this thing," Timms said. "SMPD tells me they didn't find any identification on the guy who assaulted you. Don't suppose you could save us all some time?"

"Wish I could," Andrew said. "But I've never seen him before."

"No offense," Timms said. "But that's starting to sound a little familiar."

Andrew shrugged again. "What can I tell you? I'm not from around here."

"I've got a couple of problems."

Andrew waited to hear them.

"First problem is, the gun you shot this guy with seems to have been relieved of its serial number. I'm trying to figure out how a law-abiding out-of-towner like yourself would come to be in possession of such a firearm."

"You'd have to ask the guy who pulled it on me. Like I told the other cops. He walked in with the thing."

"Yeah." Timms nodded again. "That's the second problem. Let's say for fun that you managed to disarm this rampaging intruder despite that busted wing you've got there. You look pretty tough, I'll give you the benefit of the doubt. But here's the thing. The way it turns out, the guy you say you shot with his own illegal gun happens to work for a company called Lomax Enterprises. That name mean anything to you?"

"I'm becoming familiar with it," Andrew said. "So who is this guy? I thought you said you didn't have an ID on him yet."

"I said Santa Monica PD didn't find identification," Timms said. "We already know him. Little homicide we're working on."

"I see."

"Look." Timms rubbed his eyes. "It's late, and I'm way past tired, and you're beat to shit, so why don't we go ahead and tip our hands. Yesterday, I'd pretty much thrown you out as a joker. Today, here you turn back up as a wild card again. Just so we understand each other, I'm only concerned with anything you have to say that may or may not be relevant to my specific investigation. I'm not concerned with unrelated . . . activities that may or may not be of interest to some other cop. That sound fair enough to you?"

Andrew looked at Timms. The codeine had long worn off, and his arm throbbed inside the new cast. He sighed.

"Whatever you're looking for me to tell you," he said, "somebody hired a snoop to find it first. When that didn't work, they sent somebody to beat it out of me. And I still don't know what I'm supposed to know."

He wasn't entirely sure why he'd decided to lie. He had no particular need. Was it a higher-brain decision, or was this simply his basic instinct? Was he indulging in what Heather Lomax had called self-destructive pattern behavior?

He decided to spend some time thinking about it between now and the follow-up call he planned to pay on Mr. Doren Lomax. Maybe it was possible to change yourself, and maybe it wasn't.

In the meantime, somebody was going to pay for Caroline's goddamned screen door.

Timms didn't look particularly disappointed. He didn't look particularly surprised.

He said, "Have it your way."

Before he could say more, the door to the room opened again. A stocky fellow with graying temples, wire-rimmed glasses, and a solid-looking belly came right in. He wore a short-sleeved Dodgers jersey and what looked to Andrew like pajama bottoms. He stood a head shorter than Timms and carried himself like a bulldog.

"Ah," he said. "Here we all are. Detective Timms, nice to see you again. Hope I'm not missing anything important yet."

Timms looked over his shoulder at the man who had come through the door. They obviously knew each other. Timms took one last look at Andrew and shook his head. He offered the newcomer a polite nod.

"Pete," he said. "Been a while. How's the softball team this year?"

"Sucking hind tit, thanks. You should come back out one of these summers. We need the bats."

Pete leaned over, reaching across his body to shake Andrew's good hand. "Peter Jeffries. You're Andrew."

"You're right," Andrew said.

"This goddamn heat." Jeffries shook his head. "Summers like this, the lunatics run the asylum. So, come on, Aid. What's the story? You were a homicide cop last I knew. SMPD's boy just pulled through surgery. Should be coherent enough to book anytime now. I'm not clear on Parker Center's interest here."

"Intersecting investigations," Timms said.

"Has my client been charged with anything?"

Andrew wondered who he was talking about.

"We were just having a chat," Timms said. "When did you start defending again, Pete?"

"If I were defending again, I'd be with the other guy." Jeffries smiled. "As it is, I've been retained by Caroline Borland to counsel Mr. Kindler as we move forward with questioning. That is, if Mr. Kindler wishes to accept my services."

Timms and Jeffries both looked at Andrew.

Andrew shrugged. "Knock yourself out."

Jeffries clapped his hands and rubbed them together.

"So listen," he said. "Adrian. My client has been severely beaten. The attending says he was in shock on arrival. He's obviously exhausted. And I understand he's been given narcotics for pain."

Timms crossed his arms and listened to the drill. He appeared to be waiting for the man to wear himself out.

"Mrs. Borland has agreed to provide alternate lodging until my client's current place of residence is no longer a crime scene," Jeffries went on. "Naturally, my client is more than willing to provide any information he can. But I think we'd all be best served if he's able to do so with a clear head. If there aren't charges forthcoming, considering the circumstances, I'd like to propose that we allow Mr. Kindler to get some needed rest."

Timms yawned.

"I'm sure my client and I—assuming no scheduling conflicts with the Santa Monica police—could meet you downtown in the morning. Mr. Kindler will be prepared to volunteer a full account of this evening's events at that time. Did you have a time in mind?"

"I'll see you at eight o'clock, Pete. Sharp."

Jeffries smiled again. "We'll make every attempt. I'll get in touch if something changes on our end."

On his way out the door, Timms looked back at Andrew. "Rest that arm. Don't leave town and all that."

"My client wouldn't think of it," Peter Jeffries said.

33

THEY lay on their backs in the sand and watched the dark, clear sky above. David had always loved the beach at night.

Heather did, too.

The drug dealer behind the dummy corporation who owned the condo only used the place when he needed a place to use, and he didn't need it at the moment. But once upon a time, one of the dealer's top sales associates had spent three years as a guest of the California Institution for Men instead of giving up his boss's name.

Benjy had driven her to the place, all the way down in Oceanside. He'd dropped her off with a key and went somewhere else to wait for her to call him back for a ride.

Here with her brother, at last, Heather felt almost as if she'd stepped back into a time that had never really existed. It seemed so distant now. But they used to do this all the time as teenagers, after they'd gotten their first cars, take turns driving to the beach. They'd talk, listen to the ocean, watch the stars awhile.

They'd spent the afternoon walking this one. They'd walked this beach for hours. Same ocean, different sand.

Different world.

"Why didn't you *talk* to me?" she said. "Before any of this went so far? I don't understand why you didn't talk to me."

David lay beside her, elbows out, hands behind his head. Heather had the brief, awful thought that if he'd been on his stomach in the same position, he'd look a lot like a criminal, waiting for cuffs.

"How long have you known?" He nudged her ankle with his toe. "I mean shit, sis, when did you find out?"

"I never found out," she told him. "I've never *known*. I suspected. Girl thing, maybe. I don't know."

He looked at the sky. "Why didn't you ever say anything?"

"Because I knew how you'd react," she said.

"Come on."

She propped up on an elbow, looked up the beach, down the beach, all around them. She looked back toward the condo in the distance behind.

"Okay," David said. "Point taken. You can cut the drama."

Heather settled back again. "It didn't matter anyway. Mom was happy. She deserves that. Besides, it was none of my business."

"None of your business!"

"That's right," she said. She scooted a little closer, snugged her hip against his. "You know she and Dad haven't really been . . . together for a long time."

"He loves her. Don't give me that."

"Of course he loves her," Heather said. "But not like a wife. He loves her like a responsibility."

They watched the sky. For their eighteenth birthdays, when they'd still been goofy and epic, they'd bought each other stars. You paid the international registry fifty bucks, and they let you name a star, then sent you the coordinates for it in the mail. You couldn't see either of them without a telescope.

Heather hadn't looked in years. She'd once heard that you could see the light long after a star burned out. She wondered if either of theirs was still up there.

"We've always talked," she said. "We've always talked about everything."

David kept quiet. She waited.

"I needed to hear it from them," he finally said. "I wanted to put them in a goddamned room together and make them look me in the eye." He shrugged a little. "Dad wouldn't meet. When Greg didn't show up either, I went to his house. He wasn't getting off that easy, not the mood I was in. That's where I found him."

"That's what I don't understand."

"It was my fault," he said. "If I hadn't . . ."

"You didn't *do* anything."

"I called Benjy," he said. "I don't know why. Panic. I don't know. He asked me what I wanted to do. I told him. And it was done."

"David . . ."

"He said he still knew a few people who know people. Who know people. People who clean things up. I didn't ask, he didn't say. He asked me again if I was sure, I told him I was. So he made a call, and we left. And that was it."

He looked at the sky.

"I couldn't go to work. Couldn't face Dad, not then."

"David . . ."

"I stayed home and tanked, slept for three days. Dad and I didn't speak to each other at all."

"David, just . . ."

"When they found Gregor's . . . when they found him, I freaked. Took off driving, just couldn't deal. Couple of days, somewhere in Arizona, I turned around and started back. I was almost home when Benjy called me on the cell. Told me they'd found my badge at the house, said it looked bad. Must have fallen out of my pocket, I don't know." He looked at her, looked back at the sky. "Guess I must have had blood on my hands."

"David!" She sat up and stared down at him. "*Why?* Why didn't you call the police? When you found Gregor, why didn't you just call the *police?*"

He turned his face back to her, hands still behind his head. In the starlight, he looked ten years younger. Or ten years older. She couldn't decide.

"What if they found fingerprints? Anything? What if he'd left something behind? Jesus, Heather. What if I'd never gone to him in the first place? I'm the one who lit the fuse. So Dad knew about Gregor and Mom. Obviously he could live with it. But when he knew I'd found out, when he knew Gregor wasn't going to live with the lie anymore . . . maybe Dad went to confront him after all, lost his temper. Maybe he didn't know he'd actually killed the guy. I don't know. I don't think he could have . . . but after all this . . . how much do we really know? That's what I keep asking myself. How much do we really know about our own family?"

"Jesus, David, *Dad didn't kill Greg!*" She felt her voice getting away from her now, carrying on the breeze. She dropped it to a hiss. "Dad didn't kill Greg. He thinks you did. Our father actually believes you killed a person, and he thinks it's his fault, and it's wrecking him. That's why he's been keeping quiet to the cops. That's why Uncle Cedric—Jesus, *Uncle* Cedric, I can't stop saying it. Don't you see this? He's not trying to protect himself. He's trying to protect *you*." She clenched her fists. Unclenched them. She wanted to pound the daylights out of him. She wanted to pound everything back into place. "Jesus, what a mess. What a mess. What a *mess*."

David didn't move or say much. He stayed on his back, looking at the sky for a long silent while. Heather tried to get calm. She tried to make her heart stop pounding.

Neither of them asked the obvious question. She just looked at him.

Eventually, he sat up and looked back.

"Benjy's probably bored out of his mind by now," he said. "Think we should call him?"

"I could kill him," Heather said. "I really could. Knowing where you were the whole time . . . going along with me, keeping me busy . . . hiring that goddamned private investigator . . . I could just kill him. Both of you."

"One murder suspect in the family's enough," David said. "Besides. Benjy was just doing what I asked him to do. Be pissed off at me if you want."

"I am," she said. "Both of you."

David wrapped his arms around his knees. "So what do you think?"

"I think it's time to go home. I think it's time to go home while there's still a chance."

David looked out over the water.

"I wonder," he said.

Timms found Drea outside post-op, talking with Ron Hill from the SMPD robbery table. He rubbed his eyes and rolled his shoulders and joined them.

"There's the hotshot." Hill looked him up and down. He shook his head. "I'd ask how life in the majors is treating you, Adrian, but that just seems cruel. When's the last time you slept three hours in a row?"

"The AC's out at my place," Timms told him. He nodded at the heavy-duty evidence bag in Hill's left hand. "What's in the Hefty?"

Ron held up the bag.

Drea said, "Still don't know what it is, but I'm guessing you'll probably be able to get a *really* big discount now."

Timms peered through the plastic. He saw chain, the duct-taped skullcap, the iron weight.

"You're kidding," he said. He looked at Ron. "He rolled on Kindler with that thing?"

Ron Hill nodded. "Yup. Went Gladiator on the guy."

Timms whistled.

"Lucky all he's got is a broken arm," Hill said. "According to Kindler, the swinger was headhunting."

Drea put her hand under the bag, hefted it. "Could have left a mark."

"Could have left a big wet ditch," Hill said. He glanced at Timms, did a double-take. "Hey. Hotshot. What's the matter? You look like you saw a hypnotist."

Timms just kept looking at the bag. He reached out his hand. "Ron, you mind?"

"Be my guest."

Timms took the evidence pack and held it in both hands, feeling the weight of it. He pressed the plastic around the edges of the iron plate, finding its boundaries with his fingers.

He looked at Drea.

"Hey," he said. "Who's that computer tech down at SID who keeps asking you to lunch?"

Drea crinkled her brow. "Webster? He's not my type. Why?"

"Find his home number, call him up, and get him to meet us at the shop in an hour."

"It's two in the morning."

"I bet if you asked him nice."

"What's up?"

Timms handed the evidence bag back to Hill. "Ron, good seeing you. I'll get in touch in the morning. Give Shirley and the kids a kiss for me."

"I can do that." Hill cocked his head. "Get a bingo?"

"We'll see," Timms said.

He fished out his cell and held up a finger to Drea: *one hour.* He used the same finger to dial the home number of Doren Lomax as he walked back down the hall.

34

THE software Marcus Webster showed them had originally been developed by a plastic surgeon right here in
Los Angeles. The doctor had been using it in his own
practice for years to show patients how beautiful they
could be with just this much here, this much there.

The same principles of computer-aided 3-D mod-
eling could also show you what you'd look like with,
say, an exit wound. Or a bashed-in skull.

Timms had heard about the stuff last spring when SID
had started a pilot evaluation of the software in-house.
The programmer who had created the software for the
plastic surgeon now moonlighted as a subcontractor to
the LAPD, working with SID to tailor the program
specifically toward forensic applications.

"So something like this," Timms said, handing Webster the item he'd collected from the Lomax Enterprises

building a half hour ago. "How long would it take to put that in the computer?"

Webster yawned. His computer screen provided the only light in the lab. He reached out and flipped on the desk lamp, weighing the iron plate on one palm.

"Weigh it, take the dimensions, CAD it up, render it." He yawned again. "Not a long time. What do you want me to do with it?"

"I want you to check it against the autopsy data you've got for Gregor Tavlin." Timms read him a series of DR numbers. "You can do some voodoo with the model of the object and the models of the head wound, right?"

"I can crunch a probability based on the dimensions and the fracture points," Webster said. "But it'll only be rough. Not sure what good it'll do you."

"Rough works," Timms told him. "I'm just scratching an itch."

"Oh, well, in *that* case," Webster said. "Glad I hopped out of bed in the middle of the night and hauled my butt to the office. I mean I wouldn't want you to stay awake *itching* or anything."

Timms patted him on the shoulder. "We'll owe you one."

Drea said, "Where'd you get that?"

"Lomax building," Timms said. He nodded at Webster. "I pulled a commissioner out of bed too, if that makes you feel better."

"It's a real privilege."

Drea said, "Let's hear it."

"I remembered seeing one like it on Todman's desk this morning," Timms told her. "Didn't really register. Lomax junior and Lomax senior have 'em, too. This is senior's."

Drea took the barbell plate from Webster and hefted it the same way she'd hefted the one in Ron Hill's evidence bag.

"To the Max," she said, turning it over. "Doren Lomax."

"Lomax says he had these made up for his managers. For the ten-year anniversary of the cable show."

Drea got interested. Webster stifled another yawn.

Timms opened up the case folder he'd grabbed from his desk on the way down.

"Something's been bugging me about this for three days," he said. "Didn't lock on it until we were standing around at the hospital."

He pulled out the copy of *Health & Fitness* magazine, opened it up to the "Bold Behind the Beautiful" spread. He put the magazine on Webster's desk under the light of the lamp and tapped a finger on one of the sidebar photos: a tight shot of Tavlin in his office at home.

"See it? Trophy shelf, just over his left shoulder. It's on a little display tripod. The focus is soft, but you can still tell what it is."

Drea leaned in. "Okay."

"Web," Timms said. "You've got access to the photo banks from this terminal?"

"I have access to the photo banks from this terminal."

Timms gave him another DR number. "Pull that one up, will you?"

Webster went to the keyboard. He tapped for half a minute and sat back again.

"Okay," Timms said. "This is one of the digitals from the house search. Web, can you enlarge this area here?"

Web drew a square on the screen with the mouse. More tapping. He sat back.

Timms nodded to Drea. "Same trophy shelf. What don't you see?"

She took a couple minutes.

"Okay, I'm with you," she said. She sounded like she wanted to be optimistic but couldn't quite commit. "But they'd had their tiff by that time. Tavlin was probably pissed off. Maybe he just took it down."

"Maybe," Timms said. "Maybe somebody else did."

Drea chewed on it some more. "Okay. Say you found our weapon in theory. We still haven't *found* it."

"Right," Timms said. He was starting to feel the juice. Sometimes a little sleep deprivation did wonders for the powers of association. "But I'm thinking about everything else we didn't find."

SID's workup of Gregor Tavlin's home had been notable in one respect: the place was clean. Extremely clean. You expected to find a certain amount of human residue in any residence, crime or no crime. Fingerprints, hair, fibers, flakes of skin. On doorknobs, telephone receivers, in the carpets and cushions.

The main traffic areas in Gregor Tavlin's house had been uncommonly free of such common leavings. But Tavlin had employed a maid service that came in three times a week, and they'd been there on the afternoon of July 30. The techs had chalked it up to thorough housekeeping.

"Suppose somebody else did a little mopping up," Timms said.

Drea nodded along, going with it. "We could do it again. Fine-tooth that sucker, top to bottom, interiors and exteriors. The whole works. Hit that office hard. Sinks, drains. If there was a mess, whoever cleaned it up had to miss a spot somewhere. Especially if SID did."

Timms smiled. "It's like you're reading my mind."

"Hey, do me next," Webster said. "What am I think-ing?"

Drea looked at him. Timms saw the corner of her mouth twitch.

"Enough to get slapped," she said. "But not enough to really piss me off."

Marcus Webster dropped Timms a wink. "Matter of time."

He cracked his knuckles and went to work.

35

DENNY Hoyle hated the smell of a hospital in the morning.

It smelled like sick people. Wasn't any way to start off a day. Plus, you never knew where the hell you were going in these places, and the nurses all looked sideways at you if you asked.

Denny didn't even know why he was making the effort. Goddamn Luther. They give him his phone call, and who does he dial?

Denny didn't care if Luther *was* shot. And arrested. After the way he had dodged him all day yesterday—pretty much confirming what Denny had heard from Rod—the guy had some goddamn nerve.

It was almost 9:00 A.M. by the time Denny finally found where they were keeping him. Private room way the hell on the other side of the first floor. Uniform cop outside the door. Denny walked up on him.

"Hey, partner. Luther Vines in here?"

The cop didn't say yes or no. He just hooked his thumbs in his belt like a tough guy. "Sorry, sir. No visitors."

"What you talkin' about? No visitors. He's in custody, he ain't contagious. Least as far as I heard."

"Sorry, sir." The cop looked him up and down. "No offense, but you don't look like immediate family. So unless you're his lawyer, you'll have to come back some other time."

"Yeah, well, I'm his lawyer. Stand aside, Barney."

"You're his lawyer." The cop nodded. "Is that right?"

"That's right. You got a problem with that?"

"You don't look like a lawyer."

Smirking prick.

"Oh, yeah?" Denny looked the cop over. "How long you been on the job, rookie? Four months? Six?"

"A year in September. Sir."

"Hey, shit. A whole year! I bet you just about seen it all. Tell me something. What's a lawyer look like?"

"I don't know, sir. Do you have some ID?"

"I'll do you one better." Denny pulled his wallet. He fished out the business card of the guy who'd gotten a bullshit agg assault charge thrown out of court for him a few years back. "Go ahead and keep that. Gimme a call next time you're under review."

The cop looked at the card. He looked at Denny.

"Do you have a driver's license I can match with this, Mr. Wunderlich?"

"I don't drive. Puts holes in the ozone."

"Tell you what," the cop said. "Say something legal."

Playing around with him now.

"E pluribus fuck you," Denny said. He took back the card and snatched the gold pen out of the cop's shirt pocket before the flat-footed rookie doofus even moved.

He scribbled six random digits. "Here's my association number. Tell you what I'm gonna do. I'm gonna stand right here while you truck your green ass around the corner to that courtesy phone and check me out with the state bar. Then when you come back, we'll go over Miranda. Just as a review. How's that sound, Officer Lowell, badge number 949?"

The cop's cheeks went red. His eyes faltered a minute before hardening up again.

"Why don't you come with me to the telephone, Mr. Wunderlich. We'll get this sorted out."

"I'll wait right here and make sure nobody else with a gun and a badge comes around to violate my client's rights. But thanks, you go on ahead."

The cop eyed him. He looked at the number on the card.

"Right here outside this door," he said, pointing like he was training a puppy. "*Outside* this door, Mr. Wunderlich."

"Aye-aye, Barney." Denny snapped a salute. "Believe me, I won't want to miss seein' your face come back around that corner."

The cop took one last look at him. He seemed to be having trouble making a decision.

He finally took the card and strode off down the hall, gun belt creaking with authority. Denny waited for him to round the corner. Gave it a count of five.

Went on in.

Luther was in bed, inclined about halfway. His eyes were closed, and he had a couple tubes sticking out of him. Plus oxygen in his nose, an IV dripping away, one of those heart monitors beeping softly off to the side. He looked like he didn't feel good.

"Yo, Luthe," Denny said.

Luther opened his eyes.

"Got yourself shot, huh? That's a bummer."

Luther tried to sit up, winced, sagged back again.

"Can't stay, gotta get to work. Tape day. Plus that cop oughta be back pretty quick. But you called, so here I am. What'd you want?"

He said something, but Denny couldn't make it out.

"Say what?"

Luther motioned for water. Denny grabbed the plastic cup on the bedstand and bent the straw so Luther could get his lips around it without raising his head. Luther said something else, but Denny still couldn't hear him.

"Man, you gotta speak up." He bent down over the bed, across the railing, putting his ear closer to Luther's mouth.

This time he heard what Luther was going on about. He didn't understand much of it, but he heard most of it. He straightened.

"Hip sack. In the front seat?"

Luther nodded.

"In this pay lot you're talkin' about."

Luther nodded again.

"You don't think the cops found your car by now? Shit, dude. They probably already impounded it."

When Luther started moving his lips again, Denny bent down one more time. He listened to Luther go on.

When he finally stood up, he just couldn't help smiling.

"Todman did that?" He almost had to laugh. "No shit."

Luther just lay there like he was all out of strength. He closed his eyes.

"That's a bitch." Denny leaned down, put his elbows on the bed rail. "Kinda funny, though."

Luther opened his eyes again and looked at him.

"Hey, don't worry. I'll go check it out. See what I see. Your car's still there, and I can get into it. I'll grab this disc you're talkin' about. What are friends for, right?"

Luther kept watching him. Denny reached out and tipped him some more water. While Luther sipped on the straw, Denny leaned down further and whispered into his ear.

"Too bad you had to go and sell me out at work, though. I guess maybe we ain't friends after all."

Luther finally managed to speak in an audible tone. It wasn't much. His voice was hoarse, kind of weak-sounding. It didn't really sound to Denny like his old pal Luther at all.

"Fuck," he croaked, "you talkin' about?"

Denny just patted Luther's knee through the bed-sheet. "Don't die or nothin'. I hear prison ain't so bad. You behave, keep up your yard privileges, you get to work out all you want inside."

Luther tried to grab Denny's wrist, but he didn't have much of a reach with the IV needle spiked in the back of his hand. He coughed, made another pained face, and had to stop and wheeze a little. The quiet little beeping machine beeped a little faster.

Denny put the water cup back down on the stand. He pressed the nurse call button next to the bed. Then he went ahead and got out of there before Officer Barney came back around.

36

ANDREW woke up to the smell of home.

At first, he didn't know which pulled harder: the aroma of a fresh pot of coffee brewing downstairs, or Caroline's guest sheets. They smelled just like Aunt Judy's. Andrew could remember the first morning he'd woken up in their house after the night of the fire. He wondered if it was the detergent, or the fabric softener, some kind of potpourri she kept in the linen closet. He couldn't imagine. But it was uncanny.

He stayed in bed for a while.

It had been after three in the morning by the time he'd finished telling Caroline everything. They'd sat up together for a while after that. He didn't know what time he'd finally hit the sack, but he couldn't have slept more than three or four hours, tops.

Still, Andrew hadn't woken up feeling quite this rested in a long time. He was stiff all over. His hip bone was tender as bruised fruit, and his arm ached like somebody had pounded the hell out of it with a heavy iron plate. But all in all, he'd felt worse.

He finally hauled himself out of bed at a quarter of ten. Downstairs, he found Caroline in the sunroom. She sat with a glass of orange juice, looking out the window. She'd gone out to get the newspaper, but it didn't look like she'd opened it yet. Their little color television played on the counter in the kitchen.

Andrew poured himself a cup of coffee and joined her at the table. He kissed the top of her head and sat down.

"Mm," she said. "Morning. How did you sleep?"

"Like the dead. You?"

"Only mostly dead." She yawned. "How are you feeling?"

"I was about to ask you."

Caroline smiled a little but didn't answer the question. "Jeffries called. He wants you to call him back and let him know when you want to meet downtown."

"Right." Andrew sipped his coffee. "Downtown."

"Are you going?"

"Don't see why not." He shrugged, tried a grin. "That's what you regular citizens do, isn't it?"

She didn't say anything.

"Where's hubby this fine morning?"

"Out at the house," she said. "With the insurance adjuster. I think they're taking pictures of bullet holes while they're still fresh."

They shared a little chuckle over that. It was nice, but it wasn't much.

"Hey. Kiddo." He looked at her. "Are you okay?"

She took a moment to think about it.

"I can't decide," she said. "It was touch and go last night, but this morning . . . I don't know, Drew. Shooting somebody isn't as hard as I would have thought it should be. I think I might have serious problems."

"I'm your only serious problem," Andrew told her. "Other than that, you're just fine. Trust me."

She looked at him and smiled, and reached across the table. She grabbed the pinky finger poking out of his cast and gave it a squeeze.

"I'm glad that man didn't die," she said. "I'm glad he didn't die, and thank God I don't have to live knowing I actually killed anybody. But I'd shoot him again in a heartbeat. You know that, don't you?"

He smiled. Nodded. He knew.

She curled her little finger around his. Andrew curled back and sat with her.

When he finished his coffee, Caroline got up. She took his mug and her empty juice glass and headed back to the kitchen to fill them up again.

While he waited, alone at the table, Andrew reached out and took up the newspaper. He wondered if they'd made the morning edition. As he browsed the local section, he noticed he wasn't hearing much activity from the kitchen. He paused to listen.

"Well, I'll be damned."

Andrew put down the paper and got up to see what was going on. He found his kid cousin standing at the counter, watching the television.

"What's the matter?"

"Shh. Just watch."

He stood beside her and watched. The morning show had gone to the local news segment. He recognized the reporter right away. It was none other than the intrepid Carla Sheppard, KTLA5 News.

Sheppard stood outside a building with her trusty microphone. The text bar across the bottom of the screen read *Parker Center—Live on Location.* He caught something about early this morning before the segment went to tape.

The taped footage showed a small knot of people moving into the same building. Andrew caught a glimpse of Heather Lomax's face. He couldn't be sure, but he thought he saw the back of Benjy Corbin's head. He saw a familiar shock of thick silver hair somewhere in the middle.

He spotted Detective Timms blocking reporters on the periphery.

"What is that?"

"I'll be damned," Caroline repeated.

"What?"

Carla Sheppard came back briefly, promised updates throughout the day. Then the segment cut to another reporter with smoke in the far distance behind him, followed by aerial wildfire footage.

"Well," Caroline said. She shook her head. "There you have it."

"There I have what?"

"The prodigal son returneth," she said. "David Lomax turned himself in an hour ago."

"You're kidding."

"I'm not either."

"I don't believe it."

"They just said so on the TV. You were right here beside me."

Andrew stood and pondered this development.

Caroline looked at him. "What are you thinking?"

"I don't know."

But it wasn't exactly true.

He was thinking about everything that had happened since he'd first heard the name David Lomax four days ago. Andrew realized he'd begun to feel strangely bound to this missing stranger over the course of this strange week. Now he wasn't missing anymore. Just like that.

It seemed anticlimactic.

Caroline slipped an arm around his waist. "So what now?"

Andrew stood beside her and thought about it.

"I guess I call my lawyer," he said.

37

THROUGHOUT her statement to Detectives Joe Reese and Ruben Carvajal, Iris Warner insisted she'd never meant anybody to come to harm. She said she'd prayed for exactly the opposite.

She'd been employed by Mountain View Supported Living for nine years; she'd cared for Barbara Lomax on a live-in basis for nearly eight of them. The bonds that developed under such circumstances were different than those that normally developed between a nurse and a long-term patient, Warner said. Most people wouldn't understand, nor could they be expected to.

At first, when Barbara's period stopped coming, both women had assumed she'd reached her menopause. She was, after all, fifty-one years old. Warner claimed she'd only run the pregnancy test to ease Barbara's irrational worry that she might be with child.

When the first test came up positive, and so did the

follow-up, Warner said she'd been unable to bring herself to tell Barbara Lomax of the heartbreaking result.

Warner said she'd feared what the news would do to her patient and friend, who responded to emotional stressors unpredictably. She said she'd feared the reaction of Doren Lomax when he learned that his wife's caregiver had been secretly allowing Tavlin's visits for years. She even feared the depth of Gregor Tavlin's devotion. For all the same reasons.

She'd only wanted to protect Barbara.

Lost, and growing desperate for direction, she'd turned to the only person she could think of who might be able to provide some guidance under the circumstances. The only person, short of her children and her lover, who had visited Barbara with regularity.

This person had told her she'd done the right thing. This person had made the arrangements.

After it was over, of course—after the panic had cleared and she could see again—Iris Warner had realized they'd done something unforgivable.

Barbara Lomax had believed she'd undergone a basic menopausal examination. She'd believed her regular gynecologist had been ill that day.

It was routine to sedate her for her annual checkups, as she found them difficult and physically uncomfortable. The doctor who had made this particular house call had used midazolam hydrochloride, a powerful preanesthetic sedative commonly used during invasive procedures for its memory-impairing qualities.

Barbara had never even known she was pregnant.

But Iris Warner couldn't forget. Her conscience sliced away at her days and nights, she said. And Gregor Tavlin?

Somehow, Gregor Tavlin had sensed the lie. Warner claimed it was as if he could smell the guilt on her skin.

When Barbara suddenly began menstruating again, he'd cornered Iris alone. And then he knew.

"Warner stated that she called two people after Tavlin left the premises on the morning of July thirty," Timms told the group. "The first call went to Craig R. Robbins, OB/GYN, of South Pas. Suspended license. Late yesterday, Ruben Carvajal tracked Robbins to a rented villa on Grand Cayman. Seems the good doctor has been taking sabbatical there since August three. We're in touch with the Royal Cayman Island Police. Dolan and Levinger are running the financials."

Kevin Dolan from Team One flipped a short salute.

Timms took a moment to let the information settle, met a few gazes around the room. All eleven detectives from Teams One and Two were gathered around the conference table, including Aaron Keene, who maintained a stiff but swollen upper lip.

Meanwhile, Captain Graham conducted an unscheduled press conference in the auditorium, assuring the media swarm that nobody, including Commissioner Doren Lomax's son, David, had been taken into custody in association with the Gregor Tavlin investigation at the present time.

Present being the operative word. Timms had begun to allow himself a little optimism.

"According to Ms. Warner," he said, "the second call went to a Lomax Enterprises exec named Todd Todman. Todman's official title is Director of Corporate Identity, but he's basically a glorified PR manager. It's not clear whether he's one-hundred-percent inner circle, but he's trusted, and his job description seems to cover a lot of ground. We've got squads on the way to Todman's home and office now. Search warrants in the works. If anybody from the press gets you in a corner, we're bringing him in as a witness and not a suspect. But as far as we're concerned internally, this guy is climbing the charts. We'll approach him accordingly."

Timms nodded to Detective Ben Carlton, Team One's point man. Carlton's partner, Vaughn Chester, sat by.

"Detectives Carlton and Chester will coordinate the rework of the Tavlin residence between us and SID. Drea Munoz will coordinate deep background on Todman." Timms took off his reading glasses and tossed them onto the table. "Anybody have questions?"

Nobody did.

They went to work.

The Playa del Rey location was basically a low clifftop overlooking a sandy inlet with big rocks that sent every third or fourth wave shooting up into the air. Denny drove straight there from the beach lot in Santa Monica.

He was plenty late.

But not *that* late. Denny was surprised to find the crew already in the process of packing up by the time he arrived on the set. He saw a line of guys with dreadlocks passing stuff to each other in a kind of bucket brigade. The steel-drum band who came in to do live music every other week. They loaded their gear into a van with a bright crazy paint job. Denny didn't even see the craft services crew who supplied the water and Gatorade. Everybody else kind of stood around, talking and leaning against the breeze.

At first, Denny thought one of two things: Either this Lomax thing had queered the schedule, or maybe they'd called off production on account of conditions. It was damned hot and windy to be taping outside at this time of the day. Five minutes out of the car, his shirt stuck to his back. He already had sweat running down his leg from behind the plastic CD case tucked in his waistband.

He'd found Luther's hip sack in the Buick, right in the front seat where Luther had said it would be. Had to pay eight bucks just to get in the damned lot.

But it all worked out. He'd slim-jimmed the door, swiped the disc, left the fanny pack where he'd found it, and met a blue-and-white cruiser and a city wrecker coming into the lot as he made his way out. He was on a roll so far.

Now all he had to do was find Rod. Guy was gonna love this.

Denny asked around.

Most of the crew guys were too busy trying to break down their equipment and keep it from blowing away to pay him much attention. He spotted Cammie and Vivian hanging out with some of the other extras under a gigantic, flapping shade umbrella that looked just about ready to give over to the wind.

"Hey. Vivian." He hustled over. "How you doin'? Damn, you're lookin' great. Say, what's the deal, anyway? Where's everybody going?"

She pretended she didn't even see him standing there. She looked sexy as hell in her new *To the Max* sports bra/top thingy and bun huggers. Denny thought she also looked kind of peeved.

He turned to the taller one, Cammie. He was kind of starting to get a little wood just thinking back. But he forced himself to stay on task.

"Hey," he said. "Where's Rod, anyway?"

Cammie glared at him. "Piss up a rope."

Denny leaned back. This was kind of starting to sting.

"Jesus, what's you guys's problem?"

Cammie turned her back on him and mumbled something. One of the pretty boys stepped to him.

"I don't think she wants to talk to you, there, Security. Take the hint, huh?"

Denny looked the guy in the face and had to work hard to restrain himself. Especially the way the guy said the word *Security*. Like it was some joke. He wanted to bust a hint off this nutless Ken doll's pearly white teeth for him.

But he had more important things to do at the moment. He left the umbrella, walked around, finally found one of the sound guys he got along with okay.

"Yo, Jake," he called out. "What's happening?"

Jake looked up from what he was doing. He had his Oakleys on the top of his head, bright orange sunblocker on his nose and bottom lip. Denny could hear the daily Hot Spot report coming out of the little transistor sport radio Jake wore strapped on his arm.

"What isn't?" Jake picked up a patch cable and started winding it up. "You hear about Junior yet?"

"Lomax? Shit, yeah." Denny had caught it on the radio in the car on the way down. This was turning out to be some kind of day. "How 'bout that?"

"Crazy."

"That how come everybody's buggin' out? Where's Rodney? He take off already?"

"Hasn't even been here."

"No kidding?"

"Nope."

"Where's he at, anybody know?"

Jake raised his radio arm while he worked. "Packing, I figure. Packing real fast."

"Yo, Jake. You're losin' me."

"You didn't hear?"

"Hear what?"

"They're evacuating," Jake said. "Malibu to the Palisades. Fire's headed right through the middle, dude."

Denny blinked. "No shit?"

"No shit."

Denny stood there and listened to Jake's arm radio for a minute. The sun beat down, the ocean shimmered, and the hot wind blew.

"By the way, man—what's up with your buddy Vines? I heard he got caught breaking into some dude's house last night. Got shot like five times. Is that really true?"

Definitely some kind of day.

"Only got shot once as far as I know," Denny said.

"Man." Jake shook his head and started winding up more cable. "Man-oh-man. I gotta find a new job. Can you believe the shit that goes on around here?"

"Not hardly," Denny said, already turning to head back to the car.

38

ANDREW waited at a table in a room.

He'd never personally been at one of these tables in one of these rooms before now. He guessed he hadn't been missing much. There wasn't much to it.

Peter Jeffries, in a sharp-looking pale-gray suit today, waited with Andrew for all of forty-five minutes before his cell phone rang. Jeffries spoke to the caller in clipped tones at first, then in smooth reassurances.

Andrew got the impression that a higher-rolling client than himself had developed some sort of emergency. After a minute, Jeffries hung up and told Andrew they'd have to reschedule for later. He'd talk to the cops, very sorry, this thing could wait and the other couldn't.

Andrew told him he'd just as soon get it over with and get out of there. Jeffries took one look at him and seemed to intuit the futility of arguing the point. He left Andrew with instructions.

"Cooperate," he said. "But don't tell 'em anything you don't need to tell 'em. You seem like a bright guy, you ought to be fine. Call me if you need anything."

Andrew could have used a sandwich, but he didn't mention it. He watched his new lawyer leave.

He sat at the table and waited some more.

Finally, around three o'clock in the afternoon, a dark-haired, dark-eyed woman in a suit almost as sharp as the one Peter Jeffries had been wearing stuck her head in.

"Hi. You Kindler?"

Andrew said, "Hello."

She came in and shut the door. She seemed to be on her way somewhere else. "I'm Detective Munoz. Sorry for the wait."

"That's okay," he said.

"You can go ahead and go home," she told him. "We're leaving your case with Santa Monica PD. If we need to follow up, we'll be in touch."

Andrew wasn't sure what to say to that. He said, "Oh."

"Again, sorry for the inconvenience. Thanks for coming in."

"No problem."

"Normally I'd help you find your way out, but I'm a little short on spare minutes." The detective looked at him. "You're not going to hold the station hostage or set off a bomb or anything, are you?"

"I guess not," he said.

"I didn't think so. Take care."

With that, Detective Munoz opened the door and left the room again.

Andrew sat for a minute. He thought: *That was easy.*

Maybe he was going to be able to handle this regular-citizen thing after all.

He went ahead and got out of there.

———————

Last night, after the hospital, after the cops and the questions, after Andrew had told Caroline everything about these past four days, this week that stretched back ten years and beyond, his kid cousin had had a moment. She'd just sort of blurted out fat tears for half a minute or so.

Misperceiving a simple expulsion of stress for some kind of moral crisis, Andrew had tried to comfort her, calm her nerves, limp her through what he'd assumed was just a moment of reflex guilt over putting a bullet in a fellow human, center mass.

So he'd told her how lucky it was that she'd happened along when she did. He'd told her that for once this week, thanks to her, fate had been on his side.

But she'd already stopped crying by that time. It hadn't even been crying, really. She'd kissed him on the cheek and put her forehead against his.

You don't believe in fate, she'd reminded him.

He'd smiled. A damned lucky coincidence, then.

And Caroline had said: *There are no coincidences. Only moments and choices. Twenty-eight years of choices led me to that moment, Drew. In that moment, I had another choice to make, and I made it. That's all.*

Full of coincidence as this past week had seemed along the way, thinking back over specific events only seemed to prove Caroline right. Everything seemed somehow connected to something else.

Moments and choices.

That was what Andrew was thinking when he ran into Heather Lomax on his way out of the headquarters building of the Los Angeles Police Department.

What were the odds?

Sure, they both happened to be on the same floor of the same building at the same time. Hell, he'd even *known* she was somewhere in the vicinity, or at least he'd assumed so, based on what he'd seen on the news at Caroline's. Maybe part of him had even hoped he might see her. He could admit that.

But suppose Detective Munoz had shown up ten minutes sooner. What if he'd left the station with Jeffries earlier in the day?

What if he'd never called Benjy Corbin or Travis Plum? What if he'd left Baltimore and driven to Alaska instead of California? What if he'd kept his nose out of Caroline's business all those years ago?

What if he'd gotten a job mowing yards instead of going to work carrying envelopes with Larry in the first place?

What choice had he made as a child that led him to this particular moment in this hallway?

What choice had she?

He saw her down the hall, bending over a water fountain. Fitting, Andrew thought, considering it had been over a water fountain they'd first met face-to-face. She straightened and hiked her purse strap on her shoulder. She gripped her elbows and headed toward him, eyes toward the floor.

He was trying to decide whether or not to say something when she looked up and saw him.

"Oh," she said. "Hi."

The girl looked beat and sounded the same. The bags under her eyes looked like they carried more than the one on her shoulder.

"Hi," he said.

"What are you doing here?"

Andrew smiled. "Wasting my day, apparently."

She looked at his sling. "What happened to your arm?"

He thought about how to answer. If she didn't already know, he didn't see the point in telling her. She seemed to have enough on her mind.

He'd already decided, by the rational light of day, that he wouldn't be taking the matter up with her father after all. He didn't see the point of that, either.

So he told her nothing. He said, "No big deal."

Her expression seemed to grow concerned. "I didn't do that, did I?"

Andrew laughed, thinking back to the car yesterday, realizing the arm now wearing the cast was the same one she'd braced when he'd tried to grab her keyring away from her.

"No," he said. "Don't worry, I did this all by myself."

She looked sideways at the cast but didn't say anything more about it.

"You found your brother," he said.

Heather nodded. "Yeah."

"I'm glad."

She said David was still being questioned. Benjy had just driven her father to the office to meet more cops there. Something new had come up. She didn't say what, and Andrew didn't ask. She said she was just stretching her legs. Getting a drink. Going back to wait for David.

Andrew nodded back. "Well. Good luck to you, Heather. Really. I hope everything works out."

"Thank you," she said. "You, too."

It seemed like there ought to be something more, but Andrew knew it was only the awkwardness of the moment. There really wasn't much more to say.

He was glad when Heather's purse started ringing.

For some reason, he was having trouble wrapping up the moment on his own.

Heather sighed. She unshouldered her purse. She dug around, then held up her phone like a toy that had lost its novelty. She said, "Hello?"

Andrew touched her once on the shoulder and walked on down the hall, toward the elevators.

39

HE was still waiting for the doors to open when Heather Lomax came hustling around the corner.

She had her cell phone in her hand and a strange look on her face. Her expression seemed caught between confusion and concern. She stopped and looked at the floor-indicator lights above the doors. She looked at her watch. She didn't look at him.

He said, "Everything okay?"

"Hm? Yes. Everything's fine." She shook her head. "I guess. I don't know. I'm fine."

He watched her. She opened her phone and started punching in a number, then seemed to think better of it. She closed the phone again.

Andrew stood by. Common sense told him to keep standing by. Instinct agreed.

He wasn't sure which part of him went back to the

question she'd asked him yesterday in the car, on their way to the storage unit.

Do you think it's possible to change yourself?

He'd brushed off the question at the time. If she asked again, he'd do the same.

But suddenly, standing there next to her, waiting for the elevator to arrive, Andrew realized that it wasn't that easy. Because at the end of the day—at the end of your days—it was one thing or the other, period.

Is it possible?

He either believed the answer was yes, or he was kidding himself.

"Listen," he said. "Do you need anything?"

The bell dinged, and the doors opened. She finally looked at him.

"Do you mean it?"

"I wouldn't have asked."

Heather reached out and pressed the door bumper with the heel of her hand, holding the elevator.

"Would you mind letting me take this one? I'm sorry to ask. I just . . . would you mind waiting for the next?"

She spoke casually, as if they'd hailed the same cab. But Andrew looked in her eyes. What had impressed him about Heather Lomax from the first was the directness he'd seen there, the clarity. It was a cliché, but only because it was true: With people, it was all in the eyes.

Right now, her eyes were troubled, and she was trying to hide it, but she couldn't. The eyes had it.

So did he.

Moments and choices.

Andrew made one.

40

"PLEASE," she said. "I'm not kidding. Didn't you tell me you didn't want to play games?"

"I did."

"Why start now?"

"I'm not playing games," he said.

Andrew got in the passenger side of her little yellow Z3 and shut the door.

She'd put the top up. With the reflective sunshade unfolded across the windshield, and the tinted side windows, the cabin of the Beemer was like warm dusk in the middle of the blazing afternoon.

He heard her curse outside.

She slid into the leather bucket seat behind the wheel and looked at him. "What are you trying to prove?"

"Now you know how it feels. Frustrating, isn't it?"

"Give me a break." She reached over the wheel, took down the sunshade, folded it up, shoved it under her seat. She looked at her watch. "Please. I need to go."

He wouldn't have pushed it this far, all the way out here to this secured lot in back of the building, if her bluster had seemed the least bit convincing. But it didn't.

Wherever she was off to in such an uneasy rush, Andrew got the feeling that she didn't altogether mind the thought of company. Out loud, she said otherwise. Until now, he couldn't think of anything Heather Lomax had said to his face that he hadn't believed.

"Don't worry," he said. "I'm not going to twist your arm."

She didn't seem to think that was funny.

"Look." Andrew took his cast out of the sling and rested it across his lap. "As hard as it is for me to admit, when it comes down to it, you actually helped me this week. It's been weird knowing you, Heather, but the truth is it's done me some good. I owe you."

"You don't owe me anything. Please get out of the car."

"I'd like to help if I can," he said.

Heather sighed and gripped the wheel. "I don't mean any offense. Okay? You're obviously going through some kind of thing here, and maybe you think this little white knight, damsel-in-distress role-playing scenario you've got in your head might help in some way. But this is my life. It's not your self-improvement project. Okay?"

"I know you don't *need* my help," he told her. "If you really want me to leave you alone, I will."

She looked at him. She looked away. She cursed again under her breath. She shook her head.

Andrew couldn't quite decide how to read her reaction. He waited.

After sitting for a minute, seemingly locked in battle

with herself, Heather finally slammed her door and started the car.

———————————

She didn't drive far.

A few blocks from the LAPD building, on Figueroa, just past a gigantic complex Andrew took to be some kind of expo center, Heather turned into a parking garage. She took her ticket at the gate and rolled on into the structure, out of the sunlight and into the shade.

She started climbing the levels, rounding each turn and climbing on to the next. Andrew rode along quietly.

Empty slots began to appear here and there the higher they climbed. Andrew figured they must be nearing the end of the trail. The parked cars continued to thin, growing fewer and farther between.

Heather drove straight to the top level.

As they rounded the final hairpin, she sat up a notch behind the wheel. She headed toward a car sitting alone in plain view, snugged up against a large round concrete support pillar. A midnight blue Mercury Mystique. Rental plates.

Heather pulled up at an angle across the empty slots on the rental car's passenger side. She set the brake, cut the ignition, and pulled her keys.

"Will you wait here?"

"If that's what you want."

She got out of the car, leaving her purse but taking her keys. Andrew opened his door a crack and waited.

Heather walked quickly to the other car. She knocked on the window, then opened the passenger door and leaned down. Holding his door a few inches open, Andrew could hear bits and pieces of her half of the conversation with whoever sat in the other vehicle.

What are you doing here? Where's your car?

I don't think that's a good idea.

No. I won't get in. Tell me what's going on.

Andrew watched the door open on the driver's side of the Merc. He watched a man step out into the narrow space between the car and the big corner footing. The man had dark smudges under his eyes, a white strip across the bridge of his nose, and a loosened tie hanging around his neck. He motioned to Heather across the roof of the car with both hands: *Just wait one minute.*

The guy leaned back into the car, then straightened again.

Now he hobbled around the rear bumper using a golf club like a cane. One foot wore an elastic compression bandage instead of a shoe. He didn't even look toward Heather's BMW. He focused completely on Heather.

Andrew could hear both of them now. He sat and watched the show.

"Todd, what on earth happened to you?"

"I told you, sweetie. Just a little fender bender. It's nothing. I'm fine."

"The police are looking for you," she said. "They're looking for you right now."

"I know, I know . . . they were at the office when I came back from lunch. I drove by home on the way here, and they were there, too." The guy shook his head like he wouldn't have believed it himself if he hadn't seen it with his own eyes. "I'm afraid there's been a misunderstanding. A terrible misunderstanding."

"What kind of misunderstanding?"

"Heather, I can explain."

"If you can explain, why are you running from the police?"

"I'm not running from the police. Lord, what do you think?"

"I think the police are looking for you, and you know it, and instead of talking to them about whatever they want to talk to you about, you're skulking around a parking garage in a rented car like some kind of desperado."

"Heather. I know it seems strange, but I can explain everything. Please, get in the car and I'll explain everything on the way."

"On the way where?"

"Just get in the car and come with me."

"I will not."

Andrew didn't know if he should take this as a cue, but he pushed his door open and stepped out of the Beemer anyway. As he walked toward them, adjusting his sling, he watched the guy with the black eyes and the bum wheel. He spoke to Heather, but he kept his eye on the guy.

"Everything okay?"

"Everything's fine," she said. "You said you were going to wait for me."

The guy had been watching Andrew just as closely as Andrew watched him. When he spoke, his voice came out like vented steam.

He said: "You."

Andrew looked back at him. "Do we know each other, pal?"

The guy ignored him, turning to Heather.

"What are you still *doing* with him? Who *is* this guy?" He stabbed the ground once with the handle of his golf club. "I can't *believe* you're doing this to me."

"Todd, what are you talking about?" She looked at Andrew. She looked at Todd's face, at his foot. She looked at the cast on Andrew's arm. Her voice grew suspicious. "How do you two know each other?"

"We don't," Andrew said.

The guy named Todd didn't answer her question. He seemed to be getting a bit wound up. He bent his knees as he talked, emphasizing his words with body language. Andrew thought of an unhappy kid getting ready to throw one mother of a tantrum.

"This man is *dangerous*," he said. "Don't you see that? Don't you know that this is the man who shot Luther Vines?"

Heather just shook her head at him. "Who?"

"Heather. After all the years we've known each other. I can't believe you're doing this to me again."

"Todd, I swear, what are you talking about?"

"I think I've been patient," he said. "I've certainly waited my turn in line. Some of the *losers* I've had to stand behind over the years. But have I ever pushed? Have I ever been anything other than a perfect gentleman?"

"Todd."

"Tell me where I've gone wrong, Heather. Please. I've been patient, I think I deserve to know."

"Todd, this isn't fair. You're not being fair and you know it."

Todd began to pace, sort of. It was really more like hobbling in a loose circle.

Standing there watching this jilted nut with the golf club working himself into a froth, Andrew began to suspect he'd judged Heather's father hastily. Especially when he heard the name of the guy who had jumped him at the beach house last night.

Doren Lomax hadn't been the guy who sent the guy. *This* guy had been the guy who sent the guy.

"Hey," Andrew said. He nodded toward the guy's foot. "How did you say you hurt that ankle again?"

The guy snapped up his head. He glared at Andrew with focused hate.

Andrew smiled.

"I thought I'd seen you somewhere before," he said. "Do me a favor. Turn around and limp away as fast as you can. I just want to be sure I recognize you."

Heather turned to Andrew.

Andrew kept talking to Todd. "Long trip down those stairs, huh? Sorry about that. That top step's a doozy. I really should fix it."

Slowly, Heather said, "Todd?"

The guy named Todd didn't say a word. He didn't even make a sound. He just stood there. He began tapping the ground with the handle of the golf club. Andrew noticed his face seemed to be reddening, but it still seemed sudden when he finally boiled over.

In a quick convulsive outburst, the guy turned his cane around and gripped it by the handle with both hands. He swung the club down in a hard sledgehammer arc, dead-centering the rental car's trunk. The sound of the impact boomed loud in the cavernous parking structure.

The club head left a sharp dent and bounced off the trunk lid. The combination of the swing, the connect, and the high recoil sent the guy teetering for balance; he had to hop backward on one foot to keep from falling down. He panted slightly from the effort, and his eyes seemed a touch crazed.

"Shut up!" He put his bad foot down gingerly, steadying himself, and drew back the club like a baseball bat. He faced Andrew. "Just shut up and go away. Leave us be. This is family business and it doesn't concern you."

"Todd," Heather said. "What the hell are you *doing?*"

"Careful with that thing," Andrew said, walking forward. "You keep swinging it around like that, somebody's bound to get hurt."

The guy took a vicious cut with the club, about waist level. Andrew had to take a step back and away. He felt the air from the club head as it whistled past.

He was starting to get a little tired of people trying to hit him with sporting goods.

"Next time, keep your left arm straight," he advised. "And stop pulling your head."

"Take another step toward me," the guy said, "and I'll put a cast on your other arm. You want a matching set? Go ahead and take one more step toward me."

"Andrew," Heather said. "Please. Let me handle this. Todd. Jesus. Chill out."

The guy turned to her. "Come on, Heather. We're out of here."

"I told you, I'm not going anywhere. Not until you tell me what's going on."

But Todd didn't seem to want to talk anymore. He put the club handle back to the concrete and hobbled over to her. He put his free hand on her shoulder and tried to steer her to the passenger side of the Mercury.

When she resisted, he gripped her arm and tried harder.

Andrew was about to intervene when Heather saved him the trouble.

In one smooth movement, she reached across her body and grabbed the guy's paw in an overhanded grip. Then she pulled back, breaking his hold on her and twisting his palm toward the ceiling. At the same time, she kicked his golf club out from under him with the broad side of her foot.

The guy gave a sharp yell as he fell back. His voice

bounced off the concrete all around them, flat and echo-less as a duck's quack. He dropped the club and flailed for purchase with his free hand.

He found Heather's arm again, the same one he'd grabbed the first time. This time he locked on her wrist, still trying to catch his fall. Car keys jingling in her fist, Heather eased him to the concrete, straining back against his weight for counterbalance. He probably had fifty pounds on her, but she managed him fine.

Andrew would have applauded if he'd had two good hands himself.

He should have been paying closer attention.

Heather, too.

The moment she let the guy's right hand go, he pulled her wrist toward him hard with his left. Before she could recover from the jolt, he'd wrestled the car keys out of her grasp.

"Todd, knock it off," she said. "This is ridiculous."

Todd scrambled to his feet—foot—and extended his arm. Heather's keys dangled from his fist. Heather put her hands on her hips and cocked her head.

"Todd." A sharp scold. "Quit fooling around. I'm serious."

"You don't have any idea," he told her.

And without another word, he blasted her full in the face with her own pepper spray.

Andrew couldn't believe it. For a moment, he just stood there, shocked. Heather shrieked and bent at the waist. Her hands shot up to her eyes but stopped; she seemed to will them to a sudden halt, fingers hovering a few inches in front of her face. No rubbing.

Todd stood over her now, screaming at the back of her head.

"All these years!" he shouted. "Isn't it *my* turn? Isn't it my turn *yet*?"

Heather went down on one knee, coughing, choking, pounding the concrete with the flat of her hand. Andrew hustled over to her. Todd picked up the fallen golf club and hopped back a few feet.

"I would have done anything for you," he said. "Anything. You really don't have any idea, do you? *Do* you, you self-obsessed little . . ."

He stopped, oddly, as though checking himself before he said something he might regret.

Heather coughed and spat. Thick mucus streamed from her nose. Andrew used the tail of his shirt to wipe the flow away from her mouth. Her eyelids had already swollen shut.

"You even screwed the *limo* driver," Todd said quietly. "The limo driver, Heather. And a drug-running hood to boot."

His voice began to rise again.

"And now this? *This?* In all these years. All the times I've been there for you. The only time I've ever asked you for anything, and you show up with *this* asshole?"

Heather coughed so hard she gagged. Andrew held her steady with his good arm.

"Well," Todd said. "Be blind then, Heather. You've worked hard at it. As far as I'm concerned, you two can have each other."

Andrew stood up slowly. "Buddy, I'm going to show you how to hit that iron."

"Oh, yeah?" Todd ducked through the open passenger-side door of the Mercury.

Heather began screaming profanity at Andrew's feet,

clawing at her eyes without touching them. She coughed in long, rattling jags.

Andrew looked up just in time to see an object coming at his head. He moved out of reflex, caught the thing in the air with his good hand.

A water bottle.

"Tell you what, *buddy*." Todd stood on one leg, Heather's pepper spray in one hand, golf club raised in the other. "You can come try your luck, or you can help your little . . . or you can help *her*. You choose. *Buddy*. You go ahead and choose."

Andrew didn't need to choose. He quickly uncapped the water bottle and knelt down again.

"Here," he said to Heather. "Sit up. Let me see your face."

"That's what I thought," the guy said.

Without looking up, Andrew said, "You'd better hope the cops catch up with you before I do."

But he didn't think the guy heard. A car door slammed, then another. An engine roared behind them. While Andrew dumped a splash of water over Heather's face and wiped it away with his hand, he heard tires screech.

Heather's BMW zipped past. In a few seconds, a squeal of rubber echoed back to them as the car took the nearest turn hard and fast.

Andrew splashed her face again. He tried not to waste too much of the water. She sputtered and wiped it away herself this time.

He looked around, didn't see anybody. The sound of the revving Beemer faded.

Descending.

Gone.

Andrew took stock of the situation. They had no car,

no phone, no help nearby. Heather was a mess. He wasn't exactly sure what to do.

While he thought about it, he worked his legs out from under him, sat flat on his rear, leaned her back across his lap, and did his best to rinse the fire out of her eyes.

41

UNTIL the time he was fifteen years old, Todd Todman had grown up believing that real families were for other people.

He still often wondered what might have become of him if he hadn't found the Lomaxes. Or if the Lomaxes hadn't found him.

According to his own case file at the Department of Children and Family Services, he'd narrowly missed permanent adoption four different times before the age of two. The first couple on the list believed they couldn't have children of their own, then discovered that they could after all. The second couple had suffered an unexpected change in financial circumstances. The third couple opted for a little Cambodian girl instead.

The fourth couple actually completed the process. According to the file—which Todd had obtained by submitting a Declaration in Support of Access once

he'd turned eighteen—James and Crystal Todman of
Glendale had given him a name and a home before the
state of California made them give him back.

He'd been twenty-two months old when the elder
two-thirds of Team Todman was indicted in federal
court on 1,227 counts of interstate mail fraud related to
a multilevel marketing scheme.

It seemed almost comically tragic on paper, but Todd
could admit the truth. It wasn't a particular source of
humor *or* angst. He honestly didn't really remember either of them.

He remembered most of the foster families who had
traded him through the ensuing years. One of the last
had been an especially avid churchgoing clan. Before
he'd finally given up on that bunch and run away gladly,
Todd remembered being dragged to Sunday School—on
Sundays, Wednesdays, and Friday evenings—week after
God-fearing week.

He'd been the only kid in his class who refused to
memorize the 23rd Psalm. Todd simply hadn't been able
to commit to the text. He'd never felt like the Lord was
his shepherd, and he didn't see the point in lying about it.

When the teacher had tried to embarrass him into
line, forcing him to get up in front of the class and say
the words like everybody else, he'd quoted her Section
271.5 from the California Penal Code instead.

*Any parent, or other person who has lawful custody of a
minor child, 72 hours old or younger, may voluntarily surren-
der physical custody of the child to any hospital emergency
room, without fear of prosecution.*

That verse he'd had memorized for years.

Todd had been fourteen when he first met Barbara
Lomax at the Morrison Home for Boys on Slauson Avenue. She came in to teach art classes there every other

Saturday. The first afternoon Todd ever attended, she'd smiled at him, and patted his shoulder, and told him he had a gift for imagery.

He hadn't missed a single one of her classes from that day on. Some weeks, he'd been the only guy in the house who showed up. He'd never had a crush on a teacher before.

He'd never met anybody he could honestly say he would have liked for a mother, either. In a way, it was almost like being born all over again. This time, without the abandonment.

The spring he'd turned fifteen, Mrs. Lomax— Barbara—helped him enter a national contest sponsored by *Advertising Age* magazine. When his submission took first runner-up in the age group, Barbara invited him to her family's house in Beverly Hills for a celebration pool party with her own kids.

That had been the first time he'd met Heather. Todd had been lost from the first Marco Polo. She was so much like her mom that it made him ache.

Meanwhile, Barbara instructed her husband to help Todd invest his prize money in an educational IRA. That June, Doren gave him an actual job working the towel counter at the main club on Wilshire—full-time during summers, part-time during the school year—on the condition that Todd continue to invest half his earnings in the college fund. Once he'd proved himself, Lomax Enterprises began to match his contributions under the corporate junior sponsorship program.

He'd worked his way up to assistant manager at the club by the time he started his Communication Studies program at UCLA.

Todd spent his third- and fourth-year internships as a copywriter in Doren's public relations department.

Precious David had still been swapping hickeys in the
swim gym at Beverly Hills High when Todd finished
his degree and came on the company payroll full-time.

He'd been the one who helped Heather get an A on
her mass-media term project her senior year at BHHS.
He'd been the one who had driven her to the emergency
room with broken bones in her hand that summer.

He'd been the one who had helped build MHTV
and Gregor Tavlin from the ground up.

He'd even helped Doren find Mountain View for
Barbara when that time came. Precious David certainly
hadn't been required to shoulder the responsibilities of
a son. While he and his little dope-dealing pal Benjy
passed the water bong at the frat house and cut class to
go off and surf, Todd had been the one who had been
there to help do what needed to be done.

He'd spent holidays and weekends at the Lomax table
along the way. Times were good and times were bad. Together and apart, the Lomaxes had their share of both.
But no matter what, Todd had never been anywhere that
felt so much like the way he imagined a home ought to
feel.

———————————

He made reporters leap out of his way as he sped
through the open gates. Thumb still on the button of
Heather's remote, he closed the gates behind him and
stayed on the gas.

At the house, Todd slammed on the brakes and skidded to a stop in a cloud of white oyster shell dust. He
saw Rosa already waiting for him at the door.

The sight of her did Todd's soul good. It took him
back. It brought him around. He got out of the car and
limped through the dust cloud.

"Rosa, thank God you were home."

"You stay away," Rosa said.

Todd had made his way close enough now to see the look on her face. The look on her face and the kitchen knife in her hand.

"Rosa?" Todd stopped and held up a palm. "For heaven's sake, put that thing down. It's me."

"You stay away," she said again, brandishing the knife between them.

"Rosa! There's no time for this. Heather's been injured. She's in danger, we need to hurry. Did you call Doren like I asked you?"

"I called Mister Doren. He's coming with the police."

"Rosa. No."

"You don't talk about Heather." Rosa waved the knife. "You sprayed poison in her face and stole her car. I know. Mister Doren knows. Everybody knows. You left her with Mister Andrew."

Mister Andrew.

Todd couldn't believe what he was hearing. Mister Andrew? This knuckle-dragging caveman Heather had taken up with was Mister Andrew now?

They'd obviously found a phone already. Maybe her boy had a cellular. Maybe somebody had stopped to help. Todd had been focused so completely on the fine points of the story he'd tell Doren that he hadn't really considered the various possibilities in between.

It didn't really matter. It was a mistake, coming here. Todd saw that now.

He'd thought there might still be time to spin this horrible, crumbling catastrophe of a day back his way. He refused to believe that after all these years, the life he'd built here could go up in flames this easily. Heather had actually done him a favor when she'd turned on him in that parking garage. Todd could think again.

If only he could talk to Doren, he saw a couple different ways to package this thing. It was going to be a hell of a challenge, but Todd thought he could make it sell. If he could move 30,000 copies of the authorized Rod Marvalis biography, by God, he could do anything. He had ideas.

But now, in this moment, Todd realized he'd been fooling himself. Standing here—held at knifepoint by the same woman who made him tuna fish sandwiches whenever he and Doren came back to the house after company golf league on Wednesday nights—Todd realized that he'd been fooling himself for a very long time.

There really was no place like home. Not for him. Because there was no such thing.

Todd became aware of the desert heat on his skin. It was a desiccating thing. It seemed to pull all the moisture from his tissues to evaporate into shimmering air.

It was making a husk of him.

"Mister Andrew," he said flatly, "is a liar. He's a liar and a dangerous man."

"You're the liar," Rosa said. "You're the dangerous one. You don't talk to me. Stay away."

Todd could now hear the sound of cars arriving somewhere beyond the gates: the whine of revving engines, the screech of locking wheels. Doors slamming. He closed his eyes. He felt like weeping, but he didn't seem to have enough moisture left in him to produce any tears. He finally gave up trying.

Todd turned, intending to get back to Heather's car and get out of Dodge like he should have done in the first place.

But it was too late for that now. He saw Doren's Lincoln already rounding the bend of the driveway, followed by an unmarked sedan.

He turned back to Rosa. She showed him the knife again.

Todd raised the golf club and said, "I'm sorry, Rosa. I really am."

He doubted she believed him, but it was true.

42

THROUGH the haze, Denny saw the roadblock coming in time to think about what to say.

Cars crammed both lanes on the other side of the highway, all heading the other direction in a pair of long bumper-to-bumper lines. Denny could see the flares along the shoulder up ahead, a few CHiPs wearing orange vests for visibility.

When the nearest trooper waved him over, Denny rolled to an easy stop and ran his window down.

"We're going to get you turned around, sir," the trooper said. "This area is under mandatory evac. Need to have you pull over to the shoulder behind that green minivan."

"My granny's up in Sunset Mesa," Denny said quickly. He tried to sound stressed. "She called me a half hour ago, scared silly, can't get her car started. She says all her neighbors already lit out."

The CHP trooper leaned down and looked him over. He looked into the backseat of the car. Then he stood up and motioned with his arm to the guys up ahead. He leaned down again and said, "Go on and get her out of there, son. Smoke's starting to get thick up top, so drive careful."

"I will, sir. Thanks. Thanks so much."

"Don't spend any time packing up keepsakes, now. Grab your grandmother and get back on the road. An hour, hour and a half, you'll have big problems if you're not somewhere else."

"Thank you, sir. Can't thank you enough."

The trooper patted the roof of the car two times, then waved him through.

Denny turned off the highway at the next intersection and headed up into the bluffs.

The trooper hadn't been kidding about the smoke. It was thick and brown and it gave the air all around a dull yellow quality. Denny had the car buttoned up tight, and it still smelled like a campfire inside. The smoke got so thick in one spot that Denny almost missed the turn onto the winding street that led up into Rodney's cul-de-sac.

But he made it, and Rod's street finally led him out of the haze and into cleaner air. Denny parked in the driveway beside Rod's packed-up Escalade and hustled up to the front door.

He rang the bell a bunch of times, but nobody answered. He finally gave up and went around back.

Denny saw the hose and the ladder first. He followed them up to the roof with his eyes and saw Rodney there, in shorts and flip-flops and an oversize T-shirt, holding a loop of hose in one hand, a spray nozzle in the other. He was watering down the clay-tile shingles.

"Rod," Denny called out. "Shit, what you doing up there, man?"

Rod turned and saw him. He yelled something, but Denny couldn't hear what.

Denny cupped his hands around his mouth and yelled, "What?"

Rod dropped the extra loop of hose and made a hard motion with his hand. Denny looked and saw the second hose coiled in the lawn. He looked back up to Rod.

"Dude, forget about it," he shouted. "Come on down. It's time to roll outta here."

Rod yelled something else, but Denny still couldn't make it out. He looked around. He looked at his watch. He looked up at Rod.

He started up the ladder. At the top, Denny stepped over the eave and scrambled up the roof on all fours. The rounded tiles were slick with all the water. He ducked more water when Rod swung the hose around.

"Rod, man, let it go," he said. "We gotta get outta here."

"We? Who's we?" Rod gave him a look. "This is *my* house, you asshole. Don't tell me what I need to do. I've worked too goddamned hard for this to come back to a smoking goddamned hole in the ground."

Denny could hardly believe what he was hearing. He grabbed Rod's arm and pointed.

"Dude. Look over there. You see that shit? All that orange shit over the hill? That's fire. Don't be crazy. You got insurance. Let it go."

"That's three miles away." Rod pulled away, moved to a new spot, and started drenching it down. "I've still got time."

"Rod. Don't be crazy, man."

"What the hell are you doing here anyway?" Rod snapped a tangle out of the hose and kept spraying. "Did I ask for your input? Did I ask?"

"Shit, bite my head off," Denny said. "I just came to see if you needed help."

"If you want to help," Rod said, "quit wasting time, get back down that ladder, hook up that other hose around back, and start soaking down the siding. Otherwise, tuck your tail and quit bothering me."

Denny looked at Rod. He looked at his watch again. He looked out into the distance, at the puddles of orange over the hill.

He said, "Half an hour. We'll get her soaked good as we can for that long. Then we're outta here whether you wanna leave or not. I'll come back up this ladder and drag your chubby ass down if I have to. Hear?"

He didn't know if Rod heard or not. Guy didn't even look at him. Rod just moved to another spot and kept the water coming.

Some damn kind of day, Denny thought.

He dropped to his rear and scooted back to the ladder across the slick wet tiles quick as he could without sliding right over the edge.

Doren kept a loaded revolver in the locked bottom drawer of the big desk in his den. Todd promised Detective Timms that he'd shoot the housekeeper with it if anybody tried coming in.

"Believe that," he said into the receiver. "It's not a bluff. I don't want to hurt anybody. But I swear to you, if you send anybody in here, I'll shoot Rosa first, then I'll put a bullet in my own head. Have fun putting together *that* press release."

He hung up the phone. Then he unplugged it from the wall so that it wouldn't ring anymore.

Todd broke the blade of Rosa's knife prying the desk drawer open. She screamed at him in Spanish from the floor where he'd bound her with extension cords from the kitchen.

At first, he'd been afraid he'd hit her harder than he'd intended. He was afraid he'd broken her hand with the golf club. But if he had, it didn't seem to bother her now. She worked constantly at the electrical cords around her wrists and ankles, berating him at the top of her lungs the whole time.

Todd finally sat down, unwound the bandage from his ankle, and gagged her with it.

He didn't want to hurt Rosa. But even with the gag, her voice was a rasp on his nerves. He couldn't take it anymore; he needed a little peace. Just a few moments of silence. Under the circumstances, he didn't think it was too much to ask.

He hit her on the back of the head with the butt of the revolver. The thud of the gun handle on bone vibrated through his hand, up his wrist. It was a sickening feeling. Rosa grunted and fell over. Todd didn't think she lost consciousness, but at least she stopped yelling. She didn't make another sound.

"Please, Rosa," he said. "Please."

Slumped, face touching the floor, she nodded her head slowly.

Todd hopped to Doren's reading chair and fell into it. He raised his leg and rested his throbbing ankle on the footstool. He could see the fabric of the bandage still imprinted in the puffy, discolored skin of his foot. He focused on the granular patterns and tried to collect his thoughts.

From where he sat, he saw plenty of challenges. Not many opportunities. He didn't think he probably had time to sit around waiting for one to present itself.

He sat there anyway. Todd could smell the leather of the chair, the gun oil from the revolver in his hand. They were good smells, strong and soothing. Hypnotic. He was beginning to think he could sit in this spot for the rest of his life.

Todd looked around the room. He noticed one of Doren's pictures on the side table next to the chair. He picked up the frame and turned it over. He spent a while gazing at the photograph under the glass.

He was still looking at the photo when he heard the front door open.

Todd cocked the pistol with his thumb and pointed it at Rosa. She'd worked her way back up to a sitting position. When she saw the gun, her eyes widened. Then she closed them.

"Don't make me do it," he called out to whoever was listening. "I don't want to. But I will."

He waited.

Nothing happened.

He looked over at Rosa and corrected his aim. The weight of the gun kept forcing his hand to drift. He'd never held one before. Todd had no idea they were so heavy. The revolver felt like it must have weighed ten pounds.

Todd heard movement and looked up quickly. He saw Doren watching him from the doorway.

He lowered the gun.

"That's better," Doren said.

Todd raised the gun again, this time pointing it at Doren's chest. "You should have stayed outside."

Doren walked into the room. He walked straight toward Todd.

"Doren, stop. Please. I'm going to pull this trigger if you don't."

In the background, Rosa began to wail through her gag. But Doren didn't stop coming.

Doren didn't stop, and Todd didn't pull the trigger. He tried, but he couldn't seem to make his finger cooperate.

Before he could raise his other hand to help, Doren reached forward and closed his hand over the top of the revolver, wedging his thumb between the hammer and the frame. He grabbed Todd's wrist and twisted the gun away.

Todd let his empty hand fall back into his lap.

Doren stepped back and looked at him. Somehow, the expression on his face hurt even worse than the expression he'd seen on Heather's just a short while ago. Todd felt Doren's anger all the way to his center. It was almost more than he could bear.

Yet Doren was the one with tears in his eyes. He seemed to pause a moment, allowing them. Then he blinked hard, one time, and they were gone.

Doren picked up the broken knife from the carpet and went to Rosa. He used what remained of the blade to slice through the cord around her feet. He helped her up. He whispered something in her ear. Then he sent her out.

Todd knew that he should be trying harder to regain control of the situation, but he couldn't seem to muster the will. He sat in the chair, picture frame in his lap, nine iron across his knees.

Doren came back and stood over him, looking down. For a few moments, he didn't say anything. When he finally did speak, his voice had a quality Todd had never heard in Doren's voice before:

Wounded.

"We treated you like family," he said.

Todd lowered his eyes. He sat there and felt Doren's gaze from above. He sat this way for a long while.

"You know," he finally said, without looking up, "there aren't any photos of me in this room."

Silence.

"I never realized that before today."

For one unexpected, tender moment, Todd felt Doren's thick heavy hand on the back of his head. He could feel the warmth of Doren's palm on his scalp. Then it went away.

"Don't make this worse for yourself than it already is," Doren said. "You need help, Todd. Let me help."

Todd looked at the pebbled, swollen flesh of his bare ankle. He couldn't feel the throbbing anymore.

"Funny," he said. "When David needs your help, you find the best lawyers money can buy. When I need your help, you show up with the police. What member of the family *am* I, out of curiosity? A retarded cousin? Some neighborhood stray you fed a couple of times and can't get rid of?"

"Let's go outside," Doren said.

"I begged him to leave well enough alone, you know. If he'd stayed with me in the office that night, he would have had an alibi."

"It's over, Todd. You don't need to do this. Not now."

"Do you know what he told me? He told me to mind my own business."

Doren said nothing.

"I'm sorry to say it, Doren. But your son is a whining brat who has no idea how lucky he is. He's never had the first clue. If he'd listened to me, we wouldn't be here now. I had a plan, you know. I would have taken care of everything."

Todd finally looked up. The expression on Doren's face had changed. Todd didn't know which he preferred: the contempt he'd seen there at first, or the pity he saw there now.

He picked up the frame from his lap and tossed it to Doren.

"There's a family," he said. "Look at that family and answer this question: Who's not in the photo? Who isn't sitting at the table?"

Doren didn't look at the photograph. He said, "Let's go outside, Todd. I don't want to see you get hurt."

"I was taking the picture," Todd said. "That's why I'm not *in* the picture. I get it now. I guess a picture really is worth a thousand words."

He'd thought he was past emotion; he'd thought he'd gone numb through and through. Todd didn't know where the sudden anger came from, but it bubbled up and scalded him.

He grabbed the golf club and thrust himself up out of the chair. He took a few hops over to the bookcase. He drew the club back and swung it hard, clearing picture frames from one of the shelves in a crashing shower of bent metal and broken glass.

He moved to the next shelf and swung again. Todd decided he'd stop as soon as he found his own face.

He swung again. And he swung again. It turned out to take longer than he'd expected. There were pictures all over this room. The clatter was so loud in his ears that he never even heard Doren turn his back and leave.

But when he finally looked up from the mess he'd made, spent and empty, Todd saw that he was alone.

43

DENNY figured they'd just about blown it. He really didn't think they had much of a chance.

When the fire came, it came hard and fast. It came roaring down the hill through the brush behind the house like a hell-bound train. They were ringed in before Denny even realized they were in trouble.

The world had gone dark, and it glowed orange.

The wood deck on the back of Rodney's place had already started to catch by the time Denny heard the tanker passing by overhead. He didn't think there was any hope in hell the guys in the helicopter could see them up on the roof through all the smoke, but they jumped up and down and waved like maniacs anyway, slipping and stumbling around on the wet clay tiles and holding on to each other for dear life.

Denny figured they were cooked for sure.

But then that big red baby banked, and came back around, and dropped a harness line right to the roof. Rod cheered beside him. Denny whooped and waved his arms.

He helped Rod strap on the harness, then toed into the extra loop and grabbed on tight himself.

He'd gotten so used to the feel of Luther's disc in his waistband that he'd forgotten it was still there until it fell out. Denny felt the jewel case slide down his pants leg when he reached up to grab the cable above Rod's head.

He nearly lost his grip trying to grab the damned thing before it came out the cuff at his ankle.

But it was already gone. All he could do was watch it fall. The guys up above started the winch, retracting the cable, reeling them toward the belly of the chopper. While Denny and Rod went up, the disc tumbled down. Denny watched it fall away, down into the smoke below.

He damned near would have gone down with it if Rod hadn't reached out and grabbed him by the arm.

Denny grabbed back. Up they went.

In the cargo bed of the tanker, Denny collapsed in a coughing fit. Some guy in a helmet and a jumpsuit strapped an oxygen mask over his head. He gave the guy a thumbs-up and sagged back against the hull of the bird.

Across from him, Rod looked like a great big charcoal briquette. He was covered in soot and sweat; his hair hung in his face in ashy gray clumps. He sat on a low bench bolted to the hull, hunched over, holding his own clear plastic mask over his face.

He looked at Denny, lifted the mask. He pointed to

Denny's belt, pointed out the hatch. Over the wind and the thump of the props he shouted, "What the hell was that?"

Denny just rested his head back and gulped O_2 into his scorched, aching lungs.

"Never mind," he mumbled, fogging his mask.

What the hell. They were alive.

It probably wasn't all that important anyway.

Monday, September 3
"Murder Suspect Arrested"

Los Angeles: On August 17, at approximately 4:00 P.M., detectives from the Los Angeles Police Department, Robbery Homicide Division and West Los Angeles Area, responded to a call of "suspect there now" at the residence of Los Angeles Police Commissioner Doren Lomax in the 1100 block of San Ysidro Drive in Beverly Hills.

The suspect, identified as 36-year-old Lomax Enterprises employee Todd Todman, was sought by detectives for questioning in the murder of former Lomax Enterprises employee Gregor Tavlin. Todman entered the residence by force after assaulting the housekeeper, Rosa Gonzalez, age 62. The suspect held Gonzalez inside the house while LAPD personnel attempted to establish contact.

The suspect ignored repeated verbal announcements declaring the presence of uniformed police officers and detective personnel at the door. After responding to a telephonic call initiated by Robbery Homicide Division detective Adrian Timms (46 years old, 5 years with the Department), the suspect refused to respond to multiple follow-up calls.

The suspect's actions escalated the situation into a barricaded suspect scenario. Detective personnel and West L.A. Area patrol officers contained the exterior of the location. SWAT officers responded to the scene and entered the house, using less than lethal munitions (i.e., bean-bag rounds) to gain control of the suspect.

The suspect was immediately taken into custody. Los Angeles Fire Department paramedics were on scene and rendered aid to the suspect and to the injured Gonzalez.

—UPDATE—

Based on information and evidence secured as a result of an ongoing investigation, Los Angeles Police Department detectives charged Todd James Todman on Monday, September 3, for the murder of 47-year-old Los Angeles resident Gregor Tavlin.

Todman already had been in custody without bond on miscellaneous charges, including suspicion of murder and the aggravated assault of Heather Lomax, age 30, and Rosa Gonzalez, both on August 17.

For further information contact the Los Angeles Police Department, Robbery Homicide Division, at 555-525-5555 or 555-525-5579.

This press release was prepared by Public Information Officer Clark Perry, Media Relations Section, 555-525-5455.

###

44

BY the time it was over, the Calabasas-Mandeville Canyon Firestorm claimed 45,000 acres, 397 homes, 260 miscellaneous structures, and six lives.

One morning, from the lounge chair on the deck, Andrew watched fragile ash fall over the beach like snow. It lasted almost an hour. Then, somewhere, the prevailing winds must have shifted; as abruptly as it had started, the show was over.

By the end of the following week, fire and forestry department officials pronounced the last lingering edges of the wildfire fully contained.

According to the radio reports, hot spots would probably continue to smolder until the winter rains.

─────────────

Peter Jeffries told Andrew that he'd probably be called to testify in court at some point.

In the meantime, Jeffries took him where he needed to go when he needed to go there. Andrew answered the same questions a few thousand times. It was hard to satisfy the cops, particularly Detective Timms, but he didn't know what else he could tell them. Andrew had no idea who could have sent them the letter that involved him in the affairs of the Lomax family.

The cops didn't like it, but apparently they hadn't been able to get anything different from anybody else. He pretty much stuck to the truth about the rest. That seemed to work out fine, too.

Otherwise, Andrew stayed around the beach house most days. He began to let the newspapers pile up in the woodbin again.

He made one trip to the nearest Home Depot for a few tools, a few materials. While he was there, he placed an order for a new screen door.

It wasn't always easy working with the cast on his arm, but Andrew managed. He replaced the broken tread at the top of the stairs with a sturdy new piece of cedar. Then he spent three days resealing the entire deck.

He patched and painted the bullet hole he'd put in the ceiling. The crater Luther Vines had knocked in the wall was trickier; Andrew ended up cutting out the section from stud to stud and putting in a new piece of drywall. He taped the seams and mudded them smooth. He asked Caroline if she wanted to change anything as long as he was at it, and she picked a new color for the walls. He repainted them.

Andrew tried not to wonder about his old friend Larry Tomiczek. Usually he made it until the evenings, when he'd take a beer out to the deck and watch the sky turn purple over the water.

One night, he took the six-pack with him. He drank

the whole thing, then dialed Larry's number in Baltimore. He found that it had been disconnected.

He watched the mail in the mornings. He kept hoping he'd find a postcard from someplace tropical one of these days.

Stranger things happened.

———————————

But of everything that did happen over the weeks that followed his experience with Heather Lomax in the parking garage downtown, Andrew's vote for single strangest went to something that happened one day in mid-September.

Late on a Saturday morning, Caroline showed up at the beach house in a big floppy hat. She told him to shower up and get dressed and grab his sunblock. There was a food festival on the Third Street Promenade, she said. It was going to be great, and he was going with her whether he felt like it or not. He'd been spending way too much time cooped up alone, she told him. She told him he needed to start getting out of the house once in a while, like a regular person.

Andrew didn't bother resisting. He was hungry anyway.

And he had to admit, it really wasn't a bad day for it. Seventy-five and sunny, with a clean breeze off the ocean. The city had shrugged off the long, hot summer; natives and tourists alike crowded the promenade from curb to curb. The whole place pulsed with a festive, vaguely liberated vibe. The air hung heavy with the rich, mingling smells of a hundred different kinds of food.

They ate themselves silly, strolling up and back again from one sizzling, smoky sidewalk booth to the next. They laughed a lot. It felt good.

At one point, Caroline looked up from her lamb ke-bob. She tapped him on the shoulder and pointed.

"Is that guy waving at us?"

Andrew didn't think so.

But the guy came right up to them, grinning wide. He said, "Hey, man. How's it going?"

Andrew might not have placed the face at all if not for the girl who came up to stand next to the guy. The guy must have gotten a haircut. Andrew didn't recognize him without the ponytail.

The girl looked at Andrew's cast and smiled.

"Look at us," she said, holding up her own bandaged arm. "We're twins."

Andrew had to laugh, despite the alarm bells suddenly clanging in his head. What were the odds?

"Hey," he said. "Nice to see you."

"You too, man, you too," Kyle said. "I can't believe we ran into each other."

"Kyle, Sonja, this is my cousin, Caroline," he said. He slipped Sonja an extra look and said, "Caroline Borland."

He saw a quick flicker in Sonja's eyes, but she hid it well. She wasn't such a bad actress herself apparently.

"Hi," she said.

"Nice to meet you." Caroline grinned at Andrew. "You're really getting around this town, aren't you?"

"This is Kyle and Sonja," he told her. "I ran into them when I went to see Lane at the office that day. Kyle blows things up for the movies."

"Wow," Caroline said.

"I take it you two patched things up?"

"Well, you know," Kyle said. "We got to talking."

"Good for you," Andrew told them. He really meant it. "You're a real cute couple."

Sonja blushed. Kyle just shook his head.

"Man, I don't know what you did that day, but you're my hero." He reached into the pocket of his cargo shorts and handed Andrew a *Crash and Burn Productions* business card. "If you ever need anything. I mean anything, man. You give me a call. Okay?"

Caroline snatched the card from Andrew and looked at it. Her grin became a smile, then a goofy laugh.

Kyle looked at Andrew. He looked at Sonja. "Did I say something stupid?"

Caroline just handed the card back to Andrew. "See that? I told you. No coincidences."

"Don't mind her," Andrew said. "She's on a spare rib high."

"Right," Kyle said. He grinned and said, "Well, look, we gotta bust on out of here. But I'm serious. You ever need anything, you've got my number."

"I'll tack it on the fridge."

"Right on. Good running into you, man. Take it easy."

"You, too," Andrew said. "Nice seeing you again, Sonja."

Sonja waggled her fingers. They went on their way.

After they were gone, Andrew looked at Caroline, who had gone back to her kebob. She was still chuckling to herself beneath the brim of her sun hat.

"What's with you?"

"Not a thing," she told him. "I was just wondering when you were going to start thinking about finding yourself a job."

"Please tell me you're kidding," he said.

Caroline just licked her fingers and smacked her lips, still grinning. "I'm not saying another word."

———————

The cast came off the first week in October. It was about time. Andrew had been using a letter opener to scratch away the itchy dead skin underneath.

He still hadn't seen that postcard from Larry in the mail.

But one afternoon, a couple of weeks before Christmas, a delivery man came to the door. When Andrew saw the size of the package, he told the guy that it must be a mistake. But the guy checked his manifest and shook his head.

"Says Andrew Kindler," he said. He tilted the form so that Andrew could see the address. "You Andrew Kindler?"

Andrew shrugged. "I guess I am."

He signed for the package and had to use both arms to carry it inside.

Andrew opened the large flat box in the living room. Packed inside, only slightly smaller than the box itself, was an object wrapped in brown paper. Four feet by four feet square, a couple inches deep. Andrew slid the box away and leaned the object against the couch. He found a note taped to the brown paper wrapping. He pulled the note off and read the handwriting.

It said:

Andrew,

My father told me what you used to do for Cedric before you came to Los Angeles. I find that extremely bizarre.

The enclosed is a painting by my favorite artist. I took

the liberty of titling it myself. I call it "Self-Destructive Pattern Behavior."

If you haven't already, stop reading this note now and unwrap the painting. It will help the rest make sense.

Mildly astounded, Andrew followed the instructions. He put the note down on the coffee table and went to the wrapped canvas. He got a corner started with his finger and began tearing the brown paper away. When he finished, he took a step back and looked at the painting.

The first thing that struck him was the color. Swirling shades of oranges and reds and yellows covered the canvas in vibrant, fiery whorls.

As he stood there, he began to notice things. In one spot, he saw what he thought must be the joint of a large feathered wing. In another, he saw what looked like a dark round eye. He took another step back, then another. He stood some more. The longer he studied the painting, the more he began to see the shape of some great bird within the riot of flaming color.

He took the note up again.

I've heard different versions of the Phoenix legend. The one I like best says that the adult bird turned its own nest into a funeral pyre, consuming itself in flame. After the conflagration, a new Phoenix rose out of the ashes. Maybe you've heard it.

I hope you like the painting. Happy Holidays.

—Heather Lomax

Andrew read the note again before he put it down. He stood there and looked at the painting awhile. In the bottom right corner, something caught his eye. He stepped closer and bent down to look, saw the initials BL drizzled in black paint.

He stepped back again and thought, *I'll be damned.*

The painting itself really was something. Andrew didn't know much about art, but he liked it. He liked it quite a lot. He liked it more every time he walked past actually.

He tried it above the fireplace first, because it fit the space there. But something about putting it above a fireplace seemed heavy-handed, so he took it down. He tried it in the bedroom, but it didn't really go with Caroline's decor.

He tried a few other things, but he didn't like any of them, either.

Eventually, Andrew gave up and left the painting on the floor in the living room, leaning against the wall.

There just didn't seem to be a good spot for it here. But Andrew figured it would keep. It really was about time he found his own place anyway.

Hot Spots

Fire is a catalyst; it synthesizes whatever surrounds it;
it takes its character from its context.

—Stephen J. Pyne
Environmental Historian,
Arizona State University

Report

LAPD investigators never recovered a murder weapon in the **Gregor Tavlin** case. During an extensive follow-up search of Tavlin's home in Palos Verdes, SID technicians used chemical enhancement techniques to discover latent fingerprints and blood spatters on and around a fiberglass basement utility sink. Disassembly of the sink's trap pipe led to the collection of hair and tissue samples. Lab analyses calculated a one-in-six-billion chance that the DNA contained in the collected samples belonged to any person other than the victim.

Todd Todman remains in custody in the Men's Central Jail in downtown Los Angeles. Three applications for bail have been denied. He is awaiting trial in the Superior Court of the State of California, Los Angeles County.

David Lomax pleaded guilty to felony charges of accessory after the fact to murder. He was sentenced by a Los Angeles Superior Court judge to 15 to 24 months at the California Institution for Men at Chino, with credit for time served. **Benjamin Corbin** was not implicated in any criminal activity. Corbin conducted an informal primer course on life inside the Chino facility and is counseling Lomax in preparation for his first parole hearing.

After completing the oral portion of the lieutenant's

exam and placing in the top flight of candidates on the final list, **Adrian Timms** took his daughter on a weekend salmon fishing trip in Puget Sound.

Drea Munoz and **Marcus Webster** had drinks. It didn't work out.

Pursuant to section 2761(c) of the Business and Professions Code of California, and in accordance with internal disciplinary guidelines, the California Board of Registered Nursing stayed the revocation of **Iris Warner**'s license to practice with three years of probation. The Board of Directors of Mountain View Supported Living voted to continue Warner's employment provisionally based on the appeals of Lomax family members. No criminal charges were filed.

CNN, MSNBC, and local network affiliates all carried stories covering the California Department of Forestry's daring air rescue of **Rodney Marvalis** and **Denny Hoyle.** Rod Marvalis played himself in a reenactment on the Fox prime-time television series *American Catastrophes*. He is currently represented by Mitchell Towne of the William Morris Agency. He remains the sole client of Hoyle & Associates Personal Security, Inc.

Luther Vines was prosecuted and convicted on charges of assault with a weapon and laying in wait to commit bodily harm. Possession of an illegal gun and assault with a deadly weapon charges were retracted during the plea-bargaining process. Designs for The Neckerciser are patent pending.

The whereabouts of **Lawrence Michael Tomiczek,** aka "Eyebrow Larry," remain unknown. Los Angeles private investigator **Travis Plum** is tracking a lead in the Florida Keys.

And on the first day of the new year, late in the

afternoon, **Andrew Kindler** followed **Heather Lomax** from her father's home in Beverly Hills to her own house in Los Feliz. He waited at the curb for half an hour before Heather emerged, got back in the car, and left again. He followed her little yellow Beemer, not bothering to keep distance between them. He got the feeling she'd known he was there all along.

She led them north on the 405, to the 5, past San Fernando. He followed, racking miles on the odometer as they climbed gradually out of the basin, through the foothills, and into the San Gabriel Mountains. Andrew saw a sign that said Antelope Valley Freeway. Eventually, they arrived at a long driveway lined with cedars and pines.

She waited for him in the parking lot with her arms folded, head tilted, keys dangling from her hand. She wore a light sweater and faded blue jeans.

"Happy New Year," he told her.

"Same to you," she said.

"Thanks for the painting."

Heather looked at him for a while without speaking.

"Don't thank me," she finally said, smiling a little. "Just tell me what you're doing here."

Andrew smiled back. He put his hands in his pockets. He looked off toward the A-frame lodges. He looked east, thinking of a cemetery he needed to visit soon. He looked at Heather.

"I was just thinking that I never did get to meet the artist," he said. "I was wondering if you'd mind if I thanked her myself."

For a long time, Heather stood quietly. Andrew wasn't sure how to read her response. She looked off toward the A-frame lodges. Finally, she turned back to him.

"You'll like her," she said, and took his arm.

Acknowledgments

Thanks are due, as always, to the folks who helped.

First, to my wife, Jessica, who holds the unenviable job of First Reader.

Thanks one more time to Tom Fassbender and Jim Pascoe for their uncommon insight and faith.

Thanks to Brian Hodge, Victor Gischler, and Nathan Walpow for empathy and input. Thanks to Jennifer Robinson for taking a chance way back when. Special thanks to Tess Monaghan for abiding a quick storybook version of her stomping ground.

Finally, a respectful nod to the men and women of the Los Angeles Police Department, who may notice discrepancies between this work of fiction and real life on the job. Dramatic license and all.

My advice to any armchair detectives out there: leave all your important murder investigations to the professionals.

About the Author

Sean Doolittle won the gold medal in the mystery category of *ForeWord Magazine*'s Book of the Year Award for *Burn*. He is also the author of *Dirt,* an Amazon.com Top 100 Editor's Pick for 2001. The author lives with his family in Omaha, Nebraska. Visit him on the web at www.seandoolittle.com.